A DEADLY GILDED
Free Fall

CECELIA TICHI

A Deadly Gilded Free Fall

Copyright © 2021 by Cecelia Tichi

ISBNs:
979-8-9851216-4-3 (paperback)
979-8-9851216-5-0 (eBook)

Chapter One

New York City, April, 1899

SUNLIGHT FLOODED OUR BREAKFAST space, but it felt like midnight at the table. A visitor was expected later today, a law school friend of my husband's and new business partner, but the timing could not be worse. My Irish ire was up. "You were right, Roddy," I said, "I should have hired a chef for last night."

"I should have insisted," my husband replied in his calm tenor voice. "From now on, we'll commit to a chef."

Cold comfort. Last night's formal dinner for fifty guests here at 620 Fifth Avenue was to be flawless. I had pored over the menu and hired extra footmen from a reliable agency. My fifth-generation New York Knickerbocker husband, Roderick Windham DeVere—my Roddy—had approved the seating, and my silk moiré gown from Worth set off my

1

diamonds and tiara as I greeted our guests. Weeks in preparation, the dinner honored a good friend soon to embark on a scientific expedition.

"Our cook did her best," I said, "but the soup...and that lamb...." I paused between 'charred' and 'charcoal.'

"I doubt that our guests minded," my husband said softly, "and Dudley least of all." Our friend, Dudley Forster, the guest of honor, would soon sail halfway around the world in search of fossils. "I doubt that he cared one bit."

Roddy spoke smoothly, but I yanked the sash of my rose-colored sacque. "The extra footmen clattering the plates just when you toasted Dudley's expedition. And smashing that platter on the floor..." I said, "I thought Bronson and Chalmers would have a fit."

"Hard going for Bronson," Roddy agreed.

"And Chalmers too." Our two stalwart footmen, Bronson and Chalmers, coped with the hired hands who had blundered their way through all seven courses.

"To cap it off..." I went on, "*Town Topics* is certain to fill a gossipy column about our dinner. A guest is sure to tattle, and *Town Topics* will broadcast something like...'Wild West Hostess Offers Campfire Grub...Dished by Cowhands in Footman's Garb.'"

"Val, don't...." Roddy's deep blue eyes spoke his concern, and his strong jawline jutted in the chiseled look I found irresistible.

"Valentine Mackle DeVere...please stop. Our visitor will be here shortly, so let's think ahead."

"I'll try." I meant it.

Roddy's former law school classmate, Martin Coates, was due after 2:00 p.m. He had written last autumn to invite Roddy to "the City by the Lake" for talks about a problem he had not spelled out—and a solution involving a partnership with my husband.

He got the jump on Roddy by coming here last February, and the two men huddled over several days in a private club-room. My husband grew more enthusiastic each evening at our dinner table. In law school days, Roddy had concocted icy drinks with whiskey and bitters that everyone liked, and the two men had mentioned going into the bitters business one day as partners. Years later, the partnership was taking shape. A letter of intent had been signed under the laws of Illinois.

The February talks were strictly business, so no social events took place, which was just as well. A terrifying event at the Metropolitan Opera in January nearly cost me my life. Roddy swore he would never forgive himself if I had been killed. His business talks with Martin Coates proved distracting and helped take his mind off the opera fiasco. My nightmares had finally lessened.

Martin Coates's own life had also taken a sudden, tragic turn. My husband knew that Martin's father was felled by a stroke over a year ago and was immobilized for months before his death. Suddenly, however, his wife died just weeks ago in early March. Roddy learned of her passing in the law school alumni bulletin, which explained why he had not heard recently about the partnership. We sent a letter of condolence and flowers.

"Was it sudden, Roddy? Had Martin's wife been ill?" I asked this morning.

"The notice said, 'untimely passing.'" Roddy sipped his tea. "Nothing was said about her health when we planned the partnership, though you might have met Martin and his wife two years ago at the reunion banquet.... Lydia Coates, a slim lady in a big hat. We had a few words together. Remember?"

I did not, and this was no time to pretend. I murmured that a good many couples had attended the banquet to celebrate the new Columbia University Law School building on Morningside Heights. Roddy understood. This afternoon, we would dress and prepare to receive the widower Martin Coates who was due on the Lake Shore Limited from Chicago and coming straight to us from the Grand Central Depot.

Appearing calm and collected by 2 p.m., we waited for our guest in the Louis XV drawing room that Roddy favored for its natural light and bland landscape paintings. His tan sack suit and my heather afternoon dress went with the room, pleasant and subdued, one of few such spaces in the house. My husband's parents, Rufus and Eleanor DeVere, had built this French chateau eleven years ago in 1887 and stuffed it with antiques acquired in European travels. They turned it over to us when we wed and moved into the part of the house that had been Roddy's bachelor quarters around the corner, where they had a separate entrance. I found their heavy mahogany and faded tapestries depressing and so planned a major renovation in due course. A new decorator in the city, Elsie De Wolfe, was making inroads with fresh ideas, and I planned to confer with her soon. Taste deserves personal choice.

"He should be here by now, shouldn't he?"

"Any minute," Roddy said. "The Lakeshore Limited is the pride of the New York Central."

Roddy reminded me that Martin was more of an ally than a friend. "We were never close pals, Val. We were seated alphabetically in the law school classroom. He was a few years older than most of us and had studied chemistry in college. His father insisted he learn the law to safeguard the Martin family businesses from weak attorneys."

"Or double dealing 'shysters?'"

"I never asked. His family produced that popular patent medicine, Vitalene...."

"Vitalene? Why didn't you say so?" I remembered the elixir from Virginia City, Nevada, where silver miners chugged it by the case, though my papa, a "Silver King," encouraged cold water and beefsteaks. "If you don't know what's in it, Papa said, "stay dog wide of it," meaning steer clear.

We sat for another quarter hour like attendants at a wake until the butler appeared in the doorway with a figure in a black travel suit. "Mr. and Mrs. DeVere...Mr. Martin Coates."

"Martin...good to see you again." My husband shook hands warmly and introduced me to the widower who looked to be in his later thirties. Receding dark hair gave him a high forehead with touches of gray at the temples of a craggy face with heavy brows, dark eyes, a nose cut from granite, and a thick moustache. A wide mouth made him seem on the verge of a smile, but our guest was somber as he bowed to me and was led to a settee. His suit looked rumpled, as if he had worn it since leaving Chicago yesterday afternoon. He looked fatigued but nervous. We needed no reminders that this man's wife had recently died.

Roddy took the lead. "Martin," he said, "Mrs. DeVere joins me in sympathy for you and your family...your recent loss...."

The man swallowed hard, clenched his hands together, and drew a deep breath. "Thank you. I had hoped you would come to Chicago...so much has happened. Decent of you to see me on short notice." He fingered his moustache and closed his eyes.

"It's a long story..." he said, turning to Roddy. "Our plans went so well last February here in New York that I didn't feel the need to tell you, DeVere, that I was already a married man and a father in our law school days. I kept that to myself. Lydia and the children stayed behind."

"Children?" I asked softly.

"Lester and Letitia," he said, tugging at a suitcoat button. "Their mother, my Lydia...she departed this life in March... in our Oak Park home."

I nodded in sympathy for this man and his children, but he did not pause for condolences.

"Oak Park is a village on the Illinois prairie, Mrs. DeVere," he said. "Oak Parkers knew the future value of a village with trains into Chicago, and my grandfather, Phineas Coates, bought land there and speculated in property in present-day downtown Chicago."

I glanced at Roddy, who did not return my gaze. Did Martin shield himself from grief by presenting this short history? Our butler hovered just outside the room in case we wished refreshments, but our guest continued in the same vein.

"Grandfather's business supplied pork to the Union Army and then put hams on America's tables after the war, but the Coates family always lived miles from...the hogs." He cleared his throat. "Of course, the medicine business expanded. Grandfather Phineas would not allow Piper's Magical Elixir to beat our Vitalene. Nor would my late father." He looked from Roddy to me. "You know the name, Vitalene?"

Roddy shot me a glance. I would not pretend approval of the patent medicine. As it turned out, I needn't have worried.

"It's bunk, that tonic." Martin almost cried out. He clenched his hands into fists. "Worse yet, it's got poison in it.... I studied chemistry...coal tar, formaldehyde...."

Roddy murmured, "Embalming fluid...."

"Never wanted Vitalene in my house," Martin pulled at his suit coat button. "Never let my children near it." His voice lowered in prayerful tones. "I promised Lydia to put an end to it. She said it shamed our family and hurt everyone who drank it."

He blinked back a tear. "My Lydia...she said to me, 'When women get the right to vote, we will rid the country of poisonous food, adulterated milk, and patent medicines.'" His lip trembled. "...so many tributes from Hull House women when we lost her... My dear wife helped at Hull House...."

"Hull House?" I said. "The Chicago settlement house?"

He nodded. I would later explain to my puzzled husband why the name had become familiar to me.

"And so..." Martin continued, "I made Lydia a solemn promise, and that's why I decided to approach you for a partnership, DeVere. Though my father never forgave me. To his last breath, he never forgave me. The proof's in the pudding...my disinheritance...."

Roddy looked as confused as I felt, and I wished our little French bulldog might wander in for distraction. The clock chimed. No dog.

Roddy crossed his legs. "Not sure that I understand...." he began.

"The old joke in law school," Martin almost wailed. "You were 'Gentleman Roderick' winning all the cases in mock court trials in law school...me, I had chemical facts, but they did not help in the mock trials."

Very quietly Roddy said, "Law school was quite some time ago, Martin. We needn't revisit those years. And perhaps Mrs. DeVere needs to see about other household matters just now...?"

Roddy's bid to release me from this interview stopped with Martin's awkward apology and a plea that I stay to hear him out. From a window I saw tree limbs dotted with spring green shoots. Our butler was no longer in sight.

"The bitters business, DeVere..." he said. "I have every expectation that our partnership will go forward. We both signed the letter of intent. You must come to Chicago as soon as possible."

My husband frowned. Evidently, he had not told Martin of his obligations here in the city, but Roddy was often in court defending taverns from the Temperance zealots who waged war against all alcoholic drinks. Trials were scheduled, and he had to be in the courtroom. Add to that his *bon-vivant* invention of drinks in this Golden Age of Cocktails. The courtroom and the barroom, Roddy said, were his life's yin and yang,

"A visit to Chicago at an early opportunity," Roddy said, "but I have legal obligations as a defense attorney. In addition, a few clubs have called upon me for suggestions about signature drinks."

The distraught Martin was in no state to hear his future business partner say that he was in demand to devise signature cocktails for clubs, hotels, ocean liners, railroads, resorts, etcetera...but only in strict secrecy. Master bartenders got the credit, which was Roddy's requirement. He was the stealth mixologist.

"But bitters..." Martin cried in a plaintive voice. "Our plan for the partnership is based on bitters...the letter of intent...." He broke off.

"Yes, indeed," my husband hastened to say. "Nothing has changed at my end, Martin. You can count on me."

Our guest twisted his coat button again. He had mentioned a vow to his late wife and his disinheritance. He had reviled Vitalene as toxic and urged me to stay here in this room, though he did not give a reason. Why was he here? Why was I?

"I fervently hope our partnership is not in jeopardy, DeVere." Martin's tone struck a warning.

Roddy's expression grew solemn, and his eyes narrowed. "Martin," he said, "what could jeopardize our plan?'"

The suitcoat button pulled loose, and our guest gave us baleful looks. "There is a certain rumor about you DeVeres," he said. "...that you have helped to solve crimes. Is it true?"

We looked at one another and then, a bit reluctantly, both nodded.

Martin looked relieved. "In this instance," he said, "I hope you will help prove that no crime has been committed. You see, a Chicago detective is convinced that Lydia's fall was no accident. He has singled our family out. We are now, he says, 'persons of interest.' He means every adult in the Coates household is suspected of murdering my Lydia...my brother, Owen, and Sara Dow too." He swallowed. "...and me."

He looked beseechingly from Roddy to me. "I don't know where to turn," he said, "and I count on you to help us."

The moment blared with silence. The men exchanged hard glances. Both had said, "count on." From Roddy, the phrase sounded reassuring. From Martin, a vague challenge.

A clock chimed, and the light shifted from the windows. "Would you care for tea, Mr. Coates?" I asked.

"Tea?" The word seemed to break a spell. "A cup of tea," he said. I pressed an electrical switch under the carpet at my feet, Chalmers appeared, and we were soon served afternoon tea. Martin looked more crestfallen than agitated as he sipped, put the cup down, and folded his hands.

"I have a brother," he said, "and a sister who recently returned from Europe. I am the oldest...which brings me to today's visit...why I could not wait to see you in Chicago."

I nodded, and Roddy put his cup down.

My father, Harold...my late father...enlarged our holdings in Chicago, especially the real estate and the medicine business. My brother, Owen, enjoys sports and takes little interest in business affairs, and my sister, Celia, has traveled abroad for the past two years. Her engagement to a nobleman was broken off...a Czech prince she met in London."

He reached for a handkerchief and patted his forehead. "My father's will was read when Celia returned from Europe. She is now here in New York in a house on Washington Square. She bought the house with her inheritance.... Celia has never felt a financial constraint...not as yet." He reached for his cup, drank, and looked from me to Roddy.

"My father swore by the patent medicine...called my facts 'quibbles' and took a stand against me. He uncorked Vitalene bottles and dared me to drink. He waved them in front of my dear wife and taunted her, 'Liquid gold, Lydia.' I begged him to stop, but he laughed until I barred him from our home. Our arguments grew heated…father against son. The Pure Food movement is gaining ground, I told him. Chemists are the new detectives. I gave him a recent book exposing adulterated food and warned him the patent medicines will be next."

Martin tugged at his collar. "My father stopped speaking to me, made Owen his messenger. If signatures were needed for business documents, Owen brought them to me. Whatever my father requested from my office files, Owen took them…and he spent a good deal of time at my home. The children enjoyed their Uncle Owen, and he kept Lydia company. My wife's health was always delicate…and then, her accident…."

Roddy glanced my way. I softly said, "Last month…in March?"

Martin's jaw clenched. "Lydia tumbled down the stairway of our home," he said. "Sara found her…."

"Sara…?" I asked gently.

"Our good friend, Sara Dow, has been staying with us. I was working. There was nothing to be done. Doctors were summoned…nothing to be done."

He fingered the suitcoat button and drew a deep breath. "My father's stroke paralyzed him, but he 'spoke' to me in his will. He left one million dollars to Celia, and to Owen all the real estate holdings and tens of millions. To me… perhaps you could guess…?"

Martin nodded when he heard my husband murmur, "Vitalene."

We grew quiet. The afternoon light shifted, and I caught sight of our footman crossing to another room to adjust the draperies. Roddy said, "It's our plan for the partnership, isn't it, Martin? You've come to discuss phasing out Vitalene... and the bitters business is somehow tied to phasing out Vitalene?"

"Which need not disrupt our plans, DeVere."

Martin had not answered Roddy's question, but his words rushed on. "The company has the glassworks for the bottles, the imported cork, the printshop for labels... the national distribution...."

He toyed with the loose button. "And you assured me, DeVere, that cocktails are an expanding opportunity. You call this the Golden Age of Cocktails."

"I do."

"And you are certain that ladies will drink cocktails in a few years, not only wine and liqueurs but mixed drinks as well? You believe the day is coming?"

"As we discussed in February, Martin."

"Then it's settled, DeVere." He looked from Roddy to me and said, "You must come to Chicago, both of you, and prove the detective is on a witch hunt against our family and our friend. You will come to Chicago and prove that my wife was not murdered."

Chapter Two

THE EVENING LIGHT CAST our drawing room in a soft lavender, but I was in no mood for a poetic twilight. Roddy had seen Martin to the door and now joined me upstairs in our favorite Bergere chairs. The drawing room was chilly. "How do you feel, Val?"

"Buffeted," I said. "...or maybe ambushed. Your new business partner barges in and wallops us with a plea that we free his household of suspicion of murder. Papa would say we were 'knocked upside the head.'"

"And to think," I continued, "that last night I fretted about burned lamb and worried that my tiara might come loose and fall into the cream sauce."

Roddy gave me his wry glance.

"It's heavy, Roddy. Your grandmother's tiara must weigh half a pound." I resisted saying the DeVere family jewels could be a load. "So handy that Calista sewed his button on...."

My personal maid, Calista Adrianakis, had stepped in at my request, whisked Martin's suitcoat to a sewing nook, and returned with the coat button sewn and the coat pressed. She had glanced at the wrinkled trousers but wisely withdrew. A former stewardess on a coastal steamer, Calista was a godsend to me and to this house.

"And Martin made use of those extra few minutes while waiting for his button to be fastened, didn't he," I said, "inviting us to dinner so we can meet his sister and brother before he returns to Chicago."

"To meet Celia and Owen," Roddy replied, "though he did not say whether they, too, know that a detective suspects them of murder...and the live-in companion as well. No, he did not say." My husband raked a hand through his hair. "Val, we'll mull this over, but let's sit a bit and calm down."

Roddy sat sideways on the plush chair, thumbing his wedding band and looking far from relaxed.

"A big bale of trouble, Roddy," I said softly, "too much to sort out...a sudden death, grief, anger...and a detective hounding the family. What a shock."

My husband repeated, "Shock, yes...nothing so specific in the law school bulletin about her death."

"A fall down a staircase" I said, "could happen to anyone. Our stone stairs feel slick, and long skirts are hazardous." I paused. "The detective, however ...Martin did not say who. Or why."

I, too, turned sideways. "Roddy, why did you agree to a business partnership when you knew so little about Martin? And he about you?"

"Because business best avoids personal issues, Val. It's a cardinal rule."

Highly doubtful, I thought, that personal matters could be excluded, but I did not argue.

"I suppose," Roddy said, "I relied on the reputation of a law school classmate, a trustworthy fellow alum. But no question, Martin's visit puts the partnership under a cloud."

"Is your signed agreement the cloud?"

"It might be," my husband said slowly. And the plan is complicated by the Vitalene elixir. It's a familiar story because liquors are often corrupted ...whiskey and gin, brandy too."

"Oh?" This was news to me.

Roddy sat forward on the chair cushion, relieved to be on familiar territory. "I do not confide about my cocktail work, Val, but Coates's account of Vitalene rings true. Too many medicines and foods are worse than dodgy, and beverages as well. When establishments invite me to invent special drinks, I insist on the purest liquors, and I have parted company with one club and two resorts that would not comply."

"You never told me...."

"...I don't bring tales home, my dear, but a certain club bartender was happy to serve whiskey that was 'helped' by creosote, and the resorts had no qualms about cheap gin that was favored with oil of turpentine instead of juniper berries."

"Awful...."

My husband gazed into the distance. "And when I consider Wall Street," he mused, "where cheaters are heroes, and their prize horses can be 'doped,' and Society sloughs it off...."

He went to a window overlooking Fifth Avenue and Central Park. "And the men we know," he said, "men of inherited wealth, Society's 'gentlemen' who take pride in never lifting a hand." My husband turned to me. "And your Knickerbocker lawyer of a husband who refused to manage estates and trusts, but goes into the grimy city courtroom to defend bars and saloons against the Temperance mob and—"

"—and mixes cocktails as a *bon-vivant* sideline." I joined Roddy at the window and took his hand.

"Is it self-serving, Val, that I shied away from the life of an 'idle rich' gentleman or a Wall Street schemer? Is it priggish to say that I have a reputation to protect in our Golden Age of Cocktails? Am I foolish to venture into business?"

"Never!"

I laced my fingers in Roddy's and gazed into my husband's troubled eyes. Martin Coates's visit had brought up issues that pained Roddy more than I knew.

"Shall we have a fire, Val? Too late in the season?"

"Never too late for a fire."

Our footmen often laid the fires, but Roddy went to the polished black granite fireplace and reached for wadded paper, kindling sticks, and birch logs in the holder. A match was struck, touched to the paper, and in minutes flames licked at the logs. Our French bulldog, Velvet, came in to sit on the rug between us as Roddy sat down.

I said, "Much better, takes the chill off. "But bitters, Roddy..." I said, "weren't they medicines?"

"Some still are sold in pharmacies to aid digestion. The alcoholic content is high, almost fifty percent no matter what brand or flavor."

My husband named the brands. "Hostetter's Bitters promises protection from ills of swamps and rivers. And Antoine Peychaud peddled his secret formula from a pharmacy in New Orleans, but a 'few dashes' of Peychaud's are crucial for the Sazerac Cocktail. I could go on, but no bar could survive these days without a full stock of bitters. Each one adds a special tang to a drink...consider the cocktail that we sometimes enjoy before dinner, the Old Fashioned. Trust me, the drink would not taste right without Angostura bitters."

The fire snapped. "This will sound silly, Roddy, but what, exactly, is bitters? What's in it?"

"Not a bit silly, my dear...it's from plants...a distillate of herbs, flowers, fruit, roots, sometimes bits of bark...anything aromatic. Some water and sugar syrup go into the mix, but the makers keep their formulas a closely-held secret."

"So many brands..." I said, "...and are they pure? No chemicals?"

Roddy stood to push a log with the poker. "The bitters business," he replied ruefully, "is subject to the same short-cuts as the liquors, so I am vigilant."

"So, Roddy...there is room for what you and Martin will produce."

"Orange." Roddy said the word with emphasis verging on fervor. "Orange bitters with reliable ingredients and a name brand in the market in this modern age of brands. We will start with orange and then add others. That's the plan. The market is ready. We're sure of it."

So, my husband had been pondering this for some time but keeping it mostly to himself, although it made perfect sense that each of us might harbor private thoughts and feelings. Still...would it be Coates and DeVere's Orange Bitters?

"No further discussion of bitters for the moment, Val." Roddy sat beside me. "Let's give the topic a rest. I want to know about that Chicago house you seemed to know about when Martin spoke of his wife...Hall, was it?"

"Hull House, Roddy. It's a settlement center that helps new immigrant families find their way in America...learning English, childcare, jobs...very important. Miss Jane Addams is the founder, and a few women live in the house. Volunteers help. Lydia Coates evidently participated. They call it social work."

"How do you know about it...?" He stopped. "Don't tell me, it's that women's socialist club you joined, isn't it?"

"We are not socialists, Roddy. The Consumers League is about decent wages and safe working conditions, and its new executive secretary, Mrs. Kelley, has come from Chicago...from Hull House. She lived there for years, and I will definitely visit Hull House if we ever go to Chicago."

"If we ever..." Roddy echoed. The fire popped, a log shifted, and sparks flared. "Val, we haven't talked about...Chicago."

"Or the dinner at Sherry's to meet brother Owen and sister Celia."

"The Coates siblings," Roddy said.

"...the Coates heirs," I added, "and brother Martin... stuck with Vitalene."

"Stuck...and under suspicion of murder, along with his brother and a woman companion... but not the sister," Roddy said.

The fire crackled. "Roddy, the Coates family mishmash is not our affair. Is this a good idea for us? We're barely past the near-miss at the opera house last winter."

My husband bit his lip. "I would never have forgiven myself, Val. I left you out of my sight, and you were nearly pushed to your death."

"And your law school class would have read of my 'untimely passing.'" I said, "We can meet Martin's family at dinner, but he needs to know that your business partnership does not go hand in hand with freeing his household from a charge of murder."

My husband blinked and suddenly looked cornered. The fire needed no attention, but Roddy grabbed the poker and jabbed at the logs. Woodsmoke puffed into the room, and we coughed. "What's the matter?"

"Val," my husband said, "there's something you must know...."

I waited.

Roddy put the poker down, the smoke thinned, and still I waited.

"It's about Martin...Martin and me. The fact is, he saved my life."

"Saved...?" What did I hear? A figure of speech?

"In law school," Roddy began, "an accident...a runaway horse and carriage. I would have been crushed."

"I don't understand."

My husband sat, then stood. "We were on a sidewalk. My back was turned, but Martin saw it coming...a horse dragging a carriage.... Martin pulled me, yanked me...a hairbreadth escape."

"Roddy...you never told me."

My husband went to the window. "A terrible time... the horse bucking and rearing, the carriage wrecked,....law books smashed...horseshoes and carriage wheels." Roddy turned. "If it wasn't for Martin, I would not be here."

I hardly knew what to say, what to think. Roddy knew of my narrow escapes in the West, the rockslides, the fierce currents. Had he blotted this memory? Withheld a secret?

"Val, I try not to think about it. Maybe I would not have given it a thought, if...."

"If what?"

Roddy took my hands in his and sat down. "Val, please understand that Martin and I were never close friends, but after my narrow escape, I made a pact with him. I promised that if Martin ever needed help, he could call on me. I would do my utmost to help him."

"Meaning...." I went no further. The meaning was clear. The mantel clock chimed.

"One hour until dinner," Roddy said. "I don't suppose you'd care to have our usual cocktail?"

My husband's glum voice acknowledged our rupture. It was my turn to speak, or not. We could sit in silence for the next hour. Or I could berate Roddy with "How Could You?" In the days ahead, we would have plenty to say about the Coates crisis. At the moment, however, I simply said, "A cocktail…something with bitters?"

In silence, Roddy sought his wheeled cart, a tea wagon outfitted with bottles, barware, fresh fruit, an ice bucket, and glasses. "Your pleasure, my dear?"

"Your call, Roddy." Time felt suspended as ice was chipped and corks popped. At last, my husband handed me a cold goblet and tapped his own against mine. "Salud, Val."

We sipped. "Tasty," I said. "And do I detect orange bitters?"

"Two dashes… not yet a special brand."

"And does this cocktail have a name? I think it's a recipe to record."

"A name perhaps fitting for a new venture into the unknown. This cocktail is called The Beginner."

Ingredients:
- 1 ounce Russian *Kümmel*
- 1 ounce French vermouth
- 2 dashes sweet gum syrup
- 1 dash absenthe
- 2 dashes orange bitters

Directions:

1. Put ingredients into mixing glass and stir well.
2. Fill goblet with chipped ice.
3. Strain mixture into goblet, stir gently, and serve.

Chapter Three

LOUIS SHERRY'S NEW RESTAURANT, a twelve-story edifice at the corner of Fifth Avenue and Forty-fourth Street, stood directly across from its arch-rival, Delmonico's, both drawing a nightly crush of carriages. The coachmen muttered, horses whinnied, and everyone inside the carriages fumed. On the blustery evening of Wednesday, April 26, our groom assisted Roddy and me into our barouche, and coachman Noland drove our high-stepping matched black Hackneys, Atlas and Apollo, down Fifth Avenue as the wind whistled against the carriage. A gust whipped my cloak at the Sherry's portico, and Roddy held tight to his top hat.

We would soon hear Martin Coates blame the weather for his brother and sister's delay, for he alone greeted us at the fourth-floor private dining room, the Louis Sherry D'Montforte Room, reserved for the Coates party this evening.

"So very good of you to come, very kind…and my sister and brother…any minute now. Brisk weather…holdups."

Owen, we were told, had gone to Washington Square to bring Celia to the restaurant. "But my sister has never obeyed the clock. My Lydia, on the other hand…."

Martin touched his throat and paused while a butler took our wraps. We entered a small dining room paneled in scarlet silk and lighted with a rock crystal chandelier. Our host glanced at five gleaming place settings around an oval table. His evening dress fit a man in mourning, black-upon-black except for the shirtfront. He wrung his hands and murmured about the unsettled spring weather. "Might as well be Chicago…."

My husband nodded. His darkest evening dress honored the widower and, to my eye, set off Roddy's deep blue eyes and thick light brown hair and the little rogue wave that dipped over his forehead. Calista had helped me choose a blue embroidered crape dress with a scooped neck, a double strand of pearls, and an aigrette instead of a hat. We waited for our cue to be seated, but Martin kept us on our feet for the moment.

"I hope you won't mind Sherry's," he said. "My Chicago friends urged Delmonico's, but Celia and Owen…I was out-voted. It seems my brother had dined at Sherry's on one occasion, a notorious dinner…."

The small talk ceased at the sound of an elevator door and voices, the man's slightly nasal, the woman's sweeping like a harp. Martin Coates's brother and sister entered in high spirits but pulled long faces at the sight of their somber older brother. Amid introductions, Martin pointed us to the table...or rather, *at* the table, leaving us to sort ourselves out.

Instantly, Celia Coates took charge as if the hostess duty was hers. Martin was to sit at the head, she said, and Owen to my right, with Roddy on her right on the opposite side. The candlesticks, she said, were too close together and must be spaced. She stood back with narrowed eyes to measure the correct distance.

Celia's petite figure met the current "hour-glass" ideal, and her carnelian tulle dress with outsized satin bows seemed meant to add inches to her height. A piquant face with a tiny, upturned nose and dainty mouth would have suggested a demure young lady, but gray-green eyes signaled a woman of unusual intensity. Her scent, a musk perfume, powerfully stated her presence. By my guess, Celia had not yet reached her twentieth birthday.

Owen held my chair and smiled. He looked close to Martin's age, though we had been led to think of him as a "kid" brother. His hair was thicker than Martin's, his nose broader, and a certain lazy look settled in his brown eyes, as if he let the world parade before his indulgent gaze. Of medium height, he moved with muscular confidence in the Prince Henry coat that seemed quite tight.

"Very fancy..." he said, looking about as Martin signaled for dinner service. "...red silk walls... Louis Sherry outdoes himself...a ballroom, private rooms, banquet halls. He's the emperor of New York dining." Glancing at Roddy, he turned to me. "Sherry started out waiting tables. Did you know that?"

I did not.

"...studied food in Paris, catered a bit, and opened his first restaurant years ago. He's had investors, of course. They say this place is an enraged diner's revenge. Somebody backed Sherry because his wife got furious at Delmonico's. So, every night, carriages outside in a free-for-all, and the two restaurants duel." He grinned. "Trust me, Delmonico's will never beat the Billings dinner at Sherry's...the C. G. K. Billings dinner?"

Owen looked across the table, then at his brother. "Shall I tell them, Martin?" He did not wait for the answer. "A formal dinner on horseback," he said, "...surely you have heard?"

Roddy said, "Then it's true?"

Owen sipped his water as waiters brought champagne. "Leave it to Sherry...he hoisted a couple dozen saddle horses upstairs in an elevator, outfitted the waiters as grooms, and decorated with plants and little trees. And Billings's invitation called for riding britches and boots with formal jackets and ties."

He glanced at his brother. "Iced champagne in the saddlebags and trout served at the pommel...and a photographer to prove it happened. Nothing of the kind in Chicago, which is why I vote for New York."

I reached for my wine. My adopted city in triumph because a restaurant served dinner to men on horseback with champagne stowed in saddlebags? Memories rushed in...of western saddlebags filled with tools for fencing on the range and first-aid kits in case of trouble. And the horses at the dinner? Were they drugged?

Before I could ask, Celia summoned the waiter, pointed manicured fingers at the table, and called a halt until the candlesticks had been spaced inches farther apart. She smiled sweetly and said, "Ever so much better," then agreed with her brother about New York.

"Not about dining on a horse," she said to me and to Roddy. "But I, too, vote for New York. I am a collector, and my New York household awaits *l'art du salon....*"

"A collector?" I said. "Artworks? Paintings?"

"Of artists," she said, "and raconteurs...and furnishings, of course. As soon as my house is redone."

"On Washington Square, I believe," I said, picturing the blocks of brick townhouses. "A charming part of the city."

"Charm?" The word seemed to annoy her. "Charm, perhaps, Mrs. DeVere," she said, "but for the future, I foresee style...taste...spirit... *élégance.* I am working with a highly valued decorator, Miss Elsie De Wolfe."

"Oh," I said, "Miss De Wolfe...."

"In demand," Celia said, "but I stole a march on clients waiting in line. Fifth Avenue clients, Mrs. DeVere. Mansions are all the rage, but the townhouse is an Elsie De Wolfe specialty...irresistible. A decorator worth her weight in gold. You must come to Washington Square and see for yourself, Mrs. DeVere." She gave me a puckish smile. "...and no more need be said...except that London and Europe have had their day. I cast my vote for New York City."

She raised her champagne glass, toasting the city and herself. I recalled her broken-off engagement to the Czech prince. Martin Coates looked distressed. He sipped his wine. We all sipped.

The dinner began with oysters, then Russian caviar. Martin had asked Sherry's to plan the menu, and so we proceeded to the "tomatoes surprise," "watercress and cucumber salad," "aspic of ham," "spring duckling," "spring lamb," "hothouse asparagus," and on and on. Between the "half alligator pear" and the "casaba melon," Celia Coates remembered her older brother's feelings. "Martin," she said, "we don't for a minute forget your loss...the loss to us all...the children...and Sara too."

Martin said, "Thank you."

I recalled the name, Sara Dow, the family friend who was at the Oak Park home when Lydia Coates died.

"Such a shock..." Celia continued, "and so good that you let her come to me here...such comfort."

"...better all around," Martin said.

"...since Sara has her finger on our pulse and knows just what to say, what to do," Celia said.

"Woman's intuition, isn't that what it's called?" Owen sounded dubious.

I glanced at Roddy, hoping he gleaned a few clues as the Coates' conversation turned inward. Neither Owen nor Celia hinted that they and their brother might be suspected in Lydia Coates's death.

Martin looked my way. "Perhaps you recall that we spoke of Miss Dow when I visited your home?"

"Your family friend," I answered.

"...who has lived with us in Oak Park for some time," he answered, "and has joined Celia on Washington Square."

"So relieved that got settled," Celia said. "Oak Park will be starved of gossip, and Sara and I will be like two nuns in New York City."

"Celia, enough, please...."

She leaned across the table toward Owen. "And not a murmur about how you, Owen Coates, might have been the one to mourn the loss of your late wife, Lydia Anne Coates—"

"—Celia!"

"Well, it's true, isn't it?"

The table went stone silent. A waiter entered to remove dishes, and another to bring the cheese and little plates. Suggestions of a dessert followed. The siblings seemed to forget that Roddy and I were at this table.

No one spoke until Martin cleared his throat and said, "Shall we let our friends know what Oak Park has known for years...that a younger Owen Coates first courted Miss Lydia Anne Gerstle...who eventually became Mrs. Martin Coates." He gripped the cheese knife. "My late wife," he said....

"...saw the light," said Owen, "...and chose the better man."

The two brothers locked eyes. Celia lowered her gaze and toyed with a spoon. Roddy and I carefully avoided looking at one another. The red wall panels pulsed with flickering candlelight, and all eyes lowered to the pale Camembert lying beside the blue-veined Roquefort.

"We will welcome you to Gotham, my brother," Owen said at length. "Plan to visit us often."

"And do bring the children when school is out," Celia added. "Sara will love to see them...spoil them both...."

Owen thrust out his chest. "And the Coates Medicine Company is rock solid," he said, "and Vitalene has a bright future...unless...unless...."

"Go ahead, Owen, say it...unless I ruin it? Isn't that the point?"

Roddy shot me a warning glance to keep quiet. We both sat very still.

Martin's face darkened, and we watched the cheese knife stab at the Camembert. "And let's not—"

"—not bring up father? Not say he devoted his whole life to the medicine, fought for the patent, beat the competition. And groomed you to take over...sent you, Martin Coates, to learn chemistry and law." Owen's chest thrust forward. My husband eyed the knife in Martin's fist. "And the shock when you let Lydia's foolish notions—"

"—that's enough."

"—sentimental notions about Vitalene...from that bunch of do-gooder women in the slums...poisoned her mind."

"Poison..." Martin growled. "Poison for certain...."

"And father would be alive today...his stroke...."

"That...will do." Celia's harp-like tone worked like magic. Silk and steel, her voice put an end to the rancorous back and forth. "And so," she said just as two waiters appeared, "we come to the sweets of this evening." A vanilla mousse was served, and sauce poured from a pitcher as red as blood.

Chapter Four

BUNCHES OF TULIPS AND jonquils were this morning's gift of a "tiny floral treat" from my mother-in-law, Eleanor, who paid her first call of the day to Roddy and me at nine-thirty a.m. on this brisk morning. She regretted not seeing her son and supposed that I had sent him on an errand in the chill spring air. A "little bird" had told her that Roderick and I dined at the new Sherry's Restaurant last evening, but the DeVere family, she insisted, ought to remain loyal to Delmonico's on all occasions.

I might have replied that a quiet dinner at "Del's" would have been preferable. Or that we had felt too troubled after the Sherry's dinner to talk sensibly about the Coates family turmoil we had witnessed. I did say that Roderick had gone to our private stable to see our coachman about new horseshoes for Atlas and Apollo.

My mother-in-law's visit lasted the socially required twenty minutes. She eyed our dog who had retreated to a suede encampment in the corner of the *Crème* drawing room and kept a wary canine eye on the visitor. Eleanor regretted, as she often had, that we made a home for a French bulldog instead of a purebred pug and departed with instructions about the "most suitable" vase and a reminder to use freshest water. "Needn't think back to your western…sluices. 'Bye for now, dear."

The welcome scent of leather and hay wafted from Roddy's kiss when he returned just after 10:00 a.m. to find me coping with the flowers in the *Crème* drawing room. "…a gift from your mother, Roddy, and word is out that we dined last night at Sherry's."

"The city can be a village," he replied, "and we were probably recognized…and why not ask Mrs. Thwaite to arrange those flowers?"

"Because our housekeeper is visiting her sister for a few days," I said. Our household overseer, Mrs. Thwaite, had taken the train "upstate" to help her sister with spring cleaning. "Enough of this…." I reached for my mother-in-law's assigned vase, made sure all the stems were in water, and put the whole thing on top of a gate leg table that Roddy's mother had said dated from the seventeenth century.

We sat down on an Italian divan, and Velvet approached to sniff at Roddy's boots. "What did Noland say?" I asked.

"That the farrier will shoe both horses within a week. The groom saw a loose nail on Apollo's left hind shoe, and we ought to see to it that the horses are ready for the coaching parade."

"The coaching parade..." I echoed. My husband kept track of the social calendar and now brought up a parade that was looming, the New York Coaching Club's annual parade.

"I know the parade is not your favorite, Val," he said. "We will soon be on the bridle paths. Comet and Justice will be here in a few weeks. The stable will be ready. I have spoken to Noland and the groom."

"Good news," I said. Our saddle horses were cared for in South Carolina in the winter while we relied on the carriage horses, Apollo and Atlas, to take us sleighing or over the snowy or slushy streets. By June, Roddy's Arabian gelding and my buckskin quarter horse would be welcomed with pleasure.

Meanwhile, my husband read my mind about the annual Coaching Club parade. "The first Saturday in May," I said. "The annual outing for your father's beloved landau carriage...and I will wear a new summer gown and a straw 'leghorn' hat. I promise to smile all day and evening...and right now I would rather talk about horseshoes...or tulips... or anything except last night at Sherry's."

Roddy unbuttoned his jacket and patted our dog. "If Celia hadn't called a halt...."

"They would have warred on. Martin brandished the cheese knife."

"And Owen gripped the candlestick like a truncheon."

"Their sister," I said, "seems to wield some sort of power... maybe as the young lady. The brothers forgot that you and I were present at the table. Maybe they didn't care. Such rage..."

Roddy picked up Velvet and put her between us on the divan. She licked his hand. "Martin is grieving the death of his wife," Roddy said, "but his brother insulted her memory."

"He certainly did...blaming his late sister-in-law for the 'sentimental' notion that Vitalene is dangerous...."

"...even though Martin knows the cold hard facts of chemistry," Roddy said. He brushed dog hair off his cuff. "Maybe his facts lined up too well, Val. I've thought back to the mock trials in law school. I think Martin lost cases by thrusting too many facts. He forgot that others hadn't a clue about the chemists' periodic table."

I dimly recalled the science chart in the Fourth Ward School in Virginia City, Nevada, the elements, noble gases, metals...none of it in memory today. "Something else, Roddy," I said. "Owen Coates seems to resent his older brother being groomed to take over the family business. Their father sent Martin to learn chemistry and law so he could take charge of the business."

"Businesses plural, if we add the Chicago real estate," Roddy added. "Martin was headed for the top, while Owen's future was...."

"Up for grabs?"

"From what we know."

"And jolting" I said, "to hear that Lydia Coates was courted by Owen. Her first suitor was the younger brother...."

"But the 'better man' won her," Roddy said. "Once again, the older brother succeeded."

"Until the rupture with their father."

In a silent moment, our thoughts converged. "Owen hinted that their father's stroke was Martin's doing..." I said, "and his death too...."

"Caused by the elder son." Roddy ran a hand through his hair. "Not quite a charge of patricide...."

"...but close." Our dog stirred, moved her paws, and napped. "So," I said, "the father's revenge...Martin is chained to Vitalene, Owen becomes a multi-millionaire, and Celia inherits one million dollars so she can forget about the Czech prince and set up artistic housekeeping on Washington Square with a 'family friend' from Oak Park, this Sara Dow." I added, "And all three of them except Celia suspected of committing murder."

My husband's 's creased forehead should have stopped me, a sure sign of worry that I ignored. "And who is the mysterious Chicago detective, Roddy? Martin did not name him. What is the evidence? What motive?"

I rushed on. "All through the awful dinner, we got no inkling that Owen knows he is suspected of killing his sister-in-law. Or knows that Martin is suspected. Or that Celia knows anything about her two brothers being suspects...or that woman who lives with her on Washington Square."

The dog raised her head to stare at me. "Maybe it's a hoax," I said. "Maybe Martin is trying to tangle us in the

Coates family feuds? Or a scheme somehow involving your partnership? What do you think?"

In the silence, the dog licked her paw and my husband bit his lip before he quietly said, "I think we need more information."

Roddy was right. More information, however, required further contact with the Coates brothers and their sister too, not to mention the live-in friend. Unsaid between us was one basic truth—that Roddy's budding partnership could depend on sorting out the facts.

My glance shifted to the vase of flowers. The jonquils stood up straight, the tulips drooped. "Roddy," I said, "I have an idea. You might remember the home decorator's name we heard from Celia? Households are hiring Elsie De Wolfe to...to freshen up their furniture."

"Freshen?"

"Change the styles...for changing tastes. We had the *Louisa* refurbished."

"A railroad car, my dear, is not a home."

True. The DeVere's private rail car had brought Roddy and his parents to Virginia City on the V&T Railroad so that his father could see about investing in the silver mines. If Roddy had not met and married me, the DeVeres would have lost their car in a forced sale. As it was, we had the car modernized after our wedding and renamed it for my late mother, Kathleen Louise. So far, the *Louisa* had ferried us on a quick trip to Florida and would, at some point, lure us to a leisurely cross-country tour. Meanwhile, a good friend was to take the car west toward Yellowstone Park later this spring. We extended the invitation because it seemed foolish to let the *Louisa* sit on a siding when a good friend could enjoy it.

"A railroad car is not a home," Roddy repeated. The edge in his voice startled the dog, who jumped down, crossed the room, and eyed us from her bed. It was almost lunchtime, and I would keep my idea to myself lest our midday meal be spoiled by home decoration and the Coates family. I would wait for the right moment.

What moment, however, would be right? Coincidentally, Celia Coates's Washington Square house was being reworked by a decorator known to favor light over the DeVeres' drab furniture that I had lived with since our wedding. The Queen Anne style house that Papa built for us in Virginia City was now home for women teachers at the Fourth Ward School, and I gladly left all the furnishings when I put the house into the Mackle Trust for the teachers. Here in New York, I had determined that one day I would choose my own things. The vase that my mother-in-law "assigned" for the flowers caught my eye, a garish ceramic carnival of painted leaves, stems, scrolls, and salamanders. The gate leg table had too many legs, and this was not the seventeenth century.

Roddy waited for me to speak. He looked around the drawing room. I stared at the floor. "What sort of change might you have in mind?"

"I'm...not quite certain...definitely less history."

"Our furnishings..." Roddy said, "are antiques from Europe, from my family... generations of Knickerbockers...."

He broke off, and I was mindful that my husband had lived with this furniture long before we met. To him, the inky dark chairs and tables and faded tapestries meant home. To me, it was a museum.

Our dog licked her paw. The room grew quiet until Roddy said, "Suppose you were to...initiate a change. What might it be?"

How could I say that "home" harkened to mountain cabins with simple pine tables and three-legged stools in mining camps?

"You do enjoy our home...our house?" he asked, his voice growing fretful. "...take this *Crème* drawing..."

"Shhh...." I put a finger across his lips. "You know I am devoted," I said, "to the *Crème* drawing room...and this divan where we...the two of us...."

"...made love," Roddy nearly whispered. We held hands and kissed. We smiled, both recalling the divan leg that splintered from our late night "exertions" and later needed repair. The dog settled her head between her paws. "So," my husband said, "we do enjoy the *Crème* drawing room. And otherwise—?"

"Otherwise...let me count on my fingers...the conservatory with its cheerful fountain and wonderful plants and light that pours in through the glass...and upstairs with the plush Bergere chairs and the cocktails that you mix...your billiard room...and the Corinthian room, which I don't like, but the formality is useful...."

"And your boudoir?" Roddy asked. "Your bedchamber?" He cocked his head. "Surely not my suite...." I replied that my husband's suite was not in jeopardy. "Then, suppose, my dear..." he said at length, "that you were to select one room to...adjust. Which would it be?"

Without hesitation, I replied, "The *Empire* reception room with the dark varnished furniture and wallpaper that feels like a fever dream...and that table with carvings like warts. And the upholstery with the lizards."

"Mother's *Empire* room," Roddy said, pronouncing the French. "Her special favorite. She loved that room."

I had not finished. "And that gloomy oil painting of your ancestor counting gold coins. The only light in the whole space, the coins."

"The 'School of Rembrandt,'" Roddy said. "Mother and Father purchased it in the Netherlands—"

"—and would enjoy it in their apartment around the corner," I said. "Chalmers and Bronson would wrap it carefully and walk it to them."

Roddy stroked his jaw, and I folded my hands and rested my case. "Lunchtime..." I said The tender new topic could wait. Roddy had not moved. It was not furniture on his mind.

"Roddy, you're worried about the partnership. I know it. The orange bitters...."

I watched him stare into a distance beyond this space. Our silence thundered. Velvet hunched on a corner of a rug. The Coates family swirled in mind, and I finally said, "So, your partnership with Martin hinges on finding out who pushed Lydia Coates down the stairs of her home."

"Unless she simply fell," my husband said. "Fell to her death, and her family and a friend are suspected of murder.

"By a Chicago detective on a wild goose chase…or not."

"Or not…."

The moment hung. My gaze drifted to the vase of flowers, tulips and salamanders, jonquils and the gate leg table. "Roddy," I said, "you are right. Our best bet is more information. Celia invited me to Washington Square, something like, 'You must come see me,' all vague and meaningless. But I could hold her to it." I grinned. "After all, a 'Western Gal' might not be expected to know a phony invitation from the real McCoy. The 'Gal' can take the 'invitation' at face value and drop in at Washington Square—unannounced."

Chapter Five

IDENTICAL BRICK TOWNHOUSES SPANNED
the north side of Washington Square, where trees were
budding, and grassy plats turning green. Each entrance was
flanked by Ionic or Doric columns, each house boasting
white marble balustrades.

Which one belonged to Celia Coates?

Our coachman slowed the carriage before the row of
once-fashionable houses that looked untouched since the
last brick was laid decades ago. Shortly after two p.m., a
stone mason pounded paving stones near the entrance
of Number Fourteen where a delivery wagon stood at the
curb as draymen hauled bulky cartons through an opened
front door.

"Noland," I called, "this must be it." Our ruddy coachman helped me to the sidewalk like an uncle uncertain about
a niece's venture. Roddy had gone to a club, where he hoped

a late lunch with Martin Coates would let him discuss the Chicago detective who made Lydia Coates's death a case of suspected murder.

"Please drive around the Square, Noland" I said, "and meet me in front of the house where the door is open...say, an hour."

The mason held his mallet while I approached the steps, and the draymen made way as I called "Hello...." Odors of fresh plaster and paint mixed with a heavy musk perfume. "Hello," I called again, standing at the threshold with my calling card and a small gift package.

Expecting a servant, I came face to face with Celia Coates dressed in gymnasium bloomers and a sailor's blouse. Her blonde hair was pinned back, and both wrists shimmered with bracelets set with colorful stones. She looked ready to berate whoever had interrupted her.

"Miss Coates...Celia Coates...good afternoon.... So pleased to pay a call."

Irritation became caution in the intense gray-green eyes. "I don't believe we've...."

"Met? Dinner at Sherry's...the night before last...with your brothers...."

"Of course...Mrs. DeVoe..."

"DeVere," I said. "Your kind invitation to pay a call at Washington Square...and here I am." Celia frowned, gripping the door handle. "I hail from the far West, Miss Coates, and we western women like to drop in for visits. We don't stand on ceremony. May I present my card...?"

Rules of etiquette, I had learned, required that a calling card be presented and received by a servant or put into a salver or basket. Celia peered at the card as if fangs might strike. She had not noticed the small package, which I held out. "A little something," I said, "...from the Louis Sherry chocolatier. Shall we put my card on the box?"

She held the candy box with my card face up, read the Fifth Avenue address, eyed my dark blue cashmere suit, and decided it was in her interest to receive me. She had not touched the card.

We entered an anteroom with a willow chair, an hourglass Chinese chair, and a small table where she set the box. "Won't you sit down?" Her graceful hand swept the room. "Before artistry, welcome to chaos," she said. "Miss De Wolfe, my gem of a decorator, assures me it's all for the best, but we tussle. She is upstairs at this minute arguing with a plumber about steam heat...I side with the plumber."

"New arrangements," I said, "can be disruptive." Sharp voices echoed from an upper floor, but Celia offered no explanation. Musk perfume scented the space, and she rose as the draymen passed through the center hall, ordered them to "tiptoe on a cloud" and "rest" their load in the dining room. When they had "tiptoed" out, Celia closed the front door, sat beside me once again, and said, "I fear the Coates family was not at our best at dinner."

"Mr. DeVere and I appreciated the evening," I said. "And the new Sherry's is elegant. I understand that the building's upper floors are apartments...living quarters."

"...for my brother, for instance," she said. "Owen has taken a sizable suite. Didn't Martin tell you?"

"No, he didn't," I said. "Your brother was my husband's law school classmate. The dinner was meant to renew acquaintance after several years...and introduce us to Owen...and to you." I paused. "We had learned of your sister-in-law's sad passing but had had not known about the children."

"Lester and Tansy...Letitia is Tansy." Her smile flashed briefly. "How I missed them in my London years. Lester is packed off to prep school in New England, most likely to take him off Martin's shoulders." She sighed. "My brother works all the time, always did, and Lydia busied herself in a godforsaken charity in the slums, so it's just as well that she and Owen went their separate ways, even though he became a most devoted brother-in-law...utterly devoted." She tilted her head.

"Things often work out for the best," I said, staying neutral.

"In their case..." she said. "my late sister-in-law would have been a thorn in Owen's side...huge nuisance for a polo player.... 'Bleeding heart' Lydia, they called her, all pity for the ponies."

"Owen plays polo?" I asked.

"Polo...fox hunting...whatever with horses. With Martin, it was books and test tubes, but you'd find Owen in the saddle, at a horse show, at a racetrack. The family joke about Owen and Lydia was how they met in a stall. Aren't you curious?"

She gazed at me, expecting a "yes."

"We told you about them at Sherry's, remember? ...before the asparagus...or maybe the duckling.... Lydia and Owen, their 'romance'...it started when Lydia Anne Gerstle spent the night in a stall to keep a 'lonesome, ailing' horse company. Can you imagine?

She laughed. "Truer than fiction, Owen found her in the morning in a bed of straw beside the horse. The two hit it off...until the romance 'stalled.'" With a sly smile, she adjusted her bracelets. "Stall..." she said, "and 'stalled.'" She winked, and I smiled.

"Then..." I said, "it was Martin...."

"...who picked up the pieces, steady as a rock, so they thought. Our poor father—rest his soul—he did not know what to make of her or my sportsman brother...or me. He worried I might lose everything at a Mayfair roulette wheel or dash off to Monte Carlo. Or disappear with the Czech...." She sighed. "'Never fear,' I wrote, and wrote again until my secretary's fingers cramped. No confidence in my judgment or Owen's, and now here we are. But Tansy...poor dear Tansy will rattle around the big drafty Oak Park house, now that Owen is here...and Sara too. You must meet her."

"Miss Dow?" I said. "She's here?"

"At the moment, Sara is at the Tiffany studio seeing about my order...my latest order." Celia flashed her colorful bracelets. "Another two, identical to these," she said, "and inside my house, nobody would bother to swipe them. Workmen think they're colored glass."

She pointed at the colors. "Sapphires...emeralds...rubies. I like the emeralds best."

Just then, a workman tapped at the doorway, a huge wrench in one hand and a toolbox in the other. "Pardon, ma'am, maybe you need a brick mason, not a plumber. Missus Wolfe thinks a mason...I'll be going."

He thumped off with a heavy tread as light footsteps came nearer from an upper floor. Celia pushed up her sleeves . "Here we go," she said. "I will introduce you to Miss Elsie De Wolfe."

A slender woman in a coffee-colored tailored jacket and pleated skirt saw me, frowned, and struck a theatrical pose. "Miss Coates..." she said, arching an eyebrow in a face with regular features and a crown of softly curled hair. "If you might give me a moment's time, Miss Coates...?

Celia arranged her bracelets, stood, and introduced me as a "surprise" caller who was "ever so welcome."

"You must excuse my haste, Mrs. DeVere" Elsie De Wolfe said in a voice both calm and firm, "but Miss Coates and I have much work to do as the days lengthen in this marvelous springtime light. So, if I might have a few minutes?"

"As many minutes as you wish, Miss De Wolfe," Celia said. "I have not changed my mind one iota. I am set on steam heat. Americans love steam heat, and fireplaces are a dirty nuisance. If you spent time in drafty England as I have, shivering and chilled to the bone, you would think differently."

"Actually, Miss Coates," said the decorator in a cool, even voice, "I am well versed in British customs, but my recommendation stands. I am in favor of the normal heat of sunshine and open fires, especially in a smaller house such as yours, which can be easily overheated."

I was persuaded. Celia looked defiant.

"It is a distinct irritation," the decorator continued, "for a person who loves clean air to enter a room where a flood of steam heat pours out of every corner. Your ambition for a *salon*, my dear lady, will suffer terribly."

At the threat to her *salon*, Celia's bracelets jangled, as if the decorator had touched them with a live electrical wire. A startled Celia reluctantly began to yield to the idea of wood-burning fireplaces and "well-proportioned" mantels.

"...and mirrors," Elsie DeWolfe continued, "because, you see, this house is narrow in the extreme, and the secret of a successful *salon* is a renaissance of windows and mirrors—mirrors! The skillfully managed reflections hold the secret of allure!"

The decorator plucked a watch from a neck chain. "I must be going...regrets for the intrusion, Mrs. DeVere... my principles of home décor laid bare, but good taste is my mission.... Now, my hansom cab ought to be outside."

Elsie De Wolfe and I said farewell to Celia, who invited me to come again. "Your card," she said, "will tuck nicely in a new mirror frame. I won't forget...and Miss De Wolfe, don't disappoint me. I will expect you...on schedule." At the door, her shoulders back, Celia's gray-green eyes narrowed as she said, "I will expect you both."

Elsie De Wolfe and I waved farewell with our gloved hands when Celia closed her front door and walked to the curb where Noland waited with the brougham. Miss De Wolfe admired our high-stepping Hackney carriage horse, Atlas, and I mentioned that he was matched with Apollo, both horses a team, depending on carriage size. We chatted for a moment, though her hanson cab was nowhere in sight. I offered her a ride. "...to East Fifty-fifth Street?" I said. "Why, Miss De Wolfe, it's on my way." Noland assisted us both into the carriage, and for the next hour I made further acquaintance with the most sought-after home decorator in New York City.

⁂

"So, she will come to inspect our furnishings? And decide what stays and what goes?"

My alarmed husband put aside some folded papers on a sofa cushion in his study. I had changed into an evening dress of dotted tulle for the evening and burst into Roddy's study with news about Elsie De Wolfe.

Which was a mistake.

"Val, we agreed that you would visit Celia, just as I met with Martin. We both sought information, but somehow the new topic is Miss De Wolfe and our furniture?"

"Roddy, Miss De Wolfe will pay a courtesy call to see about the *Empire* room. She will make time in her busy schedule as a favor, and you and I agreed...."

"Agreed to consider it," Roddy replied, irritation in his eyes.

I had not noticed our dog lounging under a table, but her "bat" ears popped up, and I called, "Velvet...come, girl...."

French bulldogs were notoriously single minded, and my husband seemed pleased that the dog disobeyed. We were tit for tat.

Perched on a sofa arm, I eyed the folded papers on the cushion. "Are those documents?"

"Of a sort."

"Should I guess?"

"That's up to you."

I touched my pouting husband's hair, his cheek. "Where are we?" I asked softly.

"Out of sorts," he replied.

"Then…we must get ourselves into 'sorts'…on this sofa…?" His deep blue eyes slowly met my lingering gaze. "Remember, Roddy DeVere, we vowed…"

His voice softened. "…to make love in every room of this house."

"Every single one, starting with this sofa in your suite?"

Before my husband could respond, a light tap on the doorframe brought us both to startled attention. A glance at the polished shoes, the formal trousers and coat meant our butler, Sands, who apologized but wished us to know that dinner would be delayed because of "an unanticipated event in the kitchen."

"What 'event?'" I asked, but Roddy said, "Never mind, Sands. Ask a footman to bring a plate of snacks and my wheeled cart to the Green drawing room. Meanwhile, do ask a footman to take Velvet for her evening feeding."

Sands bowed out, and Roddy whispered that this sofa would be our next "favored" spot—and soon. For the moment, he would quickly dress for dinner and meet me by the Bergere chairs where he would mix us a cocktail to keep us in "sorts" while we talked over the matter of Martin Coates and his sister.

In twenty minutes, Roddy joined me in the drawing room wearing a silk dinner suit and ready for the wheeled tea wagon that had been adapted as a portable bar. A quick kiss, and I sat while he selected bottles, glasses, a lime, and ice that he plucked with tongs from a silver bucket. He soon poured two cocktails into dazzling Waterford crystal glasses, and handed one to me.

"What magic potion have we here?" I asked.

"A crystal tribute to your Irish lineage and a drink in honor of my Dutch ancestry. Presenting the Knickerbocker cocktail in Waterford crystal. Salud, my dear."

The crystal chimed, we sipped, and I said, "Delicious!"

The Knickerbocker

Ingredients

- 1 wineglass Jamaica rum
- 1 dash *Curaçao*
- 3 dashes raspberry syrup
- Juice of ½ lemon or lime
- Cracked ice

Directions:

1. Squeeze lemon or lime into mixing glass with small amount of ice.
2. Add all other ingredients.
3. Stir well, stain, and serve in fancy glass.

We sat with a tray of nuts and cheese straws. "So," Roddy said, "how fares the newest householder on Washington Square? You met with her?"

"Indeed, I did...barged in with a box of chocolates and my card. Celia answered the door, Roddy...no servant on hand. She welcomed me to the 'chaos' of a house going through remodeling, but she first took careful note of our Fifth Avenue address and my suit. I thought she might finger the fabric."

"But she recalled our dinner...?"

"She did. The Coates family were not at their 'best,' she admitted, and she expanded on the family history...described her late sister-in-law as overly sentimental about animals and a misfit for her sportsman brother who nonetheless stayed loyal to her when she married Martin."

I nibbled a cheese straw. "I doubt that Celia and Lydia were ever close, Roddy. She strikes me as stubborn and flighty...apt to chatter before thinking of the consequences... and bold. One major issue is her *salon*. Whatever her idea for a future in the city, the *salon* is first and foremost."

Roddy sipped his drink. "Did you meet Miss Dow?"

"Not this afternoon. I was told Sara Dow was representing Celia at the Tiffany studios...for jeweled bracelets. Celia's fondness for gemstones was evident on both wrists."

Roddy rubbed his cheek. "Tiffany is no bazaar. The clerks will not haggle." He took a long sip of his cocktail.

"So...so what?"

"Simply this...that Miss Dow's purpose is to curb Celia's extravagance."

"I don't understand," I said.

Roddy plucked a walnut and paused. "My lunch with Martin was... complicated. He's worried about Celia. Invested carefully, her inheritance ought to see her through, but one million dollars will not last long at the rate she spends. Martin remembers invoices from London for silver and gowns, silk rugs, a household staff.... Their father paid without a qualm."

"But he left the bulk of the fortune to Owen...."

"Martin says he can't account for it...thinks their father might have intended to 'spank' her for the Czech prince. He also imagines their father might have relied on Owen to pay her bills. The father's will contains a codicil about the Coates heirs in 'future family continuity,' but Martin did not explain what it means. Or perhaps he is not certain."

"Or else he thinks that it's none of your business?"

"That too." Roddy sipped his drink. "In any case, Martin encouraged Sara Dow to come to New York for the time being. Miss Dow is to be a steadying influence."

"The 'family friend' as a sedative? Not at Tiffany...unless Miss Dow went to cancel the order for a set of jeweled bracelets." I shifted in my chair. "What else about Martin? Did he talk about the family...situation?"

Roddy paused. "He did, both eagerly and reluctantly. He desperately wants to get rid of Vitalene...and rid of the detective who is 'hounding' the household."

"That's his term, 'hounding?'"

"He said the detective 'pesters' and 'torments,' and he flinched when I inquired about 'circumstantial evidence in the case.'"

"When you spoke as one attorney to another?"

"I tried, but Martin has let his law license expire, and his horror at the detective's investigation—as he termed it, 'witch hunt'—has apparently blurred his reasoning. He couldn't bring himself to utter the word, 'investigation.'"

"Who is this 'tormenting' detective? Did he say?"

"Only briefly...a man named Brady, who Martin thinks he might recall from grammar school in Oak Park...supposes that he joined the Chicago police, got promoted, but kept in touch with Oak Park connections, maybe with family members. He seems to think that you and I could alight in Chicago and persuade Detective Brady to abandon his 'witch hunt.'"

"But Martin has no idea why Brady suspects the Coates brothers or their woman friend of murdering his wife?"

"Claims it is 'beyond him.'"

"But Vitalene is not 'beyond?'"

"Martin is razor-sharp on that score, Val. We talked about the Pure Food Movement, and Martin is right about public alarm. All over the country, reformers are telling everyone who will listen that we need a law to protect what we eat, what we drink, and what we put into our bodies for cures and health. People are listening...and legal action is in sight. Those 'documents' you noticed in my study?"

"Yes?"

Martin gave me an envelope of them...advertisements for hair restorers, liver pills, plasters for 'malaria.' You might take a look, Val. There's Hamlin's Wizard Oil, Holloway's Ointment, Radam's Microbe Killer...."

"And Vitalene...?"

"...for 'Low Spirits' and 'Liver Complaint.' Martin admits the company has paid nearly half a million dollars on salesmen and advertising...which is also a public nuisance. You've seen the painted slogans...?"

"'*Vital Spirits with Vitalene!*' I once counted the many advertisements painted on boulders and barns from Virginia City to Reno. Papa said they defaced nature and disgraced the barns."

"All snake oil medicines," Roddy said, "but Martin pointed out 'snake oil' bitters too...Dogwood Bitters, Old Sachem Bitters.... And National Bitters...'If You Wish Life's Perfect Health.'"

I finished my cocktail. "So," I said, "Martin leaned hard, so you will not dream of withdrawing from the partnership."

Roddy put his glass down. "Val," he said, "I have thrown away countless bottles of 'Angostura' bitters. The name is a village in Venezuela, but the mixture supposedly comes from Trinidad. The contents are anyone's guess." He added, "Martin says he will not return to Chicago until I promise that we will clear up the 'misunderstanding.'"

"About the 'watch hunt?'" Roddy nodded. "And what did you say?"

"That we will consider it?"

For Roderick DeVere, the word, "consider," would have to mean something.

"Next steps…" I said. "Another lunch with Martin?"

Maybe…but first, I will invite Owen to a private sale of horses…Dutch Warmbloods, best suited to jumping and driving. And afterwards, he must join me for a drink, and we'll see. And you, my dear?"

"I will pay a call on Washington Square to meet Miss Sara Dow," I said. "I will invite Cassie to go with me. Two heads better than one."

Chapter Six

RODDY'S EYES CRINKLED AT "two heads," know-ing our friend might add insight but also sense unearthly "vapors" if she came to Washington Square. Cassie Forster (Cassandra Van Schylar Fox Forster...Mrs. Dudley Forster) had become my close friend in these East Coast years. We had met and bonded at Newport in the summertime, the Irish newcomer and the blue-blood Knickerbocker young matron and mother of two young children.

Married to a scientist whose expeditions took him across oceans for months at a time, Cassie was the head-of-household for long stretches while rearing her children in ways high Society censored. Children of her class were expected to be bathed, dressed, and presented to their par-ents only at appointed times of the day for inspection, then dismissed to the nursery to take their meals and lessons far from the adults' domains. Instead, Cassie welcomed young

Charlie and little Beatrice to the breakfast room in the mornings and gave them free rein in the Forsters' Italian Renaissance mansion on Madison Avenue—which Society found alarming.

More alarming still, Cassie was subject to "auras" and special "intuitions" that started in childhood and persisted to this day. As Mrs. Dudley Forster, my friend remained in good standing in the elite "Four Hundred." Annually invited to Mrs. Astor's ball, she was thought prone to "nervous superstition" that some thought should be treated by a specialist.

Cassie's fierce mother blamed a certain nanny from the Caribbean for "warping" her daughter, but Cassie loved Saffira of the Islands, though playmates sometimes shunned the child who fell into trances. Roddy remembered dancing school when Cassie "swooned" in the middle of a quadrille lesson.

"I might have 'swooned' at our wreck of a formal dinner the other night," I said to Roddy. "Cassie was the soul of good manners during the burned lamb...sparkling conversation with dinner companions...pretended not to hear the crash and clatter. She was poised and charming even though the dinner honored her husband's departure for the seven seas."

Roddy rubbed his jaw, and slowly said, "...if you think that Cassie is your best bet for a visit to Washington Square, Val...."

With preparation, yes," I said. Roddy still had doubts when my friend suggested a springtime afternoon outing. I agreed to go with her to fitting at an uptown dressmaker's studio, then to tea at the Palm Room. My maid asked, "Which dressmaker?"

"M. A. Connelly," I said.

"You'll want to look smart, ma'am."

How right she was. Cassie said the Irish-born Mary Connelly had dressed the ladies of Society for decades. Her "Branch Houses" blossomed from Paris to Washington, D.C., and to Newport during the summer season. The M.A. Connelly label sewn in a gown or wrap stood up to Worth or Redfern, and her hard work had made her rich.

"Ma'am," said Calista, "I suggest the *aubergine* long skirt."

"Eggplant," I said.

"And matching jacket with the Watteau fold down the front."

I loathed the neckline, which tickled and scratched. But the outfit would pass muster at Miss Connelly's, so I agreed and asked Calista to find a hat.

My friend took my arm as we set off to the Connelly salon, but she seemed lost in thought as we walked side by side on a cool and breezy afternoon. I did not probe. Privacy in friendship was our pact. If a family issue with Dudley or the children had arisen before he set sail, I would, or would not, hear about it. We spoke little before reaching the 331 Fifth Avenue studio of the renowned Irish American designer.

Seated on a plush side chair in the sizable fitting room, I tugged at the scratchy neckline of my jacket and tried to enjoy the latest fitting of my friend's gown, a confection of silk and satin, ruffles, lace, and bows in warm gold and green, cream and ivory. Cassie's natural "hourglass" figure did not require corsets, and every inch of her five feet in height fit the ideal of today's fashion. Her lustrous auburn hair and creamy complexion glowed in the studio light, but her brown eyes looked troubled.

"Madame Connelly will be with you presently, Mrs. Forster. Please do not move…remember the pins…." Smocked assistants fluttered around the carpeted platform on which my friend stood, swathed in acres of sumptuous fabrics—and a portrait of misery.

"Mrs. Forster," a supervisor intoned, "Miss Connelly for you…."

The "Irish Sensation" swept into the space with poised efficiency. Her blue eyes twinkled and judged, and she chafed her palms as if holding the fabrics in hand. The illustrious M. A. Connelly was nearing the end of her career in couture, and every Society lady had raced to make an appointment for a gown, a street costume, a wrap or bonnet. The grand finale of orders was rumored to be staggering.

Cassie's gown, ordered months ago, was ready for its final touches.

Why did she look so miserable?

Madame Connelly raised a pinkie finger, and a smocked young woman hastened to adjust the width of a panel by a smidgeon of an inch. The doyenne of couture stood back, nodded, smiled approval, and said, "Mrs. Forster, I do hope you are pleased."

Her soft Irish brogue lulled me to thoughts of the mother I had never known.

Lost in thought as Cassie was helped from the platform, I barely noticed the moments slipping by, when my friend reappeared, already in streetwear.

"Time for tea," she said.

One hansom ride, and Cassie and I were seated in the Waldorf Hotel Palm Room. Cassie requested a far table closest to a potted palm. Her voice sounded strained, and our tea and cucumber sandwiches sat untouched.

"Unless the palms have ears," she said, "we can talk. There's something on my mind...."

"Cassie," I said, "...if this is about our calamitous dinner in honor of Dudley's voyage, let me apologize...we'll have a chef in the future...."

"Heavens...." She patted my hand. "Put your mind at ease, Valentine DeVere. My Dudley was delighted, and so was I...so were all your guests." She paused. "A most pleasant evening."

My friend's face showed concern beyond the dinner. "Cassie," I said, "you know I will not pry, but if I can help...."

She took a deep breath, sipped her tea, and looked me in the eye. "Val," she said, "I fear you will dismiss what I am about to say. Promise that you will listen generously."

"I will do my best," I said. Would I hear of marital rupture? Illness? The children?

Cassie arched her fingers over the tablecloth as if she were about to play the piano. Her pink nails were shaped by a new manicure.

"Madam Riva," I murmured.

Cassie nodded. "She did my nails this morning. I asked her to come. Dudley had an appointment with a ship captain…and Cara has the children for the day."

"But you requested a manicure?"

"I needed Madam Riva's counsel."

I dreaded to ask, "Surely not for a séance…?" My friend sometimes seemed captive to her mercenary manicurist, Madam Riva, whose séances struck me as costly hocus-pocus. "…a séance?" I murmured.

"For better understanding of my 'visions,' Val…."

I signaled the waiter for hot water. "What sort of 'understanding?'"

Her fingers clutched at the tablecloth. "You have witnessed my 'spells.'"

"You sometimes get dizzy," I replied.

"It's not dizziness. It's…like entering other spaces…taken captive by auras that others do not see…or feel. Dudley worries that the children could be harmed. He has heard of a specialist in Switzerland who treats such…disorders."

"Switzerland…." I worked to keep my voice low.

"In Zurich," she said. "A treatment with cold baths and electrical currents."

"Surely not, Cassie…."

"Not right away…not until Dudley returns from the South Seas…some reefs with special fossils." She sipped her tea. "I agreed to think it over. I asked Madam Riva to help me."

How would a charlatan manicurist who pretended to be a Romanian princess and bamboozled Society ladies with nighttime séances possibly help my friend?

I had tried to tell Cassie why I resisted superstition, horoscopes, séances, the whole irrational business. I explained how my papa fought wild rumors that swirled in the silver mines, how a crew would refuse to work when one man dreamed of a collapsing shaft or a fire. Catastrophes occurred often enough, Papa said, without farfetched stories.

I said these things but admitted to myself that Cassie Forster's premonitions sometimes came to pass. I could not wholly dismiss her visions. The coincidences sometimes proved uncanny. Her feelings of physical shock at times summoned visions from the past...or foretold dire events in the future.

"Val, I am trying to say something you ought to hear."

Her "ought" stopped me. "Please..." I said.

"My visions..." Cassie said at last, "come unbidden, but I have promised Dudley to try my best to stop them. I promised to practice from now on, like this afternoon at the fitting. If I succeed, we will have no more talk of Zurich." She took a sandwich.

"So..." I said, "for the sake of harmony at home...."

Cassie nodded. "I am to go about life as usual...this afternoon's fitting for the spring ball...our tea...and soon, the Coaching Club parade." She saw my face. "Oh, sorry, Val. I forgot how you dislike it. Let's think of something else to do."

"Cassie," I said, "would you come to Washington Square with me? We could we be two ladies visiting the townhouse of Miss Celia Coates. I will introduce you, and we will meet Miss Coates's companion, a woman named Sara Dow. Let me explain...."

My husband stood over a dozen corked bottles on a zinc-topped table and reached for a brown bottle and shot glass. He did not see me come in when he lifted the bottle, measured carefully, took a sip, then emptied the shot into a little pail and reached for a bottle of water. His coat was off, his shirtsleeves rolled to the elbow.

"Hello..." I said softly, watching him push the brown bottle aside, drink the water and wink "hello." This "laboratory" space inside his suite was Roddy's "Libation Foundation" where he experimented with cocktails. I had just come from tea at the Palm Room, and the hansom cab stopped to let me off before going on to the Forster home a few blocks away on Madison Avenue.

"Trying out a whiskey Dewey Cocktail, my dear..." Roddy said, "but I think gin will be a better choice. The committee is eager. We're just a few months away...."

I nodded, well aware of the three-day celebration next September with military parades, a yacht race, and fireworks blazing over the harbor in honor of Admiral George Dewey's conquest of the Spanish fleet in Manila Bay in the

Philippines. The nation had gone "Dewey mad," and next September in New York would be the biggest and boldest celebration.

Planning the Dewey cocktail, Roddy would also need to defend taverns against the Temperance battalions. He had his hands full. For the sake of his business partnership, must he take on the Coates family's problems? Must we?

"The Dewey cocktail," I asked, "will it include bitters?"

"Dash of orange bitters, for sure," Roddy answered. I pointed to the zinc table, and my husband reached for one small bottle. "This one..." he said, "Calvertine's Best Orange Bitters."

"Is it best?"

"Others are worse" Roddy said. "Vast room for improvement. Shall we sit down?"

We sat on the pearl-gray suede sofa in Roddy's suite. The afternoon with Cassie was worrisome, from the exquisite gown to her turmoil and fears. Roddy offered to mix a drink, but I said, not yet. Tempted to ask about Martin, I held back, but his brother came into the conversation. Owen had accepted the invitation to the private sale of horses.

"The Dutch...what are they?"

"Warmbloods," Roddy said. "...full, deep chests and long, straight backs...good for the saddle, good to pull a light trap." I felt his sideways glance. "...and no, my dear, the Dutch Warmbloods are not for western ranches."

"Nothing like my Comet," I said. On the New York bridle paths, astride my buckskin quarter horse, I had given

Society a season's titillation, especially at the sight of me astride the military McClellan saddle that felt much safer than that equestrian terror, a lady's sidesaddle.

"You talked with Cassandra, Val? And she agrees to visit Washington Square?"

"She does," I said. "We will pay a call. This time, no dropping in unannounced…. Etiquette to the fullest. You know Cassie."

"I do…since she and I were raised under the same regime…dancing school with curtsies and bows. And so," Roddy continued, "you told her about the whole situation?"

"Most of it," I said.

Roddy rolled his shirt sleeves down. And what did you omit, my dear?"

"Can't you guess?"

"That Miss Coates's brothers are suspected of murder? And her friend too?"

"Cassie need not know such a thing, Roddy."

He gave me a side-eye glance. "A need-to-know basis? And what if Cassandra has one of her 'spells' in Washington Square?"

"Oh, Roddy…."

"I'm not joking. Washington Square was fashionable in our grandparents' day, and those townhouses had scandals… jilted lovers, fortunes embezzled. Suppose Cassandra sees a ghost…."

"Stop it, Roddy. Cassie does not see ghosts."

"Then, what…?"

"I...I don't know." Truly, I did not. Neither did my husband. Yet Roddy's hint that I had shaded the truth about Celia did sting. And Sara Dow...who was she? I told Cassie that I had not met her. We would pay a social call, and my friend would practice shutting down the feelings that threatened her with Switzerland.

❧

Our visit to Washington Square coincided with new, blue furniture in Celia's townhouse sitting room. A week had passed since my first visit, and the house had emerged from "chaos." Chairs and tables were set on a Persian rug patterned with tiny camels on a sea blue background.

"I have gone mad about blue," Celia said. "Forgive me, I must rave on."

Our hostess had received the calling cards that Cassie and I presented to an aproned maid who replied that Miss Coates was "at home" to Mrs. DeVere and Mrs. Forster." The maid led us to a much-mirrored sitting room decorated in vibrant shades of blue, including Celia's robin's egg blue afternoon dress with a royal blue stole over one shoulder. The seating arrangement faced a wall painted with fish and flowers in aquatic tones. The paint looked wet.

"Don't you love it?" Celia said.

"A mural..." Cassie murmured.

"...by Armand, an artist and newest friend here in the city," Celia replied. "I gave him *carte blanche* when he said that plain walls are the refuge of the artistically destitute." She touched her bosom. "Armand persuades me that a wall is a blank canvas."

"Indeed…a point of view," Cassie said. Seated on Chippendale chairs with blue cushions, we were promised tea, but so far, no sign of Sara Dow. The familiar jeweled bracelets winked on Celia's wrists. If new ones had come from Tiffany, they were not in sight.

"I trust that Miss De Wolfe has been helpful," I said.

"To a point," said Celia, "but no further. Miss De Wolfe and I have parted ways. On the topic of color, I believe the celebrated decorator is color-blind. I have dismissed her."

At that moment, the maid appeared with a tea tray, followed by a willowy woman whose sweeping glance seemed to appraise the scene with watchful calculation. Her bright red shirtwaist with flaring sleeves and a high, notched collar looked somehow oriental, as did hairpins that stuck out at angles…like lacquered sticks in her jet-black hair. A dainty mouth and narrow nose were offset by wide-set, huge dark eyes that somehow fell short of warmth. She smiled with reserve while Celia introduced us while the maid set out the tea and little buns. In moments, it was clear that Miss Sara Dow would pour the tea, making her the afternoon's hostess.

"So, you have recently come to New York, Miss Dow?" I said, accepting my cup of tea in off-white china, the only non-blue item in sight.

"New York, yes" she said, "but Washington D.C. in years past…and then the world…of course, Oak Park…Chicago."

Her voice was slightly husky. She had poured tea for Cassie, then Celia. On closer look, Sara Dow was not young.

"Sara has traveled the world," Celia said. "Tell them, Sara. Was it Constantinople before China?"

"Constantinople, then Bucharest...and Peking at last." She gave Cassie and me a small smile. "My father, you see, was an envoy...in diplomatic legations."

"Tell about the soup in China," Celia said. "I love that story. Tell what you saw when the lid was lifted."

Sara Dow only smiled and offered the buns. "Chinese cuisine," she said, "relies on frying and steaming. Please try one....do...."

Celia pouted, and Cassie hesitated, but I knew those buns from Virginia City, where Chinese immigrants relocated after they built the railroad. I reached for a bun, and Cassie followed when I said, "Delicious...red bean filling."

"Mrs. DeVere," said Sara, "you seem familiar with this 'crumpet.' Have you traveled?"

The question usually would invite a social link, but her tone sounded like fact-finding.

"Mrs. DeVere comes from the West. She told me so," Celia said, adjusting the stole over her shoulder. She signaled for a refill of tea. "Will you tell us an amusing story of the Wild West, Mrs. DeVere? Cattle rustlers?"

Cassie looked as appalled as I felt. So far, Celia blocked my efforts to learn anything about Sara Dow's connection to the Coates family. "I suggest you read Mr. Mark Twain's

Roughing It," I said, "and plan to see the Buffalo Bill show when it comes back to New York."

I sipped my tea. "Perhaps, Miss Dow," I said, "you have seen Buffalo Bill Cody's show in Chicago?"

Her eyes quickly fluttered. "I did see that mad circus," she said, "before acquaintance with Lydia...the late Lydia."

The tone changed at once, as if the blue room darkened. Celia's gaze lowered to the carpet.

"Lydia explained all about the animals...the cruelty," Sara said. "I saw the live animal markets in Peking but paid no attention. Then, Lydia Anne Gerstle changed my mind... to the day she left this earth, and her voice is ever with me."

I glanced at Cassie, who simply nodded. "So," I said, "Lydia was Miss Gerstle when you met?"

"Not for long. Celia's brother introduced us."

"Owen?" I asked.

"No, it was Martin. At the time, I traveled often from St. Louis to points distant...the mercantile life, you see."

"'Mercantile?'" asked Cassie. Gripping the cup and saucer, her fingers looked taut, her knuckles white.

My friend's tone was gentle, but Sara looked as if an insect had whined.

"Traveling salesladies spend days on trains," she said. "I traveled on behalf of Vitalene...."

Stunned, I stayed quiet. At some point after her world travel, this woman had been a traveling saleswoman for the vile elixir. How did she become a close friend of the woman who loathed it and urged her husband to give it up?

Sara offered the buns. I alone accepted. She turned to me. "Martin's father suggested that I leave the road and help Mr. and Mrs. Coates...Martin and Lydia...and so I did. Trains can be wearying...and then a wreck...a car jumped the tracks at midnight...I was fortunate."

She said no more. I nibbled the bun that was now cold and doughy. So, a near-miss on the rails drew Sara Dow to Oak Park at the urging of Martin's father. Her assignment—to quell Lydia's abhorrence of the Coates's profitable tonic and keep Martin on course as head of the business. From what we knew, her mission had failed. Yet here she was, supposedly sent to curb Celia's appetite for whatever costly trinkets caught the younger woman's fancy.

The maid tiptoed in to ask whether we might need assistance, meaning that our teatime was at an end. We offered the customary thank-you and murmured about calling once again. The off-white cups and saucers annoyed Celia, who promised that tea would soon be served on new china.

"I'm thinking Wedgwood..." she said as we were shown to the door. "... count on Wedgwood...until I see about Minton. And does Lalique make blue glass dishes? Do either of you know? Do you? Surely you know...."

Chapter Seven

"QUITE AN INTERESTING AFTERNOON...," I said as Cassie and I settled in the hansom cab that took us uptown from Washington Square. "Quite interesting..." I repeated, having learned conversational "openers" since coming from the West, where we got right to the point.

Cassie gripped the ivory handle of her parasol. "Two intriguing ladies..." she said, staying quiet as a small locomotive shrieked from the "El" in the distance and the cab moved into the Thirties...31st Street, 32nd Street...33rd.

My friend's silence continued for blocks. Her knuckles whitened on the ivory handle.

"Cassie," I said, "have you ever seen such a fanciful interior wall...fish and flowers in every shade of blue?"

Her little smile was gentle and sly. "Not since my Charlie and Bea got hold of paints and brushes to 'decorate' their daddy's study wall...I think Charlie was four, and Bea just two...."

We chuckled. Cassie described the easels and watercolor sets that Dudley gave their "artistic" children, along with a special request to let all household walls alone. "So, perhaps Miss Coates might furnish her artist friend an easel and canvasses," Cassie said. We laughed.

"And Miss Sara Dow," I said, "...have you ever heard of traveling sales ladies?"

"Not so far, Val, only sales ladies behind counters at department stores. But times are changing, aren't they? Difficult to keep up...so difficult...."

My friend lapsed into silence again, and her grip on the parasol never once relaxed the entire way to the upper East Side. Once again, I said good-by at my front entrance, and the hansom took Cassie to her Madison Avenue home, where her beloved husband feared her auras would harm their children. Cassie, I guessed, had less than one year to prove that she need not be sent to Zurich.

愉

A remark about my friend frantically clutching her teacup and gripping her parasol handle would seem unimportant to my husband, though I burst with news about Sara Dow. "Listen to this, Roddy...."

He turned from his bar cart that was wheeled into the *Crème* drawing room. "Are you listening?"

"Listening," he said. Roddy was already dressed for dinner, which was unusual.

"So," I said, "Sara peddled Vitalene until Martin's father inveigled her into the Coates home. She was to persuade Lydia and Martin that the elixir is harmless. Not only that," I continued, "her every word about Lydia was spoken in tones of endearment, almost worshipful. But the fact is, Sara Dow was Martin's father's hired accomplice."

Roddy sucked his cheek and moved tongs to the ice bucket.

"And Martin's wife called the medicine 'shameful,' Roddy. We remember he told us Lydia said Vitalene is 'shameful.'"

"He did. We remember." My husband arranged spoons and a cocktail shaker.

"But here is Sara Dow on Washington Square with Martin's approval. He sent her here to curtail his sister's spending. I don't understand...."

"We don't understand...yet."

"And Cassie was strangely silent all the way back."

"I'd guess Dudley's departure is much on Cassandra's mind, Val."

Roddy said that he hoped to learn more from Owen very soon. "Meanwhile, my dear, we have a guest."

Panic...had I failed the social calendar, again? Roddy quickly put his arm around me. "Val, sorry...no worries. Theo telephoned to suggest that he might visit to have a word about Yellowstone Park and the *Louisa.* I invited him to come dine with us...and have a drink at the cocktail hour."

Limp, that wet noodle feeling of relief. Theo Bulkeley was a good friend. He was always welcome. "You spoke with Theo on the actual telephone?" I asked.

"Clear as a bell...no pun on Alexander Graham Bell. I think the telephone is here to stay. We'll soon be using it informally...no servants involved."

"That will be...different," I said. Our telephone, installed in a back hallway, let the butler call the stable for saddle horses or a carriage. Otherwise, the "phone" connected to pharmacies or doctors' offices, even department stores. Etiquette meant the butler and housekeeper took turns speaking into the wood box mounted on a wall. I had sensed 'phone rivalry between Mr. Sands and our housekeeper, Mrs. Thwaite, who had continued to visit her sister to help with spring cleaning in a town far upstate.

Roddy's parents "bequeathed" the housekeeper to us when they abruptly moved into his former bachelor apartment. Rufus and Eleanor had hired a new butler and household staff, but Mrs. Thwaite stuck with us like glue. I suspected she was in league with Roddy's mother, a pipeline for gossip on the Wild West daughter-in-law. In her absence these few weeks, the household felt as though a drill sergeant said, "At ease, troops."

By six p.m. I had changed into a mint-green silk dinner gown when Sands announced, "Mr. Theodore Bulkeley."

Our tall, slim bachelor friend entered with apologies for elbowing in at this "unseemly" hour. Over six feet tall, with narrow shoulders and twinkling pale blue eyes, Theo Bulkeley stepped with the balance of a graceful dancer.

"Beyond generous of you to have me at this ungodly hour of the sinking sun," he said, bowing to me and warmly shaking Roddy's hand.

"So pleased that you are free to join us," I said.

"Spoken, Valentine, like the true lady that you are."

The tang in his voice edged his words with satire. Theo's cynical manner hid a warm heart and generous nature that seemed to embarrass him. For sure, he relished the world's human folly, and his sharp wit was a gift...most of the time. Theo and I shared a common bond as immigrants to Gotham. His Boston "Brahmin" lineage made Theodore Bulkeley welcome in New York Society. My "adoption," on the other hand, was forever pending.

Eyeing Roddy's bar cart, he said, "Roderick, whatever pleasure you concoct, please let it be mild."

"Mild? Not the usual gin martini for our Boston friend?" Theo shook his head firmly no. Roddy turned to the cart, and in moments corks popped, and ice chimed against glasses.

Roddy said, "I hereby present the popular mild cocktail, the Duplex."

The Duplex

Ingredients:

- 1 ½ ounces French vermouth
- 1 ½ ounces Italian vermouth
- Orange peel or orange bitters

Directions:

1. Combine vermouths in glass with ice.
2. Add squeezed orange peel or bitters.
3. Stir and serve.

"Sip it slowly," Roddy said. We nodded. "Here's to...the sunset?"

"The sinking sun?" Our friend frowned. "Oscar Wilde declares it utterly provincial to extol 'beautiful' sunsets. So, here's to friendship." He tapped his glass to ours, and we sipped the cool, slightly sweet drink. "It's a good one, DeVere. Your invention?"

"Not one of mine Theo. The Duplex has been around a while. As you see, it's on the mild side...quite mild...for someone who has the need...?" My lawyer husband gave our friend a steadfast gaze to tease out the reason behind Theo's special request.

"Lately, my dear friends," he said, "I have not been well... thought I had eaten something...."

"Our dinner..." I said. "The farewell dinner for Dudley Forster—"

"No, Valentine, absolutely not."

Actually, Theo did look pale. Ready to lament the hired footmen and ruined lamb, I stopped when he said, "It's about my Yellowstone vacation ...starting in your *Louisa*." He looked sheepish, most unusual for Theo.

"You see, I have wished to prepare. The press extols Yellowstone Park's meadows and dancing geysers, but if you read between the lines, it's nothing like Florence or Venice." He looked sharply at me. "It's the Rocky Mountains...your old Rocky Mountain West, Valentine Mackle DeVere. And I decided I must be in top physical condition."

We waited. Roddy said, "You belong to the Athletic Club, Theo."

"Handball and squash, Roderick, hardly build strength for high elevations. And so," he said, "I began a system of pills and tonics...toners...."

"What pills?" Roddy asked.

"Vegetable pills...Dr. Brandreth's 'Life-Addition Pills.'

"And what toners?" I asked.

Theo sipped his drink. "A Boston cousin suggested Dr. Hemboldt's extract...a nasty draught, but tolerable. I felt perfectly well...until the third one, a highly recommended elixir."

I held my breath as Roddy leaned close and asked our friend, "What 'elixir,' Theo?"

As if decreed, we heard him say, "Vitalene...and why do you ask?"

My lips parted and Roddy's mouth tightened, both of us speechless.

"Perhaps I overdosed," Theo continued. "The pills and toners...too much. I stopped them all."

"And...?" Roddy asked.

"...several wretched days, flat out with weak tea...but never again, I assure you...."

Tempted to weigh in, I waited for Roddy to speak. Theo was a good friend, but the Vitalene conflict was our secret.

"Theodore," Roddy said, "I have reason to believe the patent medicines have been oversold." He put his glass down. "To be precise, they can be harmful. One day soon, they may be outlawed."

Theo surprised us with a grin. "Roderick, how you do fret about the law...first, whiskey, and now medicines too. You still believe that liquor will be banned one day?"

"I do."

"...the Temperance horde marching to Congress to pass a prohibition law...the President to sign it?" Theo looked from Roddy to me. "The notion of a law against whiskey just seems...farfetched."

Not 'farfetched' at this moment was our butler in the doorframe announcing dinner. "Gentlemen, shall we...?"

Dinner began with a light soup, an egg tart, trout, chicken a la "Rosemarie," peas, and a creamed corn soufflé that reminded Theo and Roddy of boyhood meals in their nurseries. They loved it.

Over poached pears and cookies, our guest apologized for shunning a serious conversation about the Rocky Mountains and Yellowstone geysers. "I meant to ask a multitude of questions," he said, "but could my 'roughing it' inquiry be postponed?"

"By all means," we agreed.

"These days," Theo continued, "I find myself tussling over new living arrangements. I am a denizen of my favorite club, as you know, but apartments are going up...the newest thing on the west side of the Central Park. Now Louis Sherry offers suites in his new restaurant building. They're going fast. A book publisher has taken one, and an entire floor to a man from outside Chicago…. I dragged myself off to have a look, hoped to see the Chicago man's suite, but nothing doing."

Roddy and I exchanged a glance. "Did you ask the man's name?" Roddy asked.

"The book publisher?"

"No, the Porkopolis man."

We smiled at the nickname of the famous Chicago packing houses.

"…and my Boston soul says no to living above a public dining room…my Beacon Hill cousins would think it depraved…and the insane carriage traffic outside. Still, it's a possibility." He reached for a cookie. "If only one needn't employ a decorator."

"Perhaps Elsie De Wolfe?" I suggested.

"How fashionable of you, Valentine." He bit the cookie. "Miss De Wolfe, the brilliant decorator who managed her own theatre company."

"Did she? Really?"

"Quite successfully, and now promises to sweep away countless Victorian household 'cobwebs' and do everything over again…everything."

Roddy abruptly cleared his throat. "Theo, I must caution you…Mrs. DeVere has the idea that a particular room in this house begs for Miss De Wolfe's attention."

I had not said 'begs,' but after coffee, we three trooped into the *Empire* room at my suggestion. Theo would see it for the first time. Our little dog trotted along.

Velvet, however, sniffed when we entered the somber room, whined, and turned to sit outside the doorway. Standing amid the inky black varnished furniture, our friend kept a straight face while Roddy recalled boyhood afternoons playing with toy soldiers on the dark brown rug and firing cannon at the upholstery lizards.

"But your boyhood was not spent here on Fifth Avenue, Roderick. You were well past lead soldiers when the chateau was built."

"True, but the furnishings," Roddy said, "came here from Thirty-third Street." His palm swept the gloomy tables and chairs. "Mother chose the wallpaper and named this the *Empire* reception room."

Theo nodded. "And who is that?" One glance at the oil painting of the DeVere ancestor counting gold coins in a mud hut, and Theo tugged his earlobe. "Perhaps," he said, "I ought to look into a Sherry suite after all."

A grandfather clock struck the hour, and Roddy no longer reminisced about boyhood battles on the rug. "Theo," he said, "you may yet have a look at the Chicago man's suite, if you'll agree to come with me to a sale of horses. But before we go, do look up Dutch Youngbloods. You'll want to know a bit about them. And when you meet the man from Chicago, do not crack a joke about 'Porkopolis' and do not mention the fitness medicines. Above all, do not let it be known that Vitalene made you sick."

Chapter Eight

I AGREED TO MEET Celia for tea and cakes at a popular confectionery while Roddy went to the sale of the horses with Owen Coates. Six days had passed since the visit to Washington Square.

Martin wrote to us on Coates & Co. paper to say that affairs kept him here in the city, but he implored us to join him in Chicago to rid the Coates family of the "evil actor."

"Evil, Roddy?"

Martin's letter, imprinted with the familiar bottle, included hand-written capital letters in the margin. Tiny numbers and arrows pointed at the word, *Vitalene.*

I asked, "are those C's and H's and O's in Martin's letter what I think they are?"

"Chemical formulas," he said, "for...creosote and formaldehyde."

"No wonder Theo got sick."

"And how many others, Val? Martin pleads for himself and for the faithful who believe in that junk. He signals that his family's plight also endangers the public."

"So," I said, "Martin doubles down. We are to prove the Oak Park household innocent in Lydia Coates's death, while saving the country from drinking embalming fluid and coal tar. What's that scrawl across the bottom?"

Roddy frowned as he read, "'Mr. and Mrs. DeVere, our future rests in your hands alone.'"

For Roddy's sake, I tried not to fume and fuss. "Does he mean us? Or the Oak Park household? Or the U.S.A. and its Territories?"

My husband did not reply, and I refrained from questions about the bitters partnership. "When you reply," I said, "you will express support without commitment?"

"The answer is, yes," Roddy said, "on both counts." My husband's stoic face masked deep distress.

♘

The sale of the Dutch horses was to take place on the same afternoon as my hour with Celia, and I arrived early at Maillard's Luncheon Restaurant and Bonbon Store to select a table with three chairs in case Sara Dow came along. Aromas of chocolate and strawberries filled the space that buzzed with conversation and utensils dinging on marble tabletops. Cassie said that before Maillard opened the confectionery, the city's famished women shoppers endured fatigue, thirst, and desperate hopes for a comfortable chair because no restaurant would admit women without gentleman escorts.

My friend accepted this state as the natural order and was shocked when I recounted sashaying into saloons in Virginia City. I determined to "sashay" into certain gentlemen-only New York strongholds in the near future. Change was long overdue.

The sky-blue Celia Coates shimmered my way to insist on a table by the front window. "To see outside, Mrs. DeVere, or what is plate glass for...? The table is held for us, so if you please...."

At her chosen table a café curtain let top hats and feathered bonnets pass before us at eye level. A table at Maillard's was not worth a spat. As my papa said, "Pick your fights."

Across from one another, we smoothed our skirts and agreed the aromas were "divine." A Maillard "hostess" in dark gray put menu cards before us and stood back.

Celia's gray-green eyes widened. "Oh look, they have lemon cream, my favorite in London days. I must have the lemon cream."

"For me," I said, "the strawberry tart."

"And let us also have meringues," Celia continued, "and iced oranges...and the tipsy cake too...and brandy snaps...and surely another...what about these sandwiches? It says 'light and dainty' sandwiches."

The "hostess" looked fretful. There seemed no end to Celia's sudden list, no rhyme or reason for these jumbled confections. Impulse was driving her.

"...and Valencia sponge cake...and...and...."

Firmly I said, "Miss Coates, suppose we begin with the lemon cream, a strawberry tart, and tea. And then, we will see…."

She narrowed her gray-green eyes at me, and said, "If you insist."

The relieved hostess withdrew, and Celia turned to the window. A trio of top hats passed at the edge of my vision, then two bonnets with bows.

"I trust that Miss Dow will not be joining us this afternoon?"

"*Au contraire*, Mrs. DeVere." Celia abruptly plucked a little watch from the blue folds at her bosom and said that Sara Dow would soon be with us. "She is seeing about a new pet for our household."

"How nice… a kitten? Or a puppy? We have a French bulldog. She's a rescue, and if you're thinking of a dog, I highly recommend a 'Frenchie.'"

Celia flashed a coy smile. "I have another idea, Mrs. DeVere. Just now, Sara ought to be leaving the zoo at Central Park."

"The zoo…?"

"To see about peacocks."

"Peacocks?"

"Indeed! You saw my blue room…just imagine the peacock colors."

"Live birds…and so large…?"

"You sound like Armand, Mrs. DeVere. He wants to paint peacocks on another of my walls. Armand is a treasure, but I have viewed Mr. Frederick Leyland's exquisite Peacock

Room in Kensington...." She gave me an arch glance. "From the Wild West, you probably do not know London."

"Not so far."

"Then let me tell you that Mr. Leyland's dining room became the Peacock Room when James McNeill Whistler went to work...painted peacocks and more peacocks. They say the artist went mad, and Mr. Leyland was furious...took Whistler to court and ruined him." She shrugged. "The point is, why settle for paintings when live peacocks are at hand. The zoo ought to arrange it. Sara will see to it."

The tea and treats were served, the lemon cream custard and my tart. So far, I had seen an impulsive Celia, while Sara Dow seemed dispatched to tasks in her name...something of a chaperone and servant. How much did Sara "arrange" for Celia? Who paid her?

Martin?

Owen?

"I hope you will be patient with Miss Dow," I said, "if the zoo officials cannot comply."

"Nonsense, Mrs. DeVere...Sara is an enchantress. She has traveled the world...knows how the diplomats do it...treaties and such. And she was a sales lady for years. Our father said Sara Dow sold more Vitalene than his best drummers."

"The men?"

She nodded. "They scoured the country, but Father called Sara his 'Firecracker' sales lady." Celia spooned her lemon cream and sipped her tea. "And how she loved my sister-in-law."

"Lydia," I said.

"...dearest friend in all her life." She narrowed her eyes. "And you might think Sara would go her own way, now that she has the bequest."

What bequest? I tilted my head to appear puzzled and open.

"You didn't know? Martin didn't tell you?"

"Tell me...?"

"That my sister-in-law left Sara a sizable bequest. Owen called it the Gerstle fortune. We were in deep grief when it all happened...Lydia breaking her neck on those stairs... hardly thinking about a will."

"Of course...." My mouth had gone dry.

"And something for that charity in the slums.... Owen wanted to contest it."

"The bequest?"

"No, the slum charity...Lydia's money thrown into the gutter for foreign peasants. I think he dropped the idea after Father's will was read. He's sure Sara won't leave the Coates fold...says she's woven tight to us in Lydia's memory."

Celia looked at my barely nibbled tart. "Now then, we must have the Valencia sponge cake. On this, I insist." She raised a kid-gloved hand, and we soon sat before the sponge cake.

I ate a dutiful bite. Celia pushed her plate away, her slice untouched.

"Mrs. DeVere," she said, "there is one thing that Sara cannot do for me at the moment."

Ready to quip "only one?" I held back at the sight of those intense eyes. "And what might that be?" I asked.

She leaned toward me and spoke in her harp-like voice, "An invitation to the New York Coaching Club Parade."

"Oh...."

"You'll be going, won't you? You and Mr. DeVere?"

"We will," I said.

"And your guests? Mr. and Mrs. Forster...your friend Cassandra and her husband?"

I nodded.

"Well, then...?"

I put down my fork. "Miss Coates," I said, "I'm afraid this year's parade has been arranged. Perhaps next year...."

She tapped a spoon on the table. "My brother is going this year. Owen is invited. He told me so. I want to go."

"Perhaps your brother can help?"

"He can't...or he won't. I knew nothing about the parade until Miss De Wolfe told me, and I told Sara. It is an important social event, is it not?"

"To New York Society, it is important," I replied. If I remarked that 'coaching' in the West meant stagecoaches, would she reconsider? If I told her that our landau coach would make her feel queasy because Roddy's father's beloved old coach had wretched springs, would she think twice? The fierce gray-green eyes said she absolutely would not.

"So far," she said, "our efforts have come to nothing."

I began a gentle protest, but Celia raised a palm and said, "No, do not fill my ear with excuses." She crossed her arms. "The first time you 'dropped in' at Washington Square, you said western women do not stand on ceremony. I took you at your word. So, Mrs. DeVere, I will not stand on ceremony. I'm asking you and your husband to find me an invitation to the Coaching Parade. I'm counting on you."

❦

"Roddy, it sounded like an ultimatum. I don't know how the peacock dealings worked out because we left Maillard's before Sara Dow arrived. This I can say for sure...Celia Coates is impulsive. And stubborn."

My husband had arrived an hour after I returned from the confectionery. He had sunk into a Bergere chair beside me as I talked about my afternoon while our dog dozed on the rug at our feet. The peacocks amused Roddy, but Celia's demand that we finagle an invitation to the Coaching Parade brought a deep frown. I had not yet talked about the bequest to Sara Dow from the late Lydia Gerstle Coates.

The mantle clock struck five-thirty p.m. as we sorted out the day. The Dutch horse sale, it seems, had been complicated.

"Let's say, Val, that a stubborn streak runs through both brother and sister Coates."

"Didn't Owen buy the horses?"

Roddy loosened his tie. "The Dutch Youngbloods go back centuries, but the first studbook wasn't published until 1887."

"So, he didn't buy the horses?"

"Excellent animals," Roddy said, "jumping, driving... average sixteen hands high...powerful."

"Roddy...tell me."

"He'll think it over. We lunched at the men's grill, and he admitted he wants black horses bred from King Arthur... stables at Camelot."

"You're joking."

"Almost.... Owen is disappointed that the Dutch Warmbloods were not bred with Anglo stock. He went on about war horses. He wants to revive jousting."

"Like...knights in armor?"

"Sounds like it."

"Theo was with you?"

"He was."

"What did he say?"

"Theo said that a new 'Round Table' is overdue in our Gilded Age. Owen missed the reference to Twain's *The Gilded Age*, but he cheered up when Theo mentioned Sir Lancelot." Roddy crossed his legs. "Remember that Theo wants to look over Owen's suite in Sherry's new building, so he was...congenial."

"Understood."

"Would you like a cocktail?"

"Roddy, I have something important to tell you, so make us something light...something cold sober."

My husband reached for the bottles at his wheeled cart, his movements calming. The clink of ice in two glasses and the seltzer water fizz…and here were our drinks. "Val, I present the Dummy Daisy."

Ingredients:

- Pony of raspberry syrup
- Juice of 1 lime
- ½ teaspoon sugar
- Seltzer water
- Ice

Directions:

1. Put syrup and sugar into tall glass.
2. Squeeze lime juice into glass.
3. Add ample cubed or chipped ice.
4. Stir, top with seltzer, stir again, and serve.

We sipped the tangy drinks. "Fizzy," I said, "and just right…." Our dog looked up, and Roddy gave her an ice chunk to lick and chew.

"So, Val, tell me…."

I began with a disclaimer. "Roddy, I'm not sure this is true, but if it is, the question of Lydia Coates's death has suddenly become more tangled…and shocking. This came from Celia, and here's what she said…."

Roddy's frown deepened as I told of the bequest to Sara Dow, the "Gerstle fortune" that followed Lydia's fatal plunge down the stairs at the Oak Park home. His brows lowered in disbelief when I repeated Celia's account of the woman's fidelity to the Coates family in homage to Lydia.

"Lifelong faithful service in tribute to her departed friend? Really?"

"Supposedly," I said, "Owen is convinced she is 'woven' into the family."

"Nonsense," Roddy said, "or wishful thinking." He sipped. "The question is, did Miss Dow know that she would be a beneficiary in the event of Lydia's death?"

Roddy's questions were also mine. "And is Celia reliable?" I added. "The woman exaggerates…speaking of which, about the Coaching Club Parade—"

"—absolutely not, Val."

"But suppose she has more information for us? Something she might let 'slip' if we stay on her good side?"

"Val, I will not demean the DeVere family by wheedling an invitation for that woman. How dare she bully you at the soda fountain?"

"Maillard's is not a soda fountain, Roddy."

"A ladies' tearoom."

"Not exactly that either." I rattled my ice. The confectionery's "light and dainty" sandwiches could not compete against the hearty fare at men's grills. Apart from Macy's soda fountain, our one-and-only "oasis" was Maillard's in a city that offered men clubs, taverns, grills, and saloons that served free lunches for the price of a nickel beer.

My annoyance eddied as our footman, Chalmers, appeared with familiar yellow and black envelope, a Western

Union telegram. Roddy thanked Chalmers, opened the message and prepared to read aloud.

"Roddy, what is it? Bad news? Please...not bad news...."

He gave me a glance that bordered on sympathy and pity "'Arriving 10:07 a.m. Expect resume duties. S. Thwaite.'"

Our housekeeper was coming back.

Chapter Nine

THE HOUSEHOLD ATMOSPHERE CHANGED—
OR was it charged?—at midmorning when the servants' rear
entrance door opened for the housekeeper, Mrs. Thwaite.
She climbed the back staircase and refused Sands's polite
offer to carry her valise to the fourth floor. By eleven o'clock,
wearing her housekeeper's belted gray dress with its jangling
bass ring of keys, she toured the rooms like an explorer who
had come upon ruins.

"If I may have a word, Mrs. DeVere? At your convenience."

"Certainly, Mrs. Thwaite. We can speak here...and now."
I stayed seated at a small desk my mother-in-law called a
Louis *escritoire* in an anteroom off the Corinthian room.
The housekeeper frowned at our dog, who put her head
between her paws. The woman's tour of the household was
distressingly satisfying.

"I hope the visit to your sister was pleasant," I said.

Her narrow nose twitched. "By no means pleasant, ma'am. Washing curtains and walls...beating rugs and wiping grit and grime away. I stayed until the dirt was defeated, not a day longer. I intend your home to become spic and span from this hour forward."

I put a finger to my lips. The housekeeper oversaw our Irish maids, training the young immigrant women who saved their wages until better prospects beckoned. Our home was their American steppingstone, and I turned a deaf ear to Society ladies, like my mother-in-law, who railed at ungrateful servants who left domestic work. I also ignored complaints that I upset Society's "apple cart" by paying high wages.

I said, "So, Mrs. Thwaite, our house is due for a spring cleaning?"

"Indeed, I will see to it that sofa coverings are cleansed in wheat bran rubbed on with flannel. The dog hair will be brushed away. And I will instruct the parlor maid that varnished furniture must be rubbed only with silk."

"About the varnished furniture," I said, "especially in the *Empire* room...."

"Yes, ma'am, special care for Mrs. DeVere's most favorite room." To Mrs. Thwaite, Roddy's mother was the authentic 'Mrs. DeVere.'

"The *Empire* room," I continued, "will soon be evaluated for changes."

"Changes?" The key ring clanked.

"We are considering a rearrangement," I said. "An interior designer will assess the room for...refreshment. A more up-to-date style."

"And has Mrs. DeVere deliberated on this matter, if I may inquire?"

"Mrs. Thwaite," I said, "the *Empire* room is not our concern at this moment. You must be eager to be about your duties, so let me not detain you."

She huffed off, the *Empire* room storm held off for now.

Miss Elsie De Wolfe's visit was scheduled for an afternoon when Roddy was at the city courthouse for a trial. He would represent the plaintiff, a tavern owner seeking damages from a Temperance group that had smashed windows and light fixtures. The main charge against the group was malicious trespass, and Roddy expected to be in court for the afternoon, since other cases preceded his.

After lunch, Sands presented the calling card on a silver tray: "Miss Elsie De Wolfe, Interior Design and Decoration."

"Sands," I said, "please show Miss De Wolfe to the *Empire* Room. I will be at the entrance."

My skin tingled when the brisk footsteps came down the hall. "Miss De Wolfe, welcome."

"Mrs. DeVere...." The decorator once again wore a pleated skirt and jacket, this time in dark plum. "Pleased to make this afternoon available for you, and what shall we do?"

What indeed? I pronounced *"Empire"* in French ("ohm-peer") and opened the door to a room as stuffy as it was drab in the poor light. I opened the draperies. "Miss De Wolfe," I said, "please inspect the room, disregard my feelings, and be frank."

Watching Elsie De Wolfe's eyes as she circled the room, I was reminded of a Virginia City miner who had smashed his leg in three places. The surgeon at the scene looked at the leg with the very gaze I saw on Elsie De Wolfe's face.

"Disastrous," she murmured, fingering the upholstery lizards and toeing the dark brown carpet. "Why is it that people chase strange styles and periods which cast them in gloom?"

She sighed a most theatrical sigh and opened her arms wide. "This is exactly what I am always fighting in people's houses—foolish choices in slavish obedience to times long past. You see the result before you, Mrs. DeVere—a sham room."

I did not interrupt.

"And what is this varnished nonsense with reptiles on the covering?" She nudged her boot against the fat leg of an empire sofa. "I have seen too many sofas and chairs I can best describe as fevered...and, oh my heavens, the wallpaper." She shielded her eyes.

"Miss De Wolfe," I said, "I am at your service...whatever you suggest."

She folded her hands and faced me. "Suitability, Mrs. DeVere. I preach to you the beauty of suitability. The first order of business," she said, "is the process of elimination, to strip the wallpaper and rid the room of all this furniture and the bric-a-brac."

"'Figurines,' my mother-in-law calls them," I said. "Rare porcelain frogs—"

"—knicknacks, Mrs. Devere" she said. "The fireplace is handsome and will show off the room, but what is that impossible painting?"

We looked together at the portrait above the fireplace mantel "My husband's parents found it in the Netherlands," I said. "They believe it is of the 'school' of Rembrandt… ancestral."

She scoffed. "The copycat 'Rembrandt' oils I have removed from 'sham' rooms would fill a museum wall." She paused. "Do you have a telephone?"

"We do, in a back hallway."

"I suggest the portrait might be hung near the telephone, a solution pleasing to another client."

"We will have the portrait taken down and moved," I said, "perhaps into my in-laws' apartment." I had begun to feel alarmed, sensing the storm to come.

"Tranquility, Mrs. DeVere, is our goal. Once cleared, the simplicity and dignity of the room will appear, and the freed space will invite furnishings worthy of the room."

Miss De Wolfe had another appointment and declined tea. "Otherwise, Mrs. DeVere, I would happily sip tea and lament that your friend in Washington Square has rejected my ideas on 'suitability.' Mark my words, a person who says, 'Oh, I love blue, let's have blue!' is apt to treat each room in a different color and go from room to room, fretful and dissatisfied."

"Miss Coates," I said, "is a slight acquaintance."

"Terribly young to be fixed in her ways. I quite regret mentioning the Coaching Club parade. Miss Coates had the audacity to terminate my services, but she pressed me to find her an invitation."

"Somewhat headstrong," I said. "Perhaps you met Miss Dow?"

"The one whose hairpins look like Chinese chopsticks? An idea from *The Mikado*, perhaps...Gilbert and Sullivan. Yes, we were introduced." The decorator pulled on her gloves. Sands held her cloak near the front door.

"The next step?" I asked. "What is next for the room?"

"Quite simply, Mrs. DeVere, that you let me know when the room is prepared. We will thereafter shop for furnishings that grace the room and insure suitability and tranquility. Good afternoon."

ᥫᩣ

Roddy's dour mood was evident upon his late afternoon return from court when his leather portfolio smacked onto a foyer table. Words exchanged with Sands brought him to the anteroom, where I sat brushing Velvet. Our dog detested brushing, no matter how soft the bristles, and I held her chest and fed her tidbits while lightly brushing her back and sides. At the sight of my husband, she jumped to the floor, glowered at me, and trotted to him.

"My dear," said Roddy as he planted a peck on my right cheek, sat down on a hassock, and said, "Good dog."

"Disappointing trial?" I asked.

"No trial today," he said. "The case is delayed. Court was adjourned before our case could be heard. A wasted afternoon of petty theft, burglary, and public nuisance. One mildly interesting case," Roddy continued. "A fellow set his engraving machine to produce bank bills, but he tried to spend them before the ink dried."

"A counterfeiter," I said.

"An open-and-shut case, but his lawyer raised objection upon objection. each one overruled by Judge Thompkins, but the case devoured the afternoon." Roddy lifted Velvet to the hassock. "Sands mentioned an afternoon visitor."

Our butler would never volunteer such information unless requested, so Roddy must have asked.

"Miss De Wolfe," I said, "viewed the *Empire* room...and made suggestions."

"I have no doubt."

To bring up the excavation of my husband's favorite boyhood furniture? Not now. "Here's something," I said. "Miss De Wolfe says Celia Coates tried to wheedle an invitation to the coaching parade. She fired the decorator but coaxed her to 'find' an invitation."

"Shameless." Roddy stroked Velvet's ears. The dog almost purred. "The Coates brother and sister do get about," he said. "I learned that Owen is to be the Holbrooke's guest for the parade."

"So, it's true?"

Roddy nodded. "I saw George Holbrooke on the way home and had a word. It seems that Owen has looked into Holbrooke's favorite breed, Hungarian horses...the stock bred back to the Vikings and Hussars."

"And King Arthur too?"

Roddy shrugged. "Holbrooke has invited him. The Holbrooke four-in-hand will be just ahead of us with the Forsters."

I wanted no irritating details of the coaching parade lineup. For now, we decided to spend an hour upstairs in the drawing room in our favorite "cocktail hour" chairs. Roddy would suggest pleasant drinks and make them for us.

So we thought, until Sands approached with an apology and a small gift-wrapped box on a tray. "If you care to receive this just now?" he asked. "It was delivered by a lady who preferred not to linger."

"What is it?" I asked. The butler only bowed and lowered the tray so Roddy could take the box in his outstretched hand.

Sands stood by, as requested, while Roddy untied the ribbon and lifted the lid.

"What is it?"

My husband uncoiled a narrow leather strap that was inset with sparkles and had a silver buckle. "A dog collar," he said. "A jeweled dog collar." He held it up. "Val, I believe these are real diamonds. And here is a card."

"What does it say?"

He handed the card to me. "It says, 'For the well-dressed French Bulldog.'" I turned to our butler. "Sands, who delivered this?"

"She did not leave her card, ma'am, nor say her name. Not to be indiscrete, but her bonnet was secured by unusual pins...rather like twigs."

"Chopsticks," I said. "It was Sara Dow, Roddy. She delivered this for Celia, and it's a bribe. A diamond-studded dog collar for an invitation to the Coaching Club parade."

"Wait, Val...something else in the box."

"What?" My husband pulled out a tasseled string with something like little red peppers. "What are those?"

Roddy frowned. "They're firecrackers," he said, "tiny firecrackers from China."

"Whatever for?"

He shrugged. "All I know is...if lighted, they explode."

Chapter Ten

SATURDAY, MAY 7, DAWNED bright and sunny, the sky edged with spun sugar clouds. The coaching parade would start at noon, and preparations had been underway for days. The ladies tittered, horses nickered, and the men laughed heartily as we gathered at our starting point, the Brunswick Hotel on 26th Street. Roddy looked handsome in his Coaching Club uniform, the green coat, gray top hat, and a boutonniere. Even the horses had flowers behind their ears.

Membership in the Coaching Club required "the ability to drive four horses with grace and skill." My husband prepared to drive Apollo and Atlas, both hitched to a matching pair of black horses from Brown's Livery Stable. Most club members kept a sizable stable of matched carriage horses, but a few rented teams from Brown's several days before the parade.

To brush up, Roddy spent afternoons on the box with our coachman, Noland, who had washed and waxed the

DeVeres' old landau carriage for the annual parade. My father-in-law's landau seated six passengers, but the carriage needed new springs and made me seasick. The Forsters gamely agreed to come as our guests. A dozen spanking clean coaches lined up at the hotel entrance, every horse brushed and harness gleaming.

My straw "harness" of a leghorn hat disguised unease that grew as this day approached. Had Celia Coates somehow wrangled an invitation? Who else had she bribed and threatened for a ride around Central Park, then back to this hotel for dinner? I did not see her amid this swirl of spring gowns and hats trimmed with cornflowers or buttercups.

Cassie and Dudley were due any minute. I had not told my friend about the "gift" box that should have been dispatched "return to sender," but Roddy urged stowing the collar out of sight in our house. The sparkles were diamonds, an extravagant expense that Sara Dow supposedly came to Washington Square to prevent. Did Celia's companion know the full contents of the box she had delivered? Were the firecrackers her idea? Sara had traveled in China where fireworks were invented, I reminded Roddy, but my lawyer husband thought the connection too remote. He and Bronson, our footman, had set them off outdoors in the back garden—bang-bang-bang. Roddy said we were lucky. A mistake could have cost a hand or an eye.

So, here we were, and one gentleman greeting us at this moment in a snug-fitting black-and-white houndstooth jacket tipped his top hat and blustered, "Mrs. Roderick DeVere, good morning to you."

"Mr. Owen Coates," I said. "Yes, a very good morning."

He greeted Roddy and looked over our horses. His face looked flushed. "Hackneys looking fine, DeVere."

"Atlas and Apollo are high steppers," Roddy said.

Owen's gaze moved to the second pair. "And what might these other two be?"

"Plantation horses," Roddy said. I expected my husband to explain about the breed, but he said no more.

"Owen pointed to the Regency coach in front of our landau. "Holbrooke could have supplied you a pair of Hungarians...great strength and excellent movement."

Was it a juniper berry scent on Owen? Gin?

"Two pair of Hungarians, I'd wager."

"Another time," Roddy said.

Owen said he looked forward to coaching with the Holbrooke party. "Don't suppose you made room for my sister, did you?" he said. "There's always next year. I'll have my own coach, drive my own team. And you'll see me in a green coat too, DeVere, and a gray hat...boutonniere as well."

We wished Owen a fine day, and he stepped toward his host's coach just as Cassie and Dudley arrived.

I doubted that Owen heard Cassie's breath that stopped just short of a gasp. Greeting our friends, I admired the daisies on her leghorn hat, and she complimented the "keyhole" neckline of my gown. Our parasols matched our dresses.

All four of us stared at Owen's back as he helped a lady onto the Holbrookes' Regency coach.

"Friend of yours?" Dudley asked.

"A new acquaintance from Chicago" Roddy said. "I was in law school with his brother."

"Oh," Cassie almost cried, "he must be Miss Coates's brother...no wonder I felt...."

"Felt what?" Dudley asked.

Cassie took her husband's arm as if to steady herself. "My visit to Washington Square with Valentine..." she said, her voice slightly quavering. "We met Miss Coates and her friend that day." Cassie 's hand clamped on Dudley's arm, her nails digging the ridges of his corduroy jacket as she watched the brawny figure climb aboard the Holbrooke coach.

Owen slipped, regained footing, and sat down beside a lady atop the coach.

Cassie's husband peered closely at the scene. Nearly six feet tall, the trim and agile Dudley Forster combined skepticism with warmth in a temperament that fit him for science. The puzzle of the earth's past, he was sure, would be solved in the fossils he sought on expeditions to faraway islands. His wealth had never lured him to the life of the "idle rich," and his clothing deliberately snubbed fashion. Renouncing ties, Dudley wore neck scarves, and his corduroy jacket, denim trousers, and lumberman's boots made a statement about Society to Society. His love and care for Cassie and their children were never in question, and the Forsters made the most of their time together.

"Soon time to get going, yes?" Dudley counted the coaches.

"Any minute," Roddy replied.

"Good exercise for the horses," our friend said. "Quadrupeds, genus *equus*, mammals in the family *Equidae*, including *horses*, donkeys, and zebras." He looked at us and laughed. "...just thinking aloud, my friends. Let's agree the Brunswick Hotel kitchen will reward us with a fine evening meal. And I trust this year's Coaching Club cocktail is your invention, Roderick?"

"On that topic, Dudley, my lips are sealed."

"Ladies, shall I...? Dudley assisted Cassie and me into the landau, then took his place beside Roddy on the box.

My friend seemed distracted. "That man...Miss Coates's brother," she said, pointing toward the houndstooth jacket atop the Regency.

"His name is Owen...Owen Coates."

Cassie shut her eyes and gripped her parasol tightly.

"We'll probably see him at balls and parties soon," I said. "He has taken a suite in Louis Sherry's new building. He is very rich... Chicago real estate and patent medicine."

Cassie kept her eyes shut.

"Sunlight too bright?" I asked. "Roddy could raise the top. Shall we raise the top?"

"Never mind, Val," Cassie said. "It's nothing."

I did not press. Nor did I say this outing brought thoughts of stagecoaches in the Rockies, the driver in buckskins and the trips over narrow mountain ridges so harrowing for passengers, driver, and the teams. To me, the

Coaching Club parade felt fussy and trivial. What's more, crowds gathered to cheer and jeer. I could enjoy watching a parade, not being the parade.

"Do not look at the crowd," Cassie advised. "Whatever you hear, think of an athletic event, such as badminton. When we enter the Central Park drive with thick foliage on both sides...then look about and enjoy the springtime shrubs and trees."

Soon enough, the sidewalk erupted in hoots and catcalls along the avenue. Policemen raised their nightstick billy-clubs. No one dared pelt us with a stone or spook the horses.

In the park, nearing the Mall at last, a distant racket of noise and thumping grew loud. Then louder. "What's that whine? That pounding?" Cassie covered her ears.

I covered mine to see, just Inches from the coach wheels, four women standing like an armed guard. One banged a bass drum, another cranked a hurdy-gurdy, and two others held up a signboard with enormous lettering:

**BEAT THE DRUM FOR
VOTES FOR WOMEN!
HURDY-GURDY FOR
WOMEN'S SUFFRAGE!**

"Val..." said Cassie, "the woman with that hurdy-gurdy... isn't that—"

"—Annie Flowers," I gasped. "...and as she threatened...a suffrage demonstration at the Coaching Club parade."

My friend looked as stunned as I felt when our names were called out. "Mrs. DeVere...Mrs. Forster...votes for women...votes...."

I waved. Cassie looked frozen, and the landau drove on, but Roddy had stiffened at the sight of the suffrage demonstration that mocked my husband's cherished Coaching Parade, though months ago he had arranged to pay Annie Flowers's fine when the suffragist was jailed for being a "public nuisance." Cassie and I met Annie Flowers last summer, when my friend's late cousin was sheltered in the woman's Lower East Side flat. More recently, Miss Flowers embroiled me in a shameful, secret history of Central Park and turned up as a secretary to the organization I had joined, the Consumers League. All told, she was like an extra conscience.

Finally, out of range of the noise, I said, "The suffrage event is a surefire topic for the Brunswick dinner tonight."

"Much likelier, Val, that no one will say a word about it," my friend replied. "The first rule of Society: avoid everything unpleasant."

I smiled. Our lighthearted moment might have continued as the coach parade entered the part of the drive where thick trees and shrubs deterred gawkers. "We can relax now, Val. We can look about and enjoy ourselves."

So we thought.

The words had barely left my friend's lips when a rustling stirred behind a birch grove. Or was it from the rhododendrons? I would be asked in specifics in the next few days but could not remember.

Squirrels, I thought at that moment. Or maybe a fox. But no...a thickset man in a cap.

With the suffragists? Was he with them?

He burst from the foliage, and his face was masked. His head turned back and forth from the landau to the Regency coach and back again. A long moment's hesitation, and he lunged at the Regency, reaching high to yank at the houndstooth coat and pull with both arms. Bracing his feet against the side of the coach, he pulled until the houndstooth coat gave way...until Owen tumbled off the coach to land with a thud and a cry of pain.

On the ground with his victim, the man grabbed at Owen's neck, and metal flashed in his hand—a knife. But Dudley jumped off the landau, pinned his arm, and struck at his head. The attacker wrestled free, sprang up, fled into the foliage and was gone.

Like a tableau, Cassie and I sat, as did Roddy, who had had reined the horses to a halt. The lady atop the Regency clasped her hat brim, and the Holbrookes' Hungarian horses snorted. Birds twittered.

What had just happened?

What did we see?

Dudley brushed at his corduroy sleeve, and Owen struggled to his feet and showed his left wrist in an unnatural position.

"Broken," he roared. "The bugger broke a bone...worse than Chicago...he broke my bone."

Chapter Eleven

THE BRUNSWICK HOTEL DINNER shivered with news of the attack on the Holbrooke carriage and the injury of the guest, whose wrist was swathed in a while silk scarf. Owen held his wrapped wrist high in the dining room where the coaching parties were seated at round tables. Politely refusing ice or heat, he chose cognac, and a bottle of Courvoisier was at his elbow. He was becoming the guest of honor, both victim and hero in the telling and retelling of the "incident."

Oysters were served as diners relayed accounts of the attack. Eight coaches ahead of the Holbrookes' Regency had kept going with no notion that anything strange had taken place. Those behind our landau had puzzled over the short halt to the parade.

As accounts circulated, questions rose as to why a vicious assault had marred such a perfect day in a prosperous year. Wall Street was doing well, no disruptive labor strikes to speak of, and workers were "quite well fed," as a young Vanderbilt man quipped.

"And well-watered," added his cousin to light chortling around the dining room.

George Holbrooke, the elder statesman-like figure at our table, assured all within hearing that he wished to take Mr. Coates to the German Hospital, but his guest vowed he would not miss his first Coaching Club dinner "for all the world."

Dudley's action fighting off the attacker was eclipsed as Owen detailed his combat against the vicious foe. In Owen's account, he had not been pulled from the coach, but leapt at the onrushing attacker before another gentleman or—heaven forbid—a lady fell victim to the mad brute. The split seam of his houndstooth coat proved his gallantry, and several tables raised glasses in gratitude and hopes for his fast recovery. All agreed that Owen had demonstrated the courage of a gentleman.

On the Suffrage demonstration, Cassie's prediction held true: complete silence.

Dudley looked amused that his efforts were ignored as he chatted with Madeline Glendorick, the wife of the shipping tycoon, while Cassie nodded and smiled at the tycoon's every word. My friend's distress was apparent to anyone who knew her well.

Had she silently warded off eerie "vapors" all day? Would she tell me if I asked?

The dinner proceeded to *Agneau de lait Boulangere,* lamb cooked in milk sauce that reminded me of my scorched lamb. The "incident" now took turns with other topics, such as members' newfound heraldry. The shipping magnate, Edwin Glendorick, displayed a new medallion on his coach panels, since his daughter, Emily, had become the Countess of Cleave upon her marriage to a British baronet. Mrs. Glendorick tut-tutted about her husband's fancy for heraldry, but she kept mum on the sum paid to the baronet's impoverished family to royalize their daughter.

In the ladies' powder room before dessert, I found myself beside Anita Holbrooke whose pert face and bright dark eyes gave her the nickname "Sparrow." She was known to be a doting, spry grandmother.

We chatted about the day, acknowledged the "incident" with raised eyebrows, and looked forward to the summer in Newport.

"...and Valentine, let me say how much George and I enjoyed your farewell dinner for Dudley Forster. Your Roderick's tribute was eloquent, and your fine home...you must know the saying that is meant for ladies, 'Have nothing in your house that you do not believe to be beautiful.'" She turned and smiled. "Fitting for you young DeVeres, I do hope."

Anita Holbrooke's reminder of our formal dinner stung. Passing as a lady had its limits. "Anita, to be frank, our home was furnished by Roderick's parents. The décor is none of my doing...none."

The attendant had slipped away, and the "Sparrow" turned to me. "You and Roderick wed...two years ago?"

"Three, going on four."

"Well, my dear, as mistress of the house, you owe yourself the furnishings that express your personality."

Her jeweled fingers fluttered. "My dear, when Mr. Holbrooke goes on safari, he returns to find the house redone...completely redone. The men are forever the happy guests in our homes, are they not?" She pinched her cheeks to rouge them. "Tell me, does Mr. DeVere go on safari? No? Well, you must find a few weeks out-of-town, and have a go." She stood. "The dessert will be melting, so we had better...."

"One question, Anita...have you heard of Elsie De Wolfe?"

Her laugh rippled. "Fifth Avenue is mad about her. I rely on Duveen...Joseph Duveen? Never mind. Trust your own judgment. If Miss De Wolfe is for you, take your turn."

Once again at the table, my thoughts of the *Empire* room shifted to the close-of-dinner rituals, the men off to the hotel lounge to smoke cigars and sip this year's Coaching Parade Cocktail, which Roddy had devised in secret. For the hour, my husband would listen for any clue about the attack, as I would do through the ladies' cigarettes and liqueurs. The chitchat swirled around me, and the unanswered questions too.

Why did a masked man with a knife lunge at Owen Coates?

Why did he hesitate before the attack? He looked from the landau to the Regency. He was uncertain, I was sure of it but told no one of what I had seen.

The evening was over by ten p.m., and we reached home an hour later and slipped into the *Crème* drawing room to talk about the day's main event.

"Owen Coates," I said, "what a liar...the 'hero' of the dinner with a guest's silk scarf 'bandage' like a theater prop. And not a word about Dudley."

"Owen was probably embarrassed, Val. He was pulled from the coach, slammed to the ground, flat on his back. He would have wanted to strike a blow, not be rescued."

"But Dudley drove that masked attacker off. It was Dudley who grabbed his arm and cuffed him on the head. He had a knife, Roddy. He was ready to use it. I saw the knife blade flash. Did you see it?"

"No, but Dudley did, and he tried to grab it. I have a souvenir of the encounter." Roddy reached into the pocket of his Coaching Club coat. "

How disappointing to see a tattered workman's cap. "The attacker wore this," Roddy said, "and Dudley snatched it when he ran away."

We both peered at the dark blue worsted cap with a viser and a puffy top.

"Typical workman's head gear," I murmured.

"But it might be evidence at some point. Remember, next week at this time, our friend will be on the high seas in quest of fossils."

I needed no reminder.

Roddy put the cap on the table beside my leghorn hat. "Val, the Coaching Club parade has never known such disruption. Never mind the cacophonous women with that sign. It's the ambush...an ambush that did not happen at random. The masked man targeted Owen."

I remembered the moment differently. To my mind, the attacker burst from the foliage, crouched to spring, then looked back and forth from the landau to the Regency. I saw hesitation, as if he might strike at Roddy, who was busy with the reins. Back and forth he looked...should I say something now? For better or worse, I stayed silent as Roddy pointed to the cap as if the culprit were before us.

"Val," he said, "we need to ask who attacked Owen Coates—and why."

"A robbery?" I said. "Was the attacker drunk?"

"Doubtful," Roddy said. "Dudley did not smell alcohol, nor did Owen mention it in the Brunswick lounge after dinner."

"Owen," I said with a short laugh, "was soaked in gin when the parade started, and that bottle of Courvoisier cognac was halfway down when you went to the lounge. He took the bottle along, didn't he?"

"He did."

"So..." I said at last, "do we focus suspicions on the most obvious 'culprits,' perhaps brother Martin? Or Sara Dow? Or both? Is the Oak Park household reduced to two suspects in Lydia's death?"

"Martin..." Roddy said slowly, "is furious at the injustice...his disinheritance." He stroked his chin. "But is he angry enough to have his brother struck down?" My husband bit his lip. "Or possibly have him injured severely...an attack that would send a message."

"To pry loose some of Owen's millions?"

"Not unheard of, Val."

"And Sara Dow? Could she get another bequest if Owen were deceased?"

"No way to know," Roddy said.

"And now Celia..." I said. "Suppose she has realized that her one million dollars will not go as far as she thought? She was furious not to be invited to the Coaching Club parade. She might have tried to ruin the day. One of her new bohemian friends might have suggested an attack."

We sat. A clock chimed the midnight hour. "I don't suppose it's out of the question that Celia and Martin conspired against their rich brother," I said, "or that Sara Dow is somehow involved, since the Coates family is not complete without this strange companion."

I reached for my husband's hand. "Roddy, the basic question for us is, how important is the partnership with Martin? What is it worth to you? Or to us?"

My husband did not answer at once. If birch logs had crackled in the fireplace, Roddy would have poked at the fire while deciding what he thought, what he would say, and how to say it. Instead, he covered my hand with his and said, "Martin asks me to see the distillery."

At this moment, I wished that Velvet were lying on the divan so that I could scratch her back and stroke her ears. "The distillery," I said, "that produces Vitalene?"

Roddy nodded.

"But would produce bitters...convert the poisonous medicine to bitters?"

"Yes."

"In Chicago."

"Yes. Martin is determined to secure the partnership. The letter of intent could be binding."

I fastened a hairpin. "But what of his wife's death... the charge that someone in the household killed her? The Chicago detective...?"

"Martin shies away from the matter, Val."

"How could he...? Last month he begged us to help clear the Coates brothers and Sara Dow of suspicion."

"Right now," he said, "Martin seems gripped by the idea that our partnership will make amends to his wife.... and make the detective somehow disappear."

"Disappear? That's absurd." My voice turned shrill.

"Val, what I can say is...clearing the Coates household of a charge of murder would clear my debt. My longtime pledge to Martin."

"And if he proves to be the guilty one? What then?"

My husband had no answer. A mantel clock chimed. Where were we?

"Roddy," I said, "are you determined to go to Chicago?"

My husband hesitated. "I am determined to fulfill my promise. I am duty-bound to Martin."

"I won't let you go by yourself."

"But the pledge was mine, Val. The runaway horse at the law school...you were far away. You knew nothing—"

"—I know it now, Roddy. Your past is my present. We will both go to Chicago."

"Which means a close look into the death of Martin's wife," Roddy said.

Somewhere a door latch clicked, perhaps Sands closing the house for the night. My coaching parade gown had wrinkled, and a small stain puckered at the knee.

"Roddy," I said at last, "the 'close look' into Lydia Coates's death must be ours alone. We must find our own way... without Martin. Do we know anyone in law enforcement in Chicago?"

We did not.

"Then," I said, "before going, we must schedule a confidential talk with a certain detective here in New York."

"If we must."

"We must."

At those two words, Roddy consented to a meeting with a man known to us since last autumn, a senior detective in the New York City Police Department.

Chapter Twelve

"MR. COLIN FINLAY FOR Mr. and Mrs. DeVere," our butler announced.

"Please show him in, Sands."

Detective Colin Finlay entered the Corinthian room like a seaman on a rolling deck. He bowed to me with a warm smile, then gave Roddy a sober nod when my husband did not extend his hand. A grandfather clock struck six p.m.

"Detective Finlay," I said, "do sit down. So good of you to come." I first met the detective under awkward circumstances months ago. It felt like years.

The last months had not changed the man whose narrow face was underscored with fine lines under watchful gray eyes. Corn color streaked his short white hair, and long arms gave him a youthful, lanky look that belied a man approaching his fortieth year.

Colin Finlay had helped enormously when death and destruction haunted Central Park last autumn, and I was pleased to see the new navy serge suit that signaled his promotion, though the same celluloid shirt collar and cuffs were sure to chafe. He sat on a French Renaissance chair with carved arms. Roddy and I faced him on a Louis XV sofa.

"Mr. DeVere and I appreciate your time," I said.

"You must be busy these days," Roddy said. "The newspapers are full of crimes and criminals."

"And arrests and convictions too," Finlay shot back. "Gambling dens broken up, thieves caught, and killers sent swinging from a yardarm."

Yardarm, once again. Roddy and I had researched that nautical term when we heard it from Finlay last autumn. Sailors' lingo salted the man's conversation and harkened to his earlier career at sea. My husband felt annoyed to hear it. I was bemused. The two men had reached a stand-off without fellowship.

"And what might I do for you, Mr. and Mrs. DeVere?"

Roddy gestured to me. "Mrs. DeVere hopes that you might be acquainted with a member of the police force in the city of Chicago, and I join her in this request. We plan a short visit to 'The City by the Lake.'"

"The 'windy City,' isn't it?"

The come-back irked Roddy.

"I believe both nicknames are in play," I said. The men blinked at each other and gave me a patronizing glance.

"And could I ask something more about the request, Mrs. DeVere? Or should a bos'n order me to pipe down?"

Finlay's nautical terms sprang up in these crossroads moments. "Quite simply, Mr. Finlay," I said, "we would like to know the name of a Chicago police officer...that is, if you or another member of the force have an acquaintance with a patrolman. Or perhaps a detective?"

He ran a hand through his white hair. "No name springs right to mind, ma'am, but I'll think hard on it, see what's in the old sea bag...recollections, I mean."

We all began to rise from our seats. "Everything at peace hereabouts, I trust?" Finlay asked. "No hooligans afoot?"

"Not on Fifth Avenue, Mr. Finlay," said Roddy, "but the gentleman who was assaulted during the Coaching Club parade in Central Park last Saturday...do the police have leads in the case?"

Finlay cocked his head. "What assault, sir?"

Roddy hid his surprise. We had assumed that Owen reported the attack, or George Holbrooke. Dudley was too busy planning his voyage to take the time.

The detective's mouth tightened, and his gray eyes narrowed to a squint. "For a fact, Mr. DeVere," he said, "nothing of the sort was reported to the police. I would know if a report came in."

We all sat back down, and Roddy calmly related the episode in the park, describing the masked attacker and Dudley's quick action. He spelled George Holbrooke's and Owen Coates's names. He gave out the Forsters' street address on Madison Avenue.

Finlay penciled quickly in a notebook, tugged his lapels and spoke to the Corinthian columns. "As you know, silence does a disservice to the police and the public. When crimes go unreported, the police are cleated to the dock."

Roddy cleared his throat, his cheeks growing pink.

"I will file the report right away," Finlay continued, shutting the notebook as I lifted my hand.

"Mr. Finlay, one further detail about the incident," I said. "Before the attacker lunged, I saw him hesitate and look back and forth from the Regency coach to our landau carriage, as if he might choose to strike the landau."

Roddy frowned. Somehow, meetings with Detective Finlay drove a wedge between my husband and me. It had happened before. It felt familiar.

The detective looked at Roddy. "Is that your recollection, sir? The assailant might have struck at you?"

Roddy touched his necktie. "Mr. Finlay," he said, "if you have ever handled the reins of a four-horse team? A four-in-hand...have you?"

"Lines, Mr. DeVere. Landlubbers say 'ropes' and 'reins,' but seamen handle the lines. I take it that you were handling your horses, and Mrs. DeVere was free to look about. Is that it?"

Roddy murmured a sullen, "Yes."

"But Mr. DeVere has possible evidence," I hastened to say. "A hat."

Roddy said, "Actually, a cap." With a one-up glance at me, he retrieved the tattered blue cap from an antique Jacobean chest and put it into Finlay's hands. "You see, Mr. Finlay," he said, "the attacker wore this common workman's cap. He also wielded a knife. As I told to you a moment ago, Mr. Forster retrieved this, and I have it for safekeeping...a common cap."

The detective looked closely at the crown. "Not so common," he said. "This is a paddock cap. The puff top is a giveaway. Mr. DeVere, have you recently been near a little field or enclosure where horses are exercised? And has Mr. Coates or Mr. Holbrooke? Do you know?"

I thought of the sale of the Dutch horses. Surely Roddy also recalled the sale, but he chose not to mention it at that moment. I kept quiet.

"Without delay," Finlay said, "we will inspect the grove where the attack occurred, and I may request another visit to your home. For the present, Mr. DeVere, would you hold the cap for safekeeping? As you know, evidence sometimes disappears from police lockers on Mulberry Street."

The infamous New York police headquarters was known by its street name, although no one could recall a fruit tree within miles of the squat, square, weathered building in which crimes were solved and covered up.

"The cap can be stowed in your home, sir?"

"Stowed, Mr. Finlay," Roddy replied. "I will 'stow' it." The nautical echo brought the two men to their truce.

We tiptoed into our dining room for dinner that night. "Roddy," I said, "when Finlay recognized the paddock cap, you surely remembered the Dutch horse sale...?"

"I did."

"But you didn't say a word about it."

"The Dutch Warmblood sale was by invitation, Val. A member of the Union Club breeds Warmbloods, and his paddock is overseen by men properly outfitted from cap to boots. Trust me, a tattered cap would not have been tolerated."

In the next moment, I eased into a topic that should not whip up the atmosphere. "Our Chicago trip," I said, "...we'll hitch the *Louisa* to the New York Central train, and Theo will be with us, on his way toward Yellowstone Park...."

Roddy nodded, and I passed the creamed potatoes. "In Chicago," I said, "I will visit Hull House. Celia says that Hull House was her late sister-in-law's favorite charity. Lydia volunteered there."

"Something about helping immigrants, yes?"

"And matters of health and wages," I said.

I should have paid attention when my husband's brow arched. "Like that Consumers League, isn't it?" he said. "Like that club of yours where the Suffragette works, the Flowers woman?"

"Annie Flowers, yes."

"The impudence...to bang a drum and crank a hurdy-gurdy at the Coaching Club parade...to make a mockery of a private celebration."

"To support women's voting rights," I said.

"Socialists," he muttered.

"Roddy," I said in my calmest voice, "The Consumers League is not a political organization.

Expecting an outburst, I heard my husband's voice turn plaintive. "Suppose it becomes a cult, Val. That's my real fear, that my wife will be taken captive...that I will lose you."

His sudden change of mood brought me close. We found ourselves gazing at one another with eyes filmed with tears. "My dear," I said softly, "I have been taken captive by Roderick Windham DeVere." I reached for his hand. "And tonight," I said, "let us enjoy my captivity to the fullest."

And we did.

Chapter Thirteen

WE ELBOWED THROUGH THE crowd to board the *Louisa* in plenty of time for the 11:46 a.m. departure for Chicago. The Grand Central Depot along 42nd street felt choked with passengers coming and going. New York needed a much larger depot. The minutes ticked away as conductors called "all aboard."

My husband gripped his watch and paced the carpet of our car. "Where is he? It's not like Theo to be late. He has exactly nine...no, eight minutes."

I pressed a cheek against the car window to see cartmen and porters on the platform. Our friend was nowhere in sight. "Cutting it close..." I said.

"Just six minutes more," Roddy muttered. "His baggage is aboard, two steamer trunks and a carpetbag. His butler is in the galley with a cook. Where is the man?"

"No idea."

"Three minutes...three," Roddy said through clenched teeth.

Just then, a rap at the car door. "Telegram...telegram for Mr. and Mrs. Roderick DeVere...sir."

Roddy snatched the envelope, dug for small change, and stuffed the Western Union envelope in his coat pocket.

"A well-wisher," I said, "probably the Forsters."

"Or my folks." Roddy shouted, "Two minutes," as a whistle announced the *Lake Shore Limited* departure on the dot of 11:46, and a familiar figure stumbled into the car.

"Roderick...Valentine...."

"Theo...where have you been...?"

"Apologies, my dear DeVeres, my humblest apologies. Your *Louisa*...very last car on the train, I should have known." The tall, slim figure in a tweed topcoat rushed into the aisle, caught his breath, swept off his short-brimmed hat, and pointed to a large box under one arm.

"Dashed here from Abercrombie's," he said, "finished in the nick of time, a buckskin suit like Roosevelt's when he went West to hunt big game. Not that I plan to shoot a moose, but when in Rome, do as...oh, here we go. We're off."

The train pulled out slowly, the locomotive and coal car, the half-dozen Pullman sleepers, the buffet, library, smoker, parlor and observation cars, barber shop, and dining car, with the *Louisa* hitched at the rear and ready to be coupled onto other trains.

Bound for Yellowstone Park, Theo Bulkeley had invited us to go along to Chicago, the first leg of his western trip. Roddy mentioned a possible business arrangement with a man from law school days, all very preliminary. I added a wish to stroll the elegant Michigan Avenue and perhaps see the famed stockyards. The timing, we agreed, was sheer coincidence.

Roddy had changed into a cheviot sport coat, and we both let the hasty telegram slip out of mind. The Western Union messengers were a common sight at rail depots and ports as friends and families telegraphed bon voyage.

Our friend knew nothing of the Chicago policeman's name that Colin Finlay had provided in a short call at our home and penciled on the back of his New York Police Department card. Nor had Theo any idea of our inquiry into Lydia Coates's death or the suspicion that someone in her house had killed her. My letter of introduction to Hull House was tucked away and need not be mentioned.

For that matter, neither Martin nor Owen Coates had any idea that Roderick and Valentine DeVere planned to investigate the homicide charge against them and their friend, Sara Dow—all on our own.

Theo was not to know that Roddy's club connections informed him about a police station and "lockup" at West Harrison and LaSalle Streets in the famed Chicago "Loop." Roddy would visit the lockup and leave a note for the officer whose name had been plucked from Detective Finlay's "sea bag" of memory.

From Chicago, Theo would head north and west on shining rails. I could envy him visiting the Rockies of my childhood, the snow-capped peaks blessed by the sun, the soft wind whistling through pines and streams trickling through rocky clefts. Then again, the sudden drenching storms, the gloom, the frozen altitudes above the timberline where the quest for gold or silver topped everything and survival by no means certain. The grizzlies.

We sat with our friend at the cherry dining table as the train skirted the Hudson River, a steely blue in this cloudy, cool day in late May. Theo had seen the butler about lunch, which I had learned to call luncheon. The table was set with white linen, silver, and crystal. From New York to Chicago, we were to be the guests of our guest.

"So, dear friends," Theo said, "I have ordered champagne to start us off and a dish perfected at the Union League Club" He winked at Roddy. "I trust you have savored the club's Codfish Benedictine on occasion at the club, Roderick?"

Roddy chuckled, and I admired the slope of his shoulders and the lock of light brown hair that brushed his broad forehead. His rich tenor voice shaded with irony when he said, "Codfish cakes? In tribute to your New England forefathers, Theodore?"

"Bless the ancestral cod fishery," Theo quipped. "And don't forget the ice trade. The Bulkeley family owes its fortune to fish and ice. Old New England never let a frozen pond go to waste. As for you, Roderick DeVere, the heir of colonial Knickerbocker cartage and hauling...a fourth generation New Yorker, are you not? Or fifth?"

"Something like that." Roddy smiled but held my hand under the table in case this line of conversation dipped too deep. The quip about the men's club was irksome because ladies had no club of our own, not even one dedicated building where we could dine, socialize, exercise, hold meetings, or spend the night. The gentlemen had a dozen or more clubs. Roddy belonged to several, and so did Theo, who claimed he heard the news in clubrooms faster than Pulitzer or Hearst could print it.

Our friend's butler appeared with champagne, poured, and withdrew as Theo toasted us and the *Louisa*. We all sipped and peered at the river for the next few minutes, collecting our thoughts.

"So, Roderick," our friend said, "you'll bring the wisdom of New York's secret mixologist for a business proposition to the city famed for hams and bacon…beefsteaks too. Is your friend a packer?" He winked. "Or has a murder in Packingtown stirred you two armchair detectives into action?"

My smile froze, and Roddy's fingers tightened on his champagne glass. It was known in social circles that Roddy and I had taken part solving a homicide case in Newport and had done citizenly duty in the deadly Central Park fiasco. We also spent a few days in Palm Beach last winter in connection with a gruesome murder that was later solved. Otherwise, we kept close to home as winter slowly loosened its grip.

"Chasing murder in The City by the Lake, are you?" our friend quipped, his eyes merry.

"Theo," I said, "right now, a few days away from New York Society will be refreshing. There will be no risk of 'murder' in Colonel Mann's deathly gossip pages in *Town Topics*.

"Speaking of which," Theo said, "did you see his 'Saunterings' column yesterday?"

"Too busy with packing and household arrangements," I said.

"Then you missed a tidbit about your friend, Mr. Owen Coates."

"Oh?" Roddy sat forward.

"Not by name, of course, since *Town Topics* never names the names if Mann can spice his pages with guessing games about apparel. Yesterday's clue was 'a black-and-white houndstooth coat.'" A perfect fit for the gossip page, yes?"

"What about the houndstooth coat?" Roddy asked.

Theo cupped one hand as if confiding a secret. "A friend who attended the Brunswick dinner told me the houndstooth man was a hero," he said, "but 'Saunterings' says he was in his cups, fell off a coach, wallowed on the ground and couldn't get up until a man in a corduroy jacket pulled him to his feet."

Dudley, I thought, knowing Cassie was doubtless mortified to read it. "So," I said, "the hero became a stooge."

"One day," Roddy said, "Colonel Mann will go too far. The fellow in the houndstooth coat has the means to go after *Town Topics* and might ruin Mann. Time will tell."

I glanced at the river. Theo sipped his wine. We murmured enjoyment of the Codfish Benedictine as the train moved north. The trees along the river had not yet leafed out, and the shrubs looked wintry.

We had urged Theo to ask any question on his mind about the *Louisa*, since the car would be his, once we reached Chicago. He gazed at the plush chairs under the vaulted maple ceiling and eyed the wall sconces, the frosted glass shades, the tables. Finally, he said, "I'm admiring your new rustic mission style. No out-of-date Moorish fringe and tassels for the DeVeres' *Louisa*. A recent renovation?"

"Somewhat recent," I said. "The car was renewed and renamed in honor of my dear late mother."

"Very modern," Theo said, "up to date."

We should have expected the next question when our friend asked, "And what about the room you showed me a couple of weeks ago?"

He had hit a nerve.

"A reception room, wasn't it? The '*Empire*' room? Something like that?" Theo looked back and forth from Roddy to me. "Have I said something amiss?"

Roddy said, "We have decided on a tentative plan. I have been persuaded to try to fit the newest fashion."

"And let me add," I said, "that Mr. DeVere has agreed to my plan at a cost to his comfort in the near term. I appreciate his cooperation."

Theo looked at our faces, burst out laughing, then grew serious when he saw distress. "I apologize...I didn't mean...."

"Never mind, Theo," Roddy said. "Valentine will explain. So, Val, if you please...?"

The train had neared Troy, or maybe Schenectady. "As an experiment," I began, "the furnishings in the *Empire* room will be put into storage in a warehouse, and the wallpaper will be removed."

I took a deep breath. "The ancestral portrait," I said, "will be hung elsewhere in the house." I did not add that the footmen would hang it in the hall beside the telephone. Nor did I detail the face-off with Mrs. Thwaite.

"There's more, Theo" Roddy said, his voice strained. "Go ahead, please tell the rest of it."

My mouth felt dry. I sipped my water. "I have invited Miss Elsie De Wolfe to select furnishings for the room and oversee the installation...on a provisional basis."

"Oh...." Theo looked from Roddy to me. "And so, when you go home, you won't recognize...I mean, how clever."

The train whistle moaned just as the butler appeared with a tray. "The cheese course, if you will," Theo said brightly, guiding us to safer shoals. "Camembert, Leicester, and Doux de Montagne," Theo said, "but my butler couldn't locate your 'Cracker Barrel' fromage, Valentine."

We laughed. I had told Theo that Colorado trading posts stocked wheels of a dark orange cheese that was cut with a cleaver and wrapped to tote on pack mules to the mining camps. Cracker Barrel cheese, we called it. I loved it.

"To conclude our luncheon," Theo said, "we will have *Glace aux Poires*, pear ice...and coffee, though it will fall short of your legendary campfire coffee, Valentine." He looked from Roddy to me. "Now, what's this about you staying at a hotel in Chicago?"

Our friend had been surprised to learn that we would not to be houseguests of Roddy's prospective business ally, since the two men were acquainted in law school. We had reservations at a downtown hotel with the odd name, The Auditorium. Roddy explained to Theo that our comings and goings made a hotel most convenient. He did not say that we had politely declined Martin's invitation to be his guests in Oak Park.

We chatted as the *Louisa* gently swayed and the butler served pear ice and poured coffee and tea. After lunch, I read a brochure on sightseeing in Chicago's Loop, and Roddy and Theo played backgammon. I missed Velvet, but she was sure to be pampered by Calista, Sands, and the footmen. Chicagoans doubtless enjoyed dogs, but Velvet would be happier at home.

Theo went in for a nap, and I remembered the telegram in Roddy's coat pocket and went to retrieve it. We sat together in the parlor, and Roddy slit it open.

"Who wishes us bon voyage?" I asked, but Roddy's eyes darted and his jaw dropped as he showed me the glaring capital letters:

WATCH OUT. CHICAGO KILLS

"Who sent this, Roddy?"

"No idea."

"A prank?"

We stared at the letters. "Surely a prank," my husband said, but he sounded more hopeful than sincere, and my stomach churned as my fingers grew cold as ice in the warm car.

"A prank...somebody's joke," Roddy said.

"Not to share with Theo."

"Of course not."

We sat in fearful silence as the train made its way toward Lakes Ontario and Erie on the route that would take us across Indiana farm fields while we tried in vain to sleep tonight. We three dined early that evening and retired to our staterooms immediately afterwards. We would enter Indiana's industrial zones by morning.

One hour from Chicago, we gathered again at the *Louisa* dining table, the tension understood to arise as final words of advice were exchanged. Our baggage had been brought to the rear of the car, ready to be unloaded in about thirty minutes.

"Theo," I said, "Be wary of Rocky Mountain snowstorms. They come up fast this time of year and pile deep. The trail disappears before your eyes. And you'll need snowshoes. And another thing...do not stand near a geyser. The geyser gases are poisonous. Have a good time but keep a good distance from the eruptions."

Theo nodded.

"And remember," Roddy added, "that you'll be a mile high by Denver and feel lightheaded. It's normal but take it easy."

"Fair warnings," our friend said. "And let me offer you advice, my friends."

The train slowed. "Chicago had its big fire and hosted the brilliant world's fair in 'ninety-three, but be very careful what you drink. A favorite cocktail, Roderick, is the Mickey Finn…knock-out drops slipped into a cocktail to send you senseless and relieve you of your valuables."

He turned to me. "And Valentine, do take extra care. Quite daring of you to go about the strange city. I'm told its streets are jampacked with the jobless…fiercely at war with the state of things. Your household is not here, not even your maid."

He looked back at Roddy, then at me. "You two…" he said. "You don't exactly ask for trouble, but somehow trouble…."

Theo's next words were drowned in the screech and squeal of train wheels as we arrived at Chicago's Union Station. In the weeks ahead, his warning rang too true.

Chapter Fourteen

RODDY FLAGGED DOWN A porter in Chicago's Union Station, a monument to ambition with its vaulted skylight and lavish gold trim. Few passengers paused to look up, and conductors' "final call" sounded ghostly. I enjoyed the men's western Stetson hats until a porter lifted our bags onto a handcart and led us outdoors to the hansom cabs.

"The Palmer, sir?"

"No," Roddy said. "The Auditorium Hotel."

We had chosen The Auditorium for novelty. The "City by the Lake" had imagined a building that mixed business offices, a theater, and a hotel, all wrapped up in ten stories with a tall tower in the commercial hub of the city. It would be so very *Chicago.*

In the cab, our bags in back, the driver seemed bent on The Palmer, which he called the favorite of all ladies.

A gaunt man in rough wool, he held the reins of a weary dapple gray and said that "the lady" (meaning me) would be "nice" to her gentleman at The Palmer, then flashed Roddy a shameless grin.

"Welcome to Chicago," I murmured. We rode in silence, enveloped in a late-morning mist that cast the streetlamps in an orange glow while clanging, rumbling railway traffic rushed on every side. From Canal Street, we passed stout granite warehouses, a Gothic church, vacant lots, and shanties. Nearing South Michigan Avenue, the scene shifted to no-nonsense office buildings.

In architecture, this city was all business.

The Auditorium stood at the corner of South Michigan and Congress Street, a warehouse-like building despite stylish arches over the windows. Roddy registered while I eyed our bags as if they might be rifled or disappear. By noon, we were shown to a suite of rooms on the eighth floor, its heavy baroque décor just like hotel rooms everywhere. The Auditorium's novelty stopped with the usual overstuffed upholstery, tassled throw pillows, and heavy lamps...reminding me of my mother-in-law.

"May I suggest the view from the tower, the biggest thing in the city," the bellman said, and we went right to the tower where we held hands at the plate glass windows and gazed below at buildings of fourteen, fifteen, twenty stories tall.

"The Coates' real estate is somewhere down there," Roddy said, "properties from the city's earliest days...valuable."

"But the property is now Owen's, isn't it? Rents…profits, all Owen's?"

"As far as we know, not a cent for Martin."

The mist was clearing, and we quietly watched steamboats crisscrossing azure Lake Michigan that stretched to the horizon. "Beautiful," I said.

A top hatted gentleman gazing at the scene stepped toward us. "You've heard of the Great Fire of 1871?" We nodded. "Where this tower now stands," he said, "you would have stood in a bed of ashes. Not a single house standing from the lake to the Chicago River."

He stepped closer, a whiskery man with a full beard. "The truth about the fire," he said, "is that one night the O'Leary woman was too drunk to milk her cow…. It kicked over a lantern in the barn and started the blaze…." His voice filled with disdain as he stepped away. "Drunken Irish," he muttered, "men and women both…ought to be hanged."

I started after him to protest, but Roddy took my arm. "Val, don't."

"I'm furious."

"Of course you are. I'm upset too, but a squabble with a stranger won't help. We don't know the city, and we need to get our bearings. This is not New York." He turned from the window to face me. "Not New York," he repeated in a low voice, "and not the West. No jokes about Porkopolis. And remember Theo's warning about jobless men roaming the streets."

"So, first thing" I said, "we had better try to meet the Chicago policeman that Finlay recommended."

"'Recommended?'" Roddy's voice was yet lower. "A name that he scribbled on the back of a business card with a vague memory is hardly—"

"—Roddy, please. At least we do have a name."

The penciled 'Jakub Polachek' on the back of Finlay's card was our sole link to law enforcement in the city of Chicago, the thinnest thread to the detective mounting a homicide case against the Coates brothers and the live-in companion to the late Lydia Anne Gerstle Coates.

The panorama felt suddenly dizzying, the lure and fear of heights too much. I took Roddy's arm, and we returned to the elevator we shared with the top hatted man who hates the Irish. (Roddy clamped his hand over mine and silenced me with a look.)

Roddy checked his pocket watch in the suite's stuffy sitting room. "Already early afternoon...." He fingered an unmarked envelope in his coat pocket. "I'll go first to the Harrison Street "Lockup" and leave this for Officer Polachek and hope he gets it. Then it's off to Martin's office. It should take a few hours."

"And I could visit Hull House," I said. "I have the letter of introduction to the founder, Jane Addams."

Roddy looked uncertain. "Val, we don't know the city. A hotel maid can help you unpack, and room service will bring a tray. We'll see about dinner when I get back, and we'll talk about Officer Polachek."

"You think he'll take our 'bait?'"

"My note says that we bring greetings from his old ship-mate, Colin Finlay, who hopes for news about the Polachek family. I added that we plan to stroll in Jackson Park the next two mornings and—"

"—and how delighted we will if he also strolls, so we can press him about a Chicago police detective who believes that Lydia Coates was murdered."

"Now, Val."

"Now, Roddy."

We faced each other, tense and fretful on the verge of a quarrel. The strange new city, the strain of traveling, the slim odds of success. And that telegram.

Who sent it?

To scare us?

To warn us?

Roddy had put it in his luggage. We did not discuss it.

My husband drew me close. "Let's not have words, Val."

"No...let's not." With my face against Roddy's chest, I could feel his heartbeat, the steady rhythm. My Roddy....

"Val," he said softly, "I will feel much better knowing that you're safe in the hotel this afternoon. Sound reasonable?"

"Completely reasonable," I replied.

I fully intended to keep my word, unpacking the dresses and suits that Calista had chosen for a few days in Chicago. I then went downstairs to peek into the celebrated Auditorium theater. As advertised, the hall showed its forefront design with overhead lights inset in a series of tiara-like jeweled arches, rugged yet elegant.

Perhaps Roddy and I would attend a concert one evening. For now, feeling hungry and closed in, I decided to go outdoors to find a nearby café. If Michigan Avenue was the city's *Champs Elysée*, the side streets ought to cheer a woman stepping smartly in a navy tailored walking suit.

Out the door, I paused for the scent of this city. Blindfolded, I would know this was not New York. The nearby prairie scented Chicago, and the lake and stockyards too. Before me, Michigan Avenue teemed with carriages, trams, and people plunging from the sidewalk into the maelstrom. Gigantic mounted policemen kept order, each man and horse a barricade between eddying crowds.

With no tearoom or café in sight on the avenue, I sought a side street and soon stepped into deep shadows. With no café yet in sight, I should have turned back when the shadows began to stir. From dark alleys and doorways, the foundation stones began to move.

I stared. The stones were men, ragged men who stumbled toward me. Tall and short, they shuffled in my direction.

"…nickel, lady…spare a nickel…you got lost…lemme show you…lemme…."

Nearer they came, their eyes dark and vacant, their voices a low growl. My tiny pocketbook held three silver dollars. Three men, three dollars, and nothing for the others. How many did I see? Would they attack?

Not one mounted policeman would patrol this spot. Suppose I scuffled with these men, as I had a few times in Nevada when nasty drunks grabbed at me. How many could I fend off? If I went down, I'd take three or four with me.

They came singly and in pairs as if cued to a target. Six? Eight? More than eight. They came from behind to surround me. I smelled tobacco.

"…help you for a nickel…." A rawboned man blocked my path, his tattered ulster dragging on the ground. He tugged my cuff. "…for a nickel."

"No, thank you, no…."

I tripped across the walkway of broken flagstones, rippled asphalt, wood planks, and mud.

"Got a dime, lady?" I smelled whiskey.

Two men lurched, and my foot skidded in mud. These men were cadaverous, their jackets foul and tattered, broken shoes…no laces, no stockings. One clutched at a stick…no, a stub of a broom. Did he say, "Sweep?"

Sweep at what?

Just then, a uniformed figure hastened down the block and stepped to my side, his gloved hands holding a sheaf of papers. His uniform tunic, stiff collar and visored cap reminded me of the outdoor red kettles at the holidays.

"Salvation Army?" I asked.

"The Lord's work," he replied, nodding as he distributed the papers to the men. "Bread and coffee at the meeting,' he said. "First, the meeting. All are welcome."

The men grabbed the papers. Tickets to a slice of bread and coffee?

"They'll beg tonight," he said. "Any concert at the Auditorium, you'll find thirty, forty men gathered to beg."

He said it cheerfully.

"Beggars?" I asked. "Chicago's beggars?"

His sharp glance softened when he looked closely at me. "New to the city? Then you don't know about our jobless men...women too. Most from the fair...from the Columbian Exposition."

"The world's fair in 1893? But that was six years ago."

He handed a second paper to a man who had lost his in the mud. "These men," he said, "came from hither and yon for jobs at the fair. When it closed, they had no jobs, no place to live. They're all over the city, out on the street... and still they come. Vagrants...hoboes."

"Chicago winters...?"

"Worst of all," he said, "our freezing winters...and drops to the teens some of these spring nights." He closed his eyes, moving his lips as if in prayer, and then he said, "We give thick-sliced bread for the body, and for the spirit... from Second Peter, 'You will do well to pay attention as to a lamp shining in a dark place, until the day dawns and the morning star rises in your hearts.'"

He offered papers to two men who refused them. One spit his refusal. "The Salvation Army hall is close by on Harrison Street," the officer said, "but let me walk with you to Michigan Avenue, ma'am. The Avenue is the ladies' promenade. You'll be more…at ease."

Roddy found me brushing mud off my boots in the suite. "I took a short walk," I said. "Chicago ought to lay better sidewalks."

My husband moved to a stuffed chair where I had tossed my little pocketbook. Lifting it, he said, "…heavy."

"Heavier," I said, "since I stopped at the desk after my walk. I changed silver dollars for nickels."

"Nickels?"

"A Salvation Army sergeant said a nickel will buy a beer and free lunch at a saloon…."

"So, you went for a walk and plan to pass out nickels to support Chicago's breweries and saloons? I don't believe it."

I set a brushed boot on the floor. "Roddy, the nickels are a safeguard. This town is full of jobless, hungry men… women too. The Army sergeant said so. I saw men, you wouldn't believe how pitiful…."

"I would, Val. Pitiful…and also dangerous. We need to talk."

I gazed at the overstuffed sofa and chairs, the gilded and swirling woodwork that gave the eye no rest. "Let's go downstairs."

"Agreed."

We dressed for an early dinner in the wood-paneled dining room with large paintings of summer landscapes in heavy gilt frames. Offered a table by the huge windows ("our most desirable seating," said the maître d'hotel), we requested a quiet corner and faced one another over sherry and a crystal saucer of nuts.

"I am ready, Val, to hear about your afternoon walk."

"You mean, why didn't I stay put in the hotel suite?"

"To stay safe in a strange city for a couple of hours. Suppose something happened…."

"Roddy, I grew up in Colorado mining camps. I've been thrown by horses and dodged rockslides."

"Valentine Mackle DeVere, you are now in the city of the Haymarket bombing that killed seven policemen."

"Years ago, wasn't it? How many…?" I remembered the whole country was shaken by the Haymarket workers' rally when somebody threw a bomb and started a riot. My papa had struck his Big Lode about that time, and news of the bombing spread in the mining camps. Papa said the invention of dynamite had changed everything.

Roddy ignored my fingers. "To this day," he said, "I suspect Chicago is a smoking cauldron. My afternoon didn't prove otherwise."

"You saw Martin?"

"Briefly…after passing vagrants, the sort of men you saw this afternoon. I saw a greengrocer hire a man to unload crates of fruit. He offered twenty-five cents for the job, and I watched six men bid it down. 'I'll do it for twenty cents'…'for fifteen.'" Roddy fingered his wine glass. "A man settled on ten cents, one dime. Two of the losers cursed each other and started to fight. One of them grabbed a pineapple, and a bloody brawl erupted. A policeman broke it up. I think the greengrocer was embarrassed."

"But happy to save fifteen cents?"

"So it seemed."

We studied the menus. Men in business suits filled surrounding tables and cracked loud jokes. I did not see one woman guest.

"Tomorrow we'll dine in Oak Park at the Coates's home," Roddy said. "Martin apologized for his busy afternoon and mumbled something about labor troubles at the Vitalene works."

"Labor troubles?"

"He wasn't clear, and I didn't probe. The man looked harried. The distillery is enormous, Val...two adjoining brick buildings with vats and fillers, bottles marching on a conveyer belt. Martin and I spent no more than a quarter hour together because he was summoned to a department where the bottles are shipped. He told a young clerk to take me into the Vitalene salesroom.

Roddy sipped his wine. "Showcases gleaming...a museum of bottles from the earliest production, quaint-looking labels."

He put his wine glass down. I am to be ready for our 'planning' meeting in his private office on Friday."

"...about shutting down Vitalene?"

"And forging our partnership in the bitters business."

I did not reply. Four men in business suits were noisily ordering cocktails. "Gentlemen, a Mamie Gilroy.... Naughty

Mamie in *The Girl from Gay Paree*, and did you hear the one about…?"

The voices dropped. Roddy took my hand. "Val, we could go to the Palmer House."

"No, we're here." I looked at the menu. "The Great Lakes Whitefish," I said. "And tomorrow afternoon we might tour the stockyards."

"'Stockyards?' Did I hear stockyards?" The man who loudly ordered the Mamie Gilroy swiveled toward us. "Folks, you take it from me, Armour's packing plant is the eighth wonder of the world. "You like beef? Sausage? The whole operation," he continued, "…chains and hoists, and pigs squeal like they know it's all over…presto, bacon and chops. Here's to the packers!"

His friends raised their drinks, and Roddy touched his glass to theirs.

"Tomorrow," I said quietly, "let's do something else. Let's not…"

I did not finish. At that moment, street noises erupted outside on Michigan Avenue, a crashing…like angry cymbals. The dining room rose to look out the windows. The waiters stared into space.

Posters bobbed up and down outside with the word, *Arbeit*, and then whistles shrieked, and the crashing became dull thuds…then quiet. The diners sat back down.

"What does *Arbeit* mean, Roddy?"

"Work. It's German for work."

The maître d'hotel approached. "Deepest regrets for the unpleasantness," he said.

"What was that about?" I asked.

"A public demonstration of dissatisfaction, I am sorry to say." He straightened his tie. "...most inappropriate. We would like to offer a dessert of your choice this evening, courtesy of the Auditorium Hotel."

We thanked him. The Mamie Gilroy man bellowed, "Damnable striking Krauts...anarchist swine ought to go back...back where they came from...."

He kept on, louder. People stared. At Roddy's signal, I quietly rose, and we made our way to the door. At the threshold, the man's voice was blaring, curses and oaths. Among his words, "...shot dead...too good for them. String them up like hogs...every one, string up every last one."

"Welcome to Chicago..." I murmured for the second time today as we crossed the lobby.

Roddy took my arm. "I'm hungry, Val, shall we try the Palmer House?"

Chapter Fifteen

WE DINED WELL AND quietly in the Palmer House Hotel's well-named Red Lacquer Room, where the gilding and carved friezes glowed under chandeliers of red garnets and Austrian crystal. The dinners promised to be excellent. Roddy ordered French wines in French.

"Val," he said over his blue point oysters, "I could look into moving us to the Palmer House."

It was tempting. New York had talked about Mrs. Palmer's collection of unusual French paintings called Impressionist, and here were pastel waterlilies in a blurry style by an artist named Monet. And Tiffany glass was always rewarding in a church or hotel or private home.

"What do you think?" he asked. "Shall we?"

I nibbled paté with a toast point. "Not yet, Roddy. The Auditorium is a business hotel, and we are here on business."

"I'll drink to that." We took our time and left the Palmer House with a promise to return as guests.

The next morning found us at breakfast in the Auditorium dining room before eight a.m., ready for the morning in Jackson Park, where we hoped to catch sight of Officer Jakub Polachek.

"Roddy, we have no idea of what he looks like."

"No thanks to your Finlay."

The knock on "my" Detective Finlay was not worth a tiff. "The men have not seen one another for years, Roddy. We are in luck that Finlay remembered the man's name." I added, "The "Lockup" officers at the police station did find his name, didn't they?"

"But not his schedule, Val, so our Jackson Park mornings might be for nothing. Besides, the man might not follow up on my note...even if he gets it. The station seemed hit and miss, prisoners grabbed by the scruff of the neck and shoved into cells."

"Awful."

"Yes."

Businessmen at nearby tables finished their meals, gripped satchels, and hastened into the workday.

"Salesmen," my husband said, "eager and anxious."

"Like Roderick and Valentine DeVere," I said, "after the bruising first day...and that loud bunch here in this dining room. I feel we've already toured the stockyards."

"...unseemly vivid details," Roddy said.

"You know that I am not squeamish," I said. "In Colorado, I put a donkey out of his misery. I cried bitterly, but it had to be done." I sipped my coffee. "That man last night…too much glee about the animals. And the hullaballoo outside. Was it a labor strike?"

"I think a protest march," Roddy said, "probably wages, but the police put an end to it."

My husband sipped his breakfast tea and asked for morning papers. At four p.m., a train would take us to Oak Park, where we would be met by Martin's carriage and driven to the Coates' home. We would dine early and be taken to the station for the train back to the city. I sipped my coffee, not strong enough.

The waiter brought *The Chicago Sun Times* and *Tribune*, Roddy snapped open the *Sun Times.* "Here it is…headline, Val…'Pandemonium on Michigan Avenue'…'brazen labor discontent.'"

"Last night? Out front?"

"'Hurly-burly march of lawless'…," my husband read. "…'source of calamity…German printers attack machine that prints Bibles…mob swarms on Michigan…one killed….'"

"Killed?"

"'bloodshed on sidewalk…casualty of trespass, four hundred block.'"

"Roddy, the four hundred block…it's right here. We are—"

"—at number 430 South Michigan Avenue. Yes, we are."

I put my cup down. "…bloodshed," I said.

Roddy nodded. "A fatality."

"Roddy," I said, "that telegram on the train…."

A long minute passed. My husband folded the newspaper. "Should we talk about it?"

"No."

"Further thoughts?"

"None."

We both scanned the room, keeping watch for nothing.

A sallow young waiter arrived, unsure of where to put the plates and bowls. Roddy disliked my impromptu chats with waiters, but I asked, was this young man on duty last evening?

"…setting the tables, mum," he said.

"And did you notice the…the ruckus?"

He jostled the eggs, nearly spilled the porridge. "Bit of a fuss," he said. "Happens from time to time."

"Here? In front of The Auditorium Hotel?"

"Hotel, yes" he said, "but a residence too. No worries, mum, the sidewalk is scrubbed clean as a whistle." He put down the jam and fled.

"What do you make of that?" I asked.

"I think the labor protest targeted someone who is living here."

"…and a life was lost for nothing." I spooned the porridge. "Roddy, let's not linger. Let's be off to Jackson Park. And never mind the stockyards."

Before ten a.m., in bright sunshine, we arrived at the park, the site of the stupendous world's fair six years ago. The Columbian Exposition had drawn crowds in the millions, and I had yearned to ride the Ferris Wheel and see the electrified classical White City after dark and snack on new caramel popcorn called Cracker Jack.

Papa, however, thought it best that I stay with him in Virginia City to see the new machinery that was to be installed for the Mackle Mining Company. He insisted his daughter witness the latest mechanical and chemical operation that refined raw ores into silver ingots. At summer's end, he ordered cartons of Cracker Jack for the miners and me, a little prize in every box.

"How I yearned to ride the Ferris Wheel," I said to Roddy. "...every car the size of a Pullman railroad car."

"We'll ride it in 1904," Roddy said. "Mr. Ferris's wheel will operate at the next world's fair in St. Louis." He squeezed my hand. "Meanwhile," he said, "not much to see here, I'm sorry to say."

No policeman was in sight, nor a man in plainclothes who might be Jakub Polachek. Little children toddled with their nannies near beds of blooming tulips. A nurse pushed an elderly man in a wheelchair.

"That crumbling building," Roddy said, "is the former Palace of Fine Arts. I understand it might be restored and turned into a museum."

"Good use," I said. We looked at the tulips and strolled the paths in silence. A young man in a cassock and clerical collar cut across a path. "A Catholic priest," I said.

"A priest," Roddy repeated. He looked into the distance. "It's a big park," he said. "My note should have specified exactly where we would stroll today and tomorrow. If Polachek comes, he could miss us."

"Patience...," I said, which was odd for me, the impulsive one.

The sun climbed higher, and we circled the pathways. An hour had passed. Killing time, and still no sign of Polachek.

"Maybe we ought to talk about tonight's dinner with Martin," I said. "If any topic ought to be out of bounds, say the word."

A little boy dashed to a flower bed, snatched a red tulip, and thrust it at the old man in the wheelchair. The old man smiled.

"That scene," said Roddy, "will make the perfect conversation," he said. "Martin is very proud of Chicago."

"Although he chooses to live several miles outside of it?"

"...and not a word about that, Valentine Mackle DeVere. And I suggest you avoid your run-in with the vagrant men yesterday. I will keep silent about the row at the greengrocer's. And not a word about last evening's fracas in front of the Auditorium." He paused. "Also, Val...."

"Yes?"

"Your visit to Hull House...?"

"I know what you're thinking, Roddy. Not a word about Martin's late wife volunteering there. If Hull House comes up, I will say that I have promised to bring greetings to Miss Jane Addams from her friends in New York. No mention of Lydia Coates's involvement."

Robins twittered, and the sun disappeared behind a cloud. A gust of wind blew at my skirt and ruffled the tulips.

Roddy snugged his hat. The sun flared again. "Nearly high noon, Val. What do you say we...?"

"Roddy," I said, "look over there." Beyond the flower beds and past the shabby Fine Arts building stood a man in a dark tunic, helmet in hand. He looked right and left, put his helmet on, and began to walk off.

Roddy waved but was ignored.

"He didn't see you."

My husband hollered into the wind. I had never seen him run so fast, but Roddy took to his heels at a blistering pace, caught up, tapped the man's shoulder, then dodged as the man spun around to throw a punch.

Lip reading was not needed to know what the two said as they walked toward me. Chicago's police tunic was a few inches longer than New York's and the brass buttons a bit smaller. The navy blue wool? Exactly the same.

A winded Roderick DeVere introduced Officer Jakub Polachek, a stocky, thick-shouldered man who took off his helmet to reveal a shiny bald head fringed with light-colored hair. A broad face with pink cheeks and alert blue eyes offset his thin, scraggly blonde beard.

"How do you do, ma'am?"

"Officer Polachek," I replied, "I am pleased to meet you."

Roddy suggested that we all sit on nearby benches. "You are not on duty?" he asked the officer.

"Not till three o'clock...afternoon shift, three-to-eleven." We faced each other on opposite iron benches, and the officer reached into his tunic pocket, pulled out a familiar envelope, and said to Roddy, "Your letter, sir. And sorry for the roundhouse punch you almost got from this...." He held up a closed fist. "Lucky you ducked in time, but take a tip from me...you don't want to mess around in Chicago."

Roddy murmured, "I'll do my best."

"Then again," Officer Polachek said, "Finlay wouldn't know about Chicago, would he?" He waved the envelope. "Nothing doing when I coaxed him to come back here with me."

"Chicago is your hometown?" I asked.

"Chicago," he said, "by way of the Vistula River in Poland." He set his helmet on the bench. "Us Polacheks settled in 'Little Poland' on Milwaukee Avenue, but I got the idea to see the world. So, sixteen years old, I hopped a freight and shipped out of the New York Harbor. I crewed with Micks and Krauts and Wops and...." He stopped and cleared his throat. "What I mean, sailors from all over, like Finlay."

"From Ireland," I said.

"Ireland...and we sailed the Atlantic, but I said, 'Come to Chicago, Finlay. We'll crew on the iron ore boats, Wisconsin to Chicago in good weather, and winters snug and warm in the saloon with nickel beer and a free lunch.'"

Roddy and I exchanged a glance.

"But now," he said, "I patrol Whiskey Row to keep the Micks...the Irish, I mean...keep the Irish and the Poles and Germans from brawls and worse." He smiled a bit bashfully. "Two seasons on an ore boat across Lake Superior and Michigan, and it was time to settle down, raise a family.

You tell Finlay that my Anna bakes the bread we dreamed about in our hardtack days at sea. You tell him I have three strapping sons and a daughter as pretty as her mother." He leaned toward us. "Now then, what news about Colin Finlay?"

How downright embarrassing. For all the help that Detective Finlay had given Roddy and me, we knew nothing of his personal life. For all the discussions with him during the Central Park murders last fall, we had never thought to ask where he lived or whether he had a family. And the man came from Ireland, my parents' own birthplace. How negligent of me. Unforgivable.

Roddy sat forward. "Officer Polachek," he said, "you will be pleased to know that Detective Finlay is among the highest-ranking officers in the New York City Police Department. His investigations have saved lives and protected innocent people from serious harm. His excellent career continues to this day, and the Chief of Police, William Devery, holds him in highest regard. Detective Finlay wants you to know that he remembers your work at sea with affection and great respect."

Roddy's smooth lies mixed with enough facts to sound like the truth. Jakub Polachek nodded solemnly as his cheeks flushed scarlet. "Well and good,' he said, "and wears a suit like a gentleman, does he?"

"At his rank," Roddy said, "a detective wears a business suit."

The moment hung. Polachek tugged the hem of his tunic. Two red-breasted robins flew at each other, and the sun beat down.

"It's give and take in life," Polachek said slowly, "so you can tell Finlay his old shipmate goes on foot patrol to keep the peace...broken street lamps, drunks, runaway horses. Never a suit for this one."

"Honorable work, to keep the peace," I said. The birds settled down. "Officer Polachek," I said, "we have a question. Mister Finlay suggests that you might know a certain detective on the Chicago police force. His name is Brady. We would like to have a word with him. Do you know a Brady?"

Polachek ran a hand over his bald head. "...first name or last name?"

"We aren't sure," I said.

He shook his head and bit a thumbnail. "Don't know as I do." I watched him look at the ground and blink rapidly. "Don't know as I can be helpful on that score." He rubbed his hands together and looked at the sky.

A long minute passed. His lips moved as if reciting a prayer. "Tell you somebody that might know," he said at last. "...but no need to say that Jakub Polachek sent you. No need."

"We will not refer to you," Roddy said.

He looked right and left, turned to glance behind and still seemed reluctant. "All right, then...there's a fire house on Lake Street...near Kedzie. The captain, a man named Cronon...he might know. Sam Cronon knows everybody." He leaned toward us. "No need to say my name."

"No need," I echoed.

He picked up his helmet and stood. "My very best to Finlay for health and a long life," he said.

"Count on it," my husband replied with gusto I hoped might sound sincere.

Polachek bowed to me and began to walk away when he paused, turned, and said, "Ma'am, next time your mister goes on a sprint, tell him to watch out. Just remember...you don't want to mess around in Chicago."

Chapter Sixteen

A SHELLACKED COACH DRAWN by a pair of chestnut bays took us from the train depot to the village of Oak Park in the early evening hour. I guessed the coachman had been ordered to drive us in a roundabout route over Oak Park's brick-paved streets to show off its modern churches, its library, post office, and courthouse. At last, we slowed on an elm-lined block of large Victorians and stopped before a turreted house set far back from the street. The front door opened, and Martin came down the front walk to greet us at the curb.

"Good evening, Mrs. DeVere...Roderick. My thanks to you for coming out to Oak Park." He led us along the walk and up granite steps onto a broad porch.

"Welcome...." He opened the front door to usher us down a front hall past a steep, carpeted stairway with a brass newel post and brass balustrades. I slowed just long enough to eye the topmost step from which Lydia Coates most likely had plunged to her death.

"The parlor," Martin said, "if you will...."

We took seats on gloomy Sheraton chairs from the Victorian era, meaning this room had not been refurbished. Years ago, parlors like this were closed off most of the time, though final good-byes to Lydia had probably happened in this room, and respects paid near her casket. I saw no obvious space where she had lain in so-called repose. Nor did family photographs brighten the bare tables or decorative shelves. Street scenes of the Orient filled a dozen picture frames on a wall near the window, village pagodas and workers in coolie hats. Somehow, the parlor felt out of kilter. The slightly crooked pictures begged to be straightened.

Martin pressed a service button as we sat down. "A fair day in the city?" he asked. "Easy ride out to Oak Park?"

"Quite," Roddy said.

"A charming village," I added.

My father, Harold...my late father built this house. Mother prized every square foot. I grew up here with my brothers, Owen and Keenan...the late Keenan...and then Celia."

"You lost a brother?" Roddy said. "I didn't know...."

Martin cracked a knuckle. "There's a saying in Oak Park that an old man dies decorously, a young man tragically." He crossed his legs. "Keenan tried to race an oncoming train across the track. He died foolishly."

Not one second's pause let us voice regrets before Martin continued. "I was married in this parlor near the window where you are sitting, Mrs. DeVere …married to Lydia Anne Gerstle, the mother of Lester and Letitia, our children."

I glanced at Roddy, whose face showed no emotion, though his hands were tightly clasped.

"My Lydia disliked this parlor," Martin said, "but she kept everything in place for mother's sake. We entertained in other rooms and outdoors in warm weather. My Lydia loved garden parties, all the ladies in big hats and lots of laughter. Our porch and the lawn were filled with guests for the garden parties."

His voice had softened as if recalling the parties. No one spoke until an aproned woman in a maid's cap appeared with a tray of glasses that she showed to Martin for his approval. "Yes, Maja," he said, "for our guests…and do ask Tansy to come meet our friends."

Offered sherry or water, I reached for the tumbler of water as the servant, Maja, blinked as if fearing that her offerings fell short. Her cap was askew, her apron spotted, and her reddened hands trembled as she held the tray. She moved to Roddy, who lifted a thick, nubbly glass filled to the brim with sherry.

"Dinner in twenty minutes, Maja?" Martin took a time-piece from a vest pocket and put it on a table at his elbow, face up and ticking.

I sometimes thought my husband peered at his pocket watch too often, but Roddy never flouted manners as Martin did at this moment. The man was either socially awkward or timing our visit to discharge a social duty before meeting privately with my husband tomorrow at the Vitalene distillery.

"You'll meet Tansy in a minute or two," said Martin. "My Lydia called our little daughter the Coates family artist... scribbled from the time she could hold a pencil. With her brother away at school in New England, it's just Tansy and me now...Maja to help out."

I heard sorrow in his words, just as a blonde-haired young girl skipped to the parlor doorframe and paused. Her white pinafore matched a fluffy white cat that sprang from her arms, meowed, streaked across the room and leapt into Martin's lap.

"Tansy, my dear...." With a kindly smile and eyes showing warmth, he invited her into the room and stroked the cat. "Mr. and Mrs. DeVere," he said, "this is my daughter, Tansy...Letitia."

Tansy Coates looked about eleven years of age, a slender child soon to leave behind girlhood's pinafores and long flowing hair tied back with a single ribbon. She stood before us, smiled sweetly, said "How-do-you-do," and curtsied. "That is Snowbell," she said in a clear lilt. "She came as a kitten. Would you like to pet her?"

"If you think she would allow it," I said.

The child brought the cat close so I could stroke the soft fur. The young girl's fingernails were bitten to the quick. Seeing me notice, she buried her fingers in the fur.

"When Snowbell sleeps," she said, "I can draw her. But she won't pose when she's awake."

"Tansy," I said, "people can be as troublesome as pets when artists try to paint them."

"I know all about that. Auntie Sara wouldn't sit still."

"Our dear friend, Sara Dow," Martin said. "Lester and Tansy call her their 'Auntie.'"

"I drew Auntie Sara when she took a nap," Tansy said, "but I learned not to do that." She nodded solemnly. "I only draw animals now." Her fingers rose to her lips, and her father raised a scolding hand.

"Remember your promise," he said, pointing at his own nails. His daughter curled her fingers.

"I'd like to see one of your drawings," I said, "but why only animals?"

I asked for conversation's sake, but Martin cut in. "Tansy's mama spoiled her," he said. "Lydia spoiled all of us."

The moment darkened at the name of the late Lydia Coates. Tansy's shoulders slumped, and her father's eyes looked mournful. The cat arched its back. I sensed a sharp aroma from the kitchen…something burning.

"That's Maja…" said Tansy, wrinkling her nose and frowning. "When Auntie Sara comes back, she'll…."

But her father raised his palm to signal silence. "Time for your schoolwork, my dear," he said. "No more drawing pictures…and then your supper…first things first."

Tansy curtsied, said flatly how nice to make our acquaintance, lifted Snowbell from her father's arms, and was gone.

It felt as though the light had dimmed. In death's aftermath, the father-daughter warmth seemed dependent on a white housecat. Maja's days in the Coates home were numbered, I guessed, and Martin would probably seek another hapless Maja to bully and badger. The acrid odor grew stronger.

Martin folded his arms across his chest. "I cannot vouch for our dinner," he said. "We've lost cooks and housekeepers… just try nowadays to find a country girl that will bake a loaf of bread, but no, they want easy work in a department store."

I might have remarked that department store clerks toiled on hard floors for long hours for pitiful wages, but our host seemed bent on venting woes about "the servant problem," a topic that engrossed Society. I was caught off guard by the rant that followed, as was Roddy. Housekeeping seemed the least of Martin Coates's problems.

"The woman in the kitchen, Maja…she can barely keep up," he said. "Immigrants…thick-headed and stubborn. I face it downtown every day, DeVere. Men line up for jobs all over Chicago, and the Vitalene operation needs workers, just like our bitters business will need men willing to pull their weight."

He clenched his hands. "But they come with harebrained notions about unions…a carryover from the Old Country. Socialist rot, and no escaping it. Build a house on 'Gold Coast' Prairie Avenue, and they'll march to your front door with 'Death to Capitalists' signs. They'll go on strike and hold you up for ransom." He paused. "You're staying at the Auditorium…."

"We are, said Roddy.

"I sympathize, Mrs. DeVere," he said in a voice more stern than sympathetic. "Why was it that your husband did not reserve a suite at the Palmer House…but never mind. A man that operates the biggest print shop near the Loop, everything from directories to Bibles…he lives at the Auditorium, and they came after him last night."

Roddy and I exchanged a quick glance.

"I stay put in Oak Park, take the train six days a week. If this house ever needs work, I can call on a local architect… see whatever young Frank Lloyd Wright can do. I tell you, no one dies from gunshots in Oak Park. No one gets drunk in public. Hoodlums don't march for revolution, and young women can go into the village shops without fear. This is what I say to anybody that talks about the charity agency on Halsted Street in the city.

The name resounded. I said the words aloud. "Halsted Street?"

"A city slum," he said, "filled with Polish and Russian peasants and their ilk. He touched his cheek. "My Lydia thought she found her mission in life down there. Sara, now…she knew how to handle them."

"Sara Dow?" I asked.

"I believe you met Sara? Celia tells me you had tea… you and your friend."

"We did," I said.

"My late wife was never the picture of health, Mrs. DeVere. You see those Chinese pictures on that wall? Sara's father was a delegate to the Far East, and her sisters are there now, converting the heathens. They sent us pictures, and Sara hung them up with Lydia's blessing." He smoothed his moustache. "The real blessing is Sara coming to us, especially in the last two years."

"Mrs. Coates's health worsened?" I asked.

"Little by little, yes. Dr. Hemingway called here every few days, and then we switched to a new medical man that came every day. Dr. Yager showed Sara how to dose the powders and pills to steady my wife's nerves, how to inject the medicines. And things went well until...until the accident."

He touched his throat. "Lydia fell down the front hallway stairs," he said in a strangled voice. "We have the strongest railing that money can buy...that carpenters can build...but my wife tumbled down...and was gone."

Martin's timepiece ticked. "Sara blames herself," he said. "She was close to Lydia when it happened, but not close enough to prevent the fall. Afterwards, Sara could not bear to stay in this house. The accident crushed her. She was eager to join Celia in New York. That's my reading."

He swallowed. "Miss Sara Dow was a companion and nurse to Lydia, as close as a sister to my wife and a favorite aunt to Tansy and Lester too. A godsend to me...so tied up at the works day after day. I saw the woman angry just once when I called her 'Saintly Sara.' She said I blasphemed. I apologized. You heard Tansy say something about Sara coming back to us...?"

I nodded.

"My daughter's pipedream," he said. "I only hope she can curb Celia's spending. Owen promises to keep an eye out, but if it's not about horses, my brother isn't interested, although I give Owen credit...he stayed close by while my wife's health failed. He took Lester riding, and he gave Tansy enough paints and paper to last a lifetime. He took turns reading aloud to Lydia in the afternoons. First Sara would read, then Owen took his turn. Day after day, week after week, Owen did his part reading books to keep up Lydia's spirits."

What did they read? I wanted to know, but Martin gestured for me to rise. "And now, Mrs. DeVere, let me escort you into the dining room. We will do our best with whatever comes from our kitchen by way of the Halsted slum."

On Martin's arm, halfway from the parlor, I remembered why Halsted Street struck a chord. Number 800 South Halsted Street was the address of Hull House.

We dined under the glowering gaze of Martin's deceased father, Harold, who presided from an oil portrait on a wall at the end of the dining room. With bushy white brows, fierce eyes, muttonchop whiskers, and a flinty mouth, Martin's father looked ready to spring from the painting to bark orders at everyone below.

Anna nervously ladled a lukewarm soup, brought a platter of scorched meat with dense dumplings, and presented a limp vegetable dish. Could I take her aside to inquire about Hull House? Impossible. The woman barely knew English, and her employer was as terrifying as the portrait.

Martin explained to Roddy how his father expanded the company tenfold and ruined rivals, and I turned my gaze to a framed photograph on a sideboard, a studio portrait of a mother and daughter, blonde Tansy and her mother. The photograph had been tinted to add color, but Lydia's sunken eyes and cheeks told a story of struggle as a wife…as a mother. Embracing her daughter lovingly in the picture, she looked at once kindly, sick, sorrowful, and bewildered.

Martin continued a recitation on distillation, and Roddy showed interest, but my gaze was drawn again to the mother and child…the child with her invalid mother. Each time I looked, Lydia Coates appeared more resigned…to illness? To fate?

Or was I imagining things?

A seed cake dessert was served at last, and Martin turned toward me. "Apologies for so much business talk, Mrs. DeVere. Let me say that having you and Mr. DeVere—Roderick—at this dinner table is a pleasure…a rare pleasure. I hope we might dine here again. This evening, the dinner table has felt like…like a warm hearth in winter."

I thanked him and saw his hands steeple in a prayerful gesture. "But not to forget," he said, "your promise to rid this household of the troublesome Chicago detective. Eternal punishment will be too good for him."

I did not know what to say. Neither did Roddy. Martin did not speak the man's name, perhaps not to sully his home or give his tormentor the stature of an opponent.

"That photograph you see of my Lydia and Tansy...." He pointed to the sideboard picture. "Taken just two years ago in a studio here in Oak Park, a loving portrait.... Every evening sitting at this table, I see my Lydia and know that no one could wish her harm. No one."

As if in benediction, we rose from the table as Martin announced that a coach with fresh horses was ready to take us to the depot. At the doorway for farewells, he called his daughter to say good-by. The child brought a folded paper that she shyly offered to me. "A drawing for you, Ms. DeVere, as you asked." Charmed, I thanked her and hoped we might see her again.

The carriage took a more direct route to the rail depot, and we passed a livery stable, a dairy, a carpentry shop, an artesian wells driller...and then a roofing company.

"Roddy," I said, "that roofer...that sign." The carriage moved quickly, and I knocked on the side of the door to request a stop, but we drove on. "That sign," I said.

"What sign?"

"Brady..." I said. "I'm sure of it...the name of the detective...Brady Roofers. It's the name, Roddy. It's the name we are looking for. Stop the carriage."

Roddy tried, but the carriage drove on.

Chapter Seventeen

WE STARTED EARLY, BUT not before the name, Brady, sparked a short dispute the next morning. I reminded my husband that Martin said the "witch hunt" detective was possibly a former schoolmate who later joined the Chicago police but still had family in Oak Park. "The Oak Park Roofers," I said, "could be the family of 'witch hunt' Brady."

"But Val," Roddy replied, "could you really see in the darkness? The carriage moved at a good clip, so perhaps you saw 'Bradley?'"

At this, I bit the chin strap of my bonnet. The teeth marks in the strap saved us from a morning flareup. We had breakfasted and prepared for demanding days, each of us on edge. Roddy would go to the Vitalene works but first see me off to Hull House.

The Auditorium doorman helped me into a cab whose driver expected a fare to Marshall Field's department store and balked at the Halsted Street address. Street urchins would hobble his horse, he said, and his cab wheels sink in mud. Muttering, he flicked the reins, and off I went. Roddy had paid him.

The hansom driver did not exaggerate. As we went west toward Halsted Street, putrid odors of rotting garbage and drainage filled teeming streets lined with fish mongers, butchers, saloons, and peddlers with pushcarts that reminded me of the Lower East Side, a familiar scene to me. Looking left and right, the same bleak sight, not one tree or blade of grass. Two ragged boys tossed a ball...no, a scrap of trash. They cursed at the cab.

Had they cursed as Lydia passed by? Lydia had come often from leafy Oak Park. She ventured freely into this mire, breathed its stench, and somehow sought fulfillment. Could I find out more?

The cab stopped at a two-story Italian Renaissance house with a wide portico and new brick outbuildings that rose on either side to amplify the house. "Eight hundred South Halsted," the driver growled, barely giving me time to get out before snapping the reins to leave me ankle-deep in muddy water that soaked my boots and the hem of my cloak. It had rained during the night, and loose paving blocks floated in muddy puddles. Hardwood blocks had been used to pave streets, but surely not in recent times. Yet here they were, dislodged and afloat. Feeling bedraggled, I mounted the granite steps and knocked on the front door.

"Good morning. Won't you come inside?" The slender, sloe-eyed lady who opened the door seemed ready to go out of doors herself, buttoned in a smart navy coat, a hat, and gloves.

"I am Julia Lathrop," she said, "and just now going out, but may I help you?" Glancing at my boots and cloak, she laughed lightly. "One day," she said, "Halsted Street will be properly paved, but for now we button up and brave the elements in all weather."

I said my name, drew the letter of introduction from my cloak, put it into her hands, and saw a warm smile. "From our Sister Kelley," she said.

"Sister? Mrs. Kelley is your sis—?

Her laughter rippled. "We call her 'Sister Kelley,' and Hull House misses her terribly." Miss Lathrop looked more closely at me. "You must be active in the National Consumers League."

The word, "active," always made me feel deficient. "I am a member," I said. "I am hoping to meet Miss Addams."

"As are a great many other visitors these days," she said. "Miss Addams ought to be back by midday, but you might have a word with one of our volunteers...."

She drew me into the foyer where a wall chart listed names and activities. Through an archway, I glimpsed a reception room where women in black babushkas and shawls sat hunched, their heads down and hands folded as if in prayer.

"You are seeing the neighborhood women who hope Miss Addams or another of us might help in some way," Miss Lathrop said. "Perhaps a grandson has been jailed for stealing milk...or coal. Chicago desperately needs a juvenile court, but in the meantime, certain ladies of the city step in to help."

"Let me see...we have "a folk music class..." she said, "and clay ceramics...and a reading class...poetry today." Her gloved finger stopped. "Here's Mrs. Enright's name. I believe she might have time to make acquaintance and explain Hull House to you. Let me take you to the coffeehouse in our new building."

A spacious room in an adjoining building featured stout oak tables and spindle back chairs. Julia Lathrop excused herself to attend a meeting about the juvenile court, but promised, "You will in good hands with Mrs. Enright."

In moments, I shook the manicured hand of a lady whose quick brown eyes scanned the room. The buxom and rosy-cheeked Gertrude Enright introduced herself and asked, "Coffee or tea, Mrs. DeVere...but I warn you, Hull House brews a strong cup of coffee."

"All the better," I said. "I prefer it black."

From the beverage bar, she brought two mugs of hot dark coffee and sat across from me. "As a member of the Chicago Woman's Club," she said, "I volunteer here three days each week. And when visitors come knocking, I am called upon to explain Hull House, which is named for the Hull family that lived here in 1850, when this part of Chicago was a country retreat."

"A country retreat? Really?"

"Strains the imagination, Mrs. DeVere, but families like the Hulls fled, making room for Miss Addams and her friend who saw the opportunity to move in and purchase the house. They drew other like-minded young women as fulltime residents. Hull House, you see, is situated among immigrants from all over the world. We now count twenty-nine different languages, and our English language classes fill every seat."

I nodded. It would not do to interrupt Mrs. Enright's account. The volunteer's task was telling the Hull House story, and the visitor was to listen with open ears. I must not hasten to quiz Mrs. Enright about Lydia Coates.

"You must understand, Mrs. DeVere, that Hull House is not a religious or political headquarters. Miss Addams's idea has been to create ...and I quote her words, a 'center for a higher civic and social life.' Hull House promotes social democracy across all classes of neighbors, and that is crucial...neighbors helping neighbors. The term that is taking hold for similar centers in American cities is, settlement house. Miss Lathrop and others are planning a professional training school they will call social work."

Mrs. Enright sipped her coffee, as did I. She put her mug down, looked closely at me, and said, "To put the case squarely, just imagine life in the ramshackle slums on these streets...Halsted, State, Polk, Clark...not one bathtub, no piped hot water. Imagine it if you can."

I shook my head to indicate that I could not. It would not help to say that my first fourteen years of life had passed without a bathtub and that winter ice was sometimes melted over a campfire to free up wash water.

"So, Mrs. DeVere," she continued, "Hull House installed little tubs in the basement, and volunteers bathe the neighborhood infants in warm, soapy water every Saturday morning. And generous donors have come forward. We are enjoying this coffee in one of the new brick buildings. Thanks to donors' understanding of the great need, Hull House has a kindergarten and a theatre and lecture hall. A gymnasium is underway for exercise and sport."

"Impressive," I said, and meant it.

"I have given you the main points, Mrs. DeVere. We do not offer tours of the house, but I believe you glimpsed the main reception room...informal furnishings with books and pictures, comfortable chairs and sofas, scatter rugs. The same idea for the residents, such as Miss Lathrop and a few women who reside on the upper floor. What else would you like to know?"

Could I plunge into a question about Lydia? Not yet. "Mrs. Enright," I said, "it seems the volunteers, such as yourself, have become an important dimension of Hull House."

Her cheeks grew rosier, her bright eyes more alight. "Hull House has brought us together...club women, women of means. Chicago grows fast, even faster since the fire of 'seventy-one. I was a little girl, and the flames so utterly terrifying. But now our work is here, and we contribute in many ways." She looked a trifle shy, then said, "Perhaps you have heard of Enright fittings?"

Fittings? "Oh," I said, "the brass faucets?"

"Faucets, doorknobs, handles.... Mr. Enright's successful brass business has helped to build these new brick buildings...it's philanthropy, Mrs. DeVere. Until our society becomes civilized, we need philanthropy."

Spoken in passing like a well-known fact, her statement struck deep, a point to mull over in time. For the moment, her words became the wedge I needed. "It happens, Mrs. Enright, that a friend of my husband is the widower of a Hull House volunteer and philanthropic donor...the late Mrs. Martin Coates...Lydia Coates."

"Oh, our Lydia...." The bright brown eyes squeezed shut, and the manicured fingers reached for a handkerchief. "My goodness..." she said. "Dear Lydia." She dabbed t her eyes. "You knew her?"

"Sadly," I said, "she passed away before we made full acquaintance. I met her briefly at a law school reunion in New York. Mr. Coates was a classmate of my husband."

Gertrude Enright seemed uninterested in my details. "If you had known Lydia, Mrs. DeVere, you would weep at the mention of her name, knowing our loss could not be greater."

She dabbed her eyes. "All who knew her loved Lydia dearly. Her work with the children...the immigrant children who timidly came to the door...she seemed to understand them, no matter what language they spoke. Every Saturday morning, Lydia knelt at the little bathtubs and soaped their bodies and trimmed their nails. She came even when her energy flagged the last year or so.... She said it did her good. She became a particular friend of Dr. Hamilton."

"Dr. Hamilton?" I asked. "Who is he?"

Her expression changed from sorrow to perplexity, and then she laughed. "Dr. Alice Hamilton," she said, "lives here at Hull House."

"A pediatrician?"

Her facial expression told me I had blundered again. "You must know, Mrs. DeVere, that Dr. Hamilton has become an expert in industrial medicine."

I hadn't the faintest notion of what the woman meant, as she must have known from a glance across the table.

"This is not in my usual Hull House talk to visitors, Mrs. DeVere, but Dr. Hamilton has learned that workers are being poisoned by the materials they handle, especially lead. It makes them sick, too weak to work. It can kill, and Dr. Hamilton has the proof. She has found all sorts of things that make workers sick, and she has begun to give lectures and to publish the facts about workplace safety and health. Our Lydia became very interested in Dr. Hamilton's work. She asked her about medicines, and Dr. Hamilton suggested she go downtown to the Crerar Library for books and articles. I'm not sure she went. Her friend did not like the idea."

"The idea of a library visit...to look up medicines?"

"...harmful substances, whatever they may be."

We sipped our coffee, which was cold. "Mrs. Coates's friend," I said, "...would that be Miss Dow?"

She looked suddenly alert, perhaps suspicious. "It would."

"Miss Sara Dow now lives in New York," I said, trying to sound genial, "and I recently had tea with her."

I watched her mouth tighten as she shoved her handkerchief up a sleeve.

"Perhaps Miss Dow volunteered here at Hull House?" I asked.

"For a time, yes. She lectured on China. Her magic lantern pictures were interesting, but the talks did not go over well, and she soon stopped. I never saw her here on Saturdays when we bathed the little ones."

Mrs. Enright began to push back her chair, meaning our coffeetime had come to an end. I, too, must push back, stand, and allow Mrs. Enright to take me to the door.

Questions redoubled. Had Lydia talked about Vitalene to Mrs. Enright? To other volunteers? To the Hull House women? Had the detective, Brady, come to here to ask questions about Sara Dow?

Could I meet Dr. Alice Hamilton?

"So pleased to have this hour with you, Mrs. DeVere."

"...and with you, Mrs. Enright, and to learn the history of Hull House."

"Living history, Mrs. DeVere."

"Living..." I echoed, as if to parry a reproach. We stood at the open doorway of the brick building, just as a hansom cab stopped to discharge a passenger."

"You are in luck today, Mrs. DeVere."

"A cab for me," I said.

"Something far more important," she said. "See the passenger who alights…?"

I saw the figure step from the cab, a woman dressed in dark tailored clothing that fit perfectly, her head tilted forward, her hair pulled into a serviceable bun. "Another volunteer?" I asked. "Or a donor?"

Mrs. Enright's eyes shone. "A volunteer? A donor?" She chuckled softly. "Indeed, yes, you might say both together, Mrs. DeVere. Step quickly. You are about to be introduced to Miss Jane Addams."

Chapter Eighteen

THE LATE AFTERNOON HAD turned sharply cold when Roddy and I met up at the Auditorium, dressed warmly, and went on foot to West Adams Street to a new German restaurant, the Berghoff. It was my husband's idea.

I did not object. My short exchange with Jane Addams had been in mind since I left Halsted Street, her every word of hope and purpose etched deeply. What courage to anchor down in that fetid slum to help new immigrants find their way in America. She mentioned how pleasing when families prospered and moved away, making room for the newest, the poorest, the neediest. This slender, soft-spoken figure defied city officials to do the right thing. Hull House was a new kind of pioneering on the urban frontier, as a New York friend, Daisy Harriman, had said to help me adjust from the West. The phrase rang true.

These thoughts swirled in the hansom cab all the way to State Street, where I nibbled finger sandwiches in the Tearoom at the Marshall Field Department Store and was fitted for a new pair of "vici kid" boots in the ladies' shoe department.

"Comfy?" Roddy asked about my new footwear as we walked up West Adams.

I said, "Yes," which was not entirely true, but our day had been too important to squander energy talking about shoes. (Two days in Chicago had ruined a good pair.)

At six p.m., the warm Berghoff Restaurant hummed with diners and white-aproned waiters hoisting trays and huge steins of German beer.

"Herr...Dame... Wilkommen."

Roddy answered the tuxedoed host in a German phrase that sounded like "cross-cut," and we were led to a table and given enormous menus. Of the twenty-nine languages spoken in the Hull House neighborhood, German was doubtless among them. The atmosphere in this restaurant was almost boisterous. "Sauerbraten, yes," Roddy said, "and Val, I recommend a schnitzel."

"Schnitzel? What is it?"

"You'll like it," he said. "And how about beer instead of wine?"

I must have nodded, because a huge, dimpled glass mug of frothing beer was put before me in an instant, and another for Roddy, who ordered our food, clicked his mug against mine, and said, "Salud, Val."

Was he as cheerful as he seemed?

"My dear," I said, "Martin's distillery must have made a very strong impression."

Did he smile or grimace when he said, "Count on a German restaurant to lift the spirit."

I nearly asked how and why the 'spirit' needed lifting, but my husband continued, "In New York, Val, I went often to Luchow's in my bachelor days. It's a German beer garden and restaurant on Irving Place around 14th Street. At first, I'd order *Sauerbraten* or potato pancakes so I could sit long enough to learn about the Schnapps and *kirschwasser* brandy. Remember, I was tutoring myself in beverages."

He sipped his beer. "Soon enough, I went to Luchow's because it felt friendly...warmer than some of Society's doings. I became a frequent customer. The word for the feeling is *gemuetlichkeit*...."

He paused, gazed at the dining room and said, "I needed that feeling after a day at the Vitalene works." He grew quiet.

I moved a little crock of mustard closer to the salt and kept quiet.

"The other day, Val, I met Martin in his office," my husband said at last, "but today I toured the distillery with him... the furnace and vats and the bottling...the labels...the works."

Once again, Roddy paused. Should I prod with a question? I knew little of factory tours. In San Francisco, Papa took me to the Ghirardelli chocolate works where I saw cocoa beans become cocoa powder. "Our industrial age..." I said, feeling witless.

The waiter brought a basket of warm rolls and butter. Roddy offered a roll, took one himself, and seemed to study it. "Berghoff," he said, "started peddling German food from a pushcart during the Chicago world's fair. Six years later, here he is...decent jobs for cooks and waiters...supplies from farms and ranches. A pleasant place for a meal...true to his German start in life. And here we are...." He gestured at the dining room.

Somehow, my husband was pondering issues beyond this restaurant. His day at the Vitalene distillery had prompted musings that touched him deeply. I would not rush him. My thoughts about Hull House would have to wait, my impressions and suspicions as well.

Our food was served, and Roddy took up his knife and fork like a man starving for beef sauerbraten, potatoes, and red cabbage. My German-style schnitzel meant that a fried egg was on top. I began with the egg. We ate in silence.

Our main dishes finished, Roddy ordered apple strudel and coffee. When they were served, my husband sat back and said, "Now, then...that's better."

"And you're ready to talk?"

"Val," he said in a quiet, even voice, "Few days have been more trying. The chemical odors would have knocked you down. Creosote smells like hot tar, and the formaldehyde smells like...like vinegar. I held a handkerchief to my nose and felt dizzy. Martin said that everyone in the plant gets used to it."

"Who is 'everyone?'"

"The workers. If they can't deal with it, they are replaced."

"Fired? Or do they quit?"

Roddy shrugged. "Martin says they're lazy. If they say they're sick, he thinks they drank too much whiskey the night before, or maybe they ate spoiled food. If they faint, the foreman yanks them to their feet, and if they can't do the job, they're gone."

Roddy lifted his fork and put it down without touching the strudel. "It's not the odors, of course, it's the toxic fumes. The man is a chemist. He knows...he has to know that his workers are hobbled by the fumes."

"Then why doesn't he do something about it?"

Roddy's jaw tightened. "Because Martin Coates is also a businessman. I asked about ventilation, and he spit out the exact number of dollars and cents to install a modern system. His father would not hear of it, and Martin spends his workdays in the office, which is several hundred yards from the distillery. Sometimes he works in Oak Park since the telephone connects his home to the distillery."

"In other words, he's nowhere near the chemicals."

"Nowhere near." Roddy jabbed at his strudel. "Martin promises the fumes will stop when Vitalene shuts down so that the plant can be readied to open under our partnership."

"In bitters."

"Bitters, all right," Roddy said. "a damnable pun, but that's how I feel."

I sipped my coffee.

"Something else, Val...."

I waited.

"The labels," he said. "Little boys lick the labels and paste them on the Vitalene bottles."

"Lick them?"

"I watched the bottling operation. The boys stand alongside a conveyer belt, and the bottles move along in front of them. Each boy has a stack of labels and a wet sponge, but the line moves too fast, and they all resort to...."

"Licking the glue on the labels..." I said. "They ingest the glue. Did Martin see this?"

"He stood at my side."

Too rattled for apple strudel, I worked to keep my voice low. "Roddy, does Martin Coates realize the boys could be the same age as his son, Lester?

"I doubt he gives it a thought." My husband sighed. "He could pay little girls less to lick the labels, he said, but some of the boys are their families' breadwinners, so he's proud of hiring boys for the labeling."

I swallowed. "Roddy, how old are those boys?"

"Hard to say, Val. They're very thin...maybe nine years old, maybe ten, or older...or younger."

"Not one in school?"

"I mentioned school, but Martin praised the discipline... feels the work builds character."

I rolled my shoulders. "Dare I ask how many hours these boys stand at the conveyor belt?"

Roddy spoke with a forced calm. "I inquired," he said, "and Martin told me they work until each Vitalene batch is complete...from distillation to shipping. The foreman tells them when they can go. Martin ordered cork mats for the boys to stand on, so the concrete floor is easier on their feet. The expense, he said, pays off. More boys show up for the work."

"And did he tell you how much he pays these boys?"

"He did."

"How much?"

My husband put down his fork and reached for my hand. "I will tell you, Val, but please keep calm."

I promised.

"The boys are paid ten cents per hour."

"Ten cents...one dime...all those hours."

"Martin calculates the return...profit to the fraction of a cent. He says he pays the going wage."

I looked about the dining room, so merry, so festive. The waiter brought coffee and filled our cups. Roddy assured him the strudel was excellent and took a bite.

"At the end of the day," I asked, "were you and Martin still on speaking terms?"

"Barely," Roddy replied. "Our disagreement boils down to wages and workers. The boys were pitiful, Val. I told Martin that I would not employ children, and I would insist on fair wages. And the bitters distillery must have proper ventilation."

"And what did he say?"

"He called me utopian, said I had never met a payroll, which is true."

"Even so…" I said, "he's courting you for a partnership, so he ought to be… a gentleman."

Somehow, the word sounded funny. Roddy chuckled, and I smiled. "And after all this," I said, "the partnership is off?"

Roddy cocked his head. "Maybe not. Maybe 'utopian' is the way to go, Val…better wages, decent hours…safety. I mentioned that Martin's late wife would surely admire a new way of doing business….and got a very stiff reaction." Roddy's forehead creased in a frown.

"Why…?"

"Martin said that his dear wife had never once been inside the distillery, and it upset him to hear her name spoken within the industrial premises."

I paused to nudge my fork at the strudel. "Interesting, Roddy…" I said, "because Lydia somehow did learn that Vitalene is harmful. This popular elixir, so widely accepted, sold at apothecaries all over the country, and yet Lydia urged Martin to close the Vitalene works. Martin's father taunted her with it, but the elixir was banned in the Coates household when Lydia was alive. She felt it shamed the family."

"And she was right. She probably heard Martin complain about it."

"Or she did not."

My husband had turned from his strudel. "What do you mean?"

"I learned something this morning at Hull House," I said. "A woman doctor lives there, and Lydia befriended her.

The doctor is interested in workplace poisons. She advised Lydia to visit a library that has useful documents. I did not meet the doctor, but I was told that Sara Dow discouraged Lydia from going to the library. The woman at Hull House did not know whether Lydia followed the doctor's advice. The library name...it sounds like a growl." I made a deep sound.

Roddy did not mock me. "Probably the Crerar Library," he said. "Science and technics."

"But Sara discouraged her," I said. "And did Martin? What about the chemist husband who cannot bear to hear his wife's name uttered inside his distillery? Is he following an old-fashioned Victorian custom? Or is he being strategic for other reasons?"

"We don't know."

The waiter deposited the check on a corner of the table. "Lydia Coates's death," I said, "enshrines her very name. It's as though we are to tiptoe around her memory and ask no questions. As long as we do, Martin will debate the new partnership that interests you, Roddy. But what is the price of this alliance with Martin Coates?

My husband did not immediately answer, but I asked the question that overrode all others. "And what, Roddy, is the price of the promise you made so many years ago when Martin pulled you from the runaway horse? Years later, the man is on our doorstep begging us to clear the charge that his wife was murdered in their home. And he hints that public health depends on the partnership...and you are also responsible for the workers' health?"

I dug at my strudel. "Your pact drags you deeper, Roddy. It's like quicksand. It sucks you down...sucks both of us. I say, please consider getting out. Whatever the "Letter of Intent,' you can cancel it. The burden is too heavy. It might be dangerous."

My husband reached for the check and his money clip. He did not answer. We left the restaurant and stepped into the cold. "That German word for a good feeling?" I asked as we walked the Chicago city sidewalk "What is that word?"

"*Gemuetlichkeit.*"

I repeated it to myself, a word that felt foreign in Chicago.

Chapter Nineteen

THE DAPPER AUDITORIUM DESK clerk handed me two envelopes and a postal card, and he pressed an envelope with red sealing wax into Roddy's palm.

"Letters for you, Mrs. DeVere...and a card...and this came by messenger for you, Mr. DeVere, if you please."

The warm lobby was a relief after the sharp, slicing wind on every block from the German restaurant. Heads down against the wind, we hiked to the hotel and soon shed coats and hats in the steam-heated suite, turned on the electrical lights, and sat down on the overstuffed brocade furniture.

"We need to visit the firehouse, Roddy...what's the captain's name?"

"Cronon," my husband said. "Samuel Cronon. We'll go tomorrow."

"And that science library..." I said, "I want to know whether Lydia paid a visit...but first, the firehouse. If Captain

Cronon can't help us find Detective Brady," I said a little too loudly, "I will visit that roofer in Oak Park."

At times, impulse got the better of me. This morning, I let the Brady-or-Bradley reference go, but the irritant surfaced on this ugly brocade upholstery that made Roddy feel at home but reminded me of the *Empire* room. At my husband's fish-eye look, I suggested we open our mail. "Amazing that it gets here so fast," I said.

"...because workers sort the mail all night in postal railroad cars while the trains run," Roddy replied. "Efficient system...and who sent the card?"

I held up the card with earthen mounds and a river. "It's Theo," I said, "from St. Paul, Minnesota... 'Indian Mounds.' He writes, 'Indian Country already! Loving the *Louisa*!'"

"I would hope so," Roddy said. We had not told Theo that private cars were often preferred to a hotel, and the railroads provided sidings in major cities. "Theo is a good friend," my husband said. "I'm glad we could lend him the car." He broke the wax seal of the envelope, which I guessed had come from Martin.

For me, a note from Cassie in gorgeous penmanship said she hoped we were enjoying "The City by the Lake" and also hoped to see us soon at home. Dudley's ship had sailed, and she and the children saw him off. A tiny ripple in the paper looked like a dried teardrop.

An extra page with colored pictures of sailing ships were signed "Charles" and "Beatrice" in elementary script, and I propped the Forster children's ships on the mantel beside Tansy Coates's drawing of animals, a black horse atop a stepladder and a lamb asleep at the bottom. Martin and Lydia's daughter showed talent. The two animals were nicely shaded and contoured. Tansy said she only drew animals these days. Perhaps they were easier, perhaps more of a challenge. The children's art brightened the space.

Roddy read his red sealing wax message as I lifted the second envelope with an abbreviated return address from East 55th Street. I murmured, "Miss De Wolfe." Her no-nonsense handwriting reported the *Empire* room furniture was in storage, the wallpaper stripped, and the draperies removed, although we had not agreed about them. ("Over-elaborate draperies shut out light and air, so they must go....now shopping with attention to lines, fabrics, and woods.") A scratched-out phrase nearly blotted her words, but I held her letter close to a light and made out "annoyance" and "Thwaite." Those two women clashing? I bet on De Wolfe.

Whatever the messenger had brought, Roddy was absorbed. He went to the window, pushed the curtain aside, and stared into the darkness.

"From Martin?" I asked.

"No, a member of the Chicago Club learned of my visit here and hopes I might offer advice about a situation on Whiskey Row."

"Whiskey Row? Didn't Jakob Polachek say that he patrols Whiskey Row? Isn't it a figure of speech...any street with saloons?"

Roddy perched across from me. "It's an actual block bordering the packing plants, Val. After work, the men go to their favorite saloon for a shot of whiskey and a beer. And the free lunch too. Two Temperance groups want it all shut down."

"On principle...no alcohol?"

"In part," Roddy said. "The men spend their wages in the saloons, and their families need every cent. It's a family issue, and the Women's Christian Temperance Union is campaigning to shut down every saloon on Whiskey Row. The Anti-Saloon League is allied with them." He paused. "Powerful forces are in play to stop them."

"Meaning...?"

"Meaning the saloons are a 'safety valve.' If the men drink and socialize, they won't strike or riot. Chicago does not need more labor turmoil. It's in the packers' interest to keep Whiskey Row open."

"Roddy, why should you be involved?"

He shrugged. "I suspect it concerns the saloons' barrel-house whiskey."

I had no notion of his meaning.

"'Barrel-House' is the poorest quality whiskey, Val, and whoever drinks it feels rotten...really sick."

"So," I said, "you might be called upon to advise a higher quality of 'booze' for the saloons?"

My husband saw no humor in my quip.

"The effort to quiet the Temperance campaign in Chicago is none of my affair, Val. I have my hands full in the courtroom in New York. My advice is apparently sought for matters of quality…in the interest of workers' health."

It took a full minute to puzzle out the logic. "I get it," I said. "The packers want the men to drink better whiskey so they can work full steam in the packing plants."

"Now, Val…."

"Now, Roddy…."

Across from one another, we glared, then laughed, then kissed. And then we tumbled onto the bed, wrestled our clothing down and off, giggled, laughed, pulled down the covers and sank into rhythm that took us into the world that belonged to us alone, together.

❦

We set out the next morning for a long Hansom cab ride to the expanding city's west side. The wind had died down, and the day promised warmth. The sad horse seemed in no mood for a long drive, and our driver did not spare the whip.

We spoke little. Roddy said that a luncheon with the "red sealing wax" member of the Chicago Club might reveal useful information about the Coates Company and Martin. I warned against tangling with saloons and liquor dealers.

At ten-thirty a.m., we stood before a two-story brick building with "**FIRE DEPARTMENT**" and the date, **1888**, chiseled in limestone above the entrance. Since its Great Fire, Chicago had built new firehouses, and we could only hope that Captain Cronon was on duty at Lake Street near Kedzie Avenue. Weather-beaten tulips bloomed in a tiny side yard, but nobody was in sight. The hansom driver was ordered to wait down the block.

Roddy knocked on a side door, waited, and knocked again. At any moment, the bells might clang, the huge center door burst open, and horses surge to pull a steam engine to a flaming building. All firehouses promised rescue—and warned of impending disaster.

An apple-cheeked young man in denim and boots opened the door a few inches on the third knock and frowned when my husband inquired for Captain Cronon. The captain was busy, he said, but reluctantly let us into an office with a rolltop desk, a chair, three stools, and a brass cuspidor. He excused himself, opened the interior door, went inside, and left us alone.

I smelled tobacco and hay and heard a horse nicker... of course, the team stabled inside with the steam engine. Roddy suggested that I sit down. Instead, I leaned to peer at a Chicago map tacked on the wall over the desk...Lake Michigan, the downtown Loop, rail lines, a hospital.

Distracted, I barely heard the door, "Madam...Sir...

We faced a stocky, black-haired man whose suspender straps drooped below a misbuttoned tunic. "This is Engine Company Forty-four. Do you know where you are?"

"We do, sir," said Roddy. "We hope you might help us. We wish to have a word with Captain Samuel Cronon."

"You're looking at him."

Roddy quickly introduced us. "...and we won't take but a few minutes of your time, sir."

The captain pointed to the chair. "Sit yourself down, ma'am."

I did so. "Thank you."

My husband rested one hip on a stool, while Captain Cronon leaned against the wall, keeping the door open to see the station interior and his two visitors. He shifted a lump from one cheek to the other. I eyed the cuspidor.

"Captain," said Roddy, "we understand that you might be acquainted with a Detective Brady of the Chicago police. We would like to have a word with him. Perhaps you could put us in touch?"

The man did not blink.

Roddy repeated, "Detective Brady of the Chicago Police Department."

Through the open door, the captain called, "...every hose, O'Boyle...shine up the nozzles." He turned to us. "This detective's full name...what would it be?"

"We are not certain," I said. "We have heard the names Francis Brady and James Brady." Which was a lie.

"Not Mike? Michael?"

It worked. I scratched my forehead. "Come to think of it," I said, "It might be Michael Brady."

"And would this be about a recent bombing?"

"Bombing...." I shuddered, a bit dramatically.

"Captain," said Roddy, "the fewer persons that know the details, the better all around."

With a slow nod, the captain released a thin brown stream that arched to the cuspidor. He pointed to the map and said, "It used to be the furnace fires and lighted matches. Now it's just as likely bombs...dynamite."

We shook our heads.

"Tell you what I'll do," he said. "You give me the particulars, and we'll see how it goes."

We hoped for more, but Captain Cronon stood with arms locked until my husband handed a calling card from his vest pocket. "Mrs. DeVere and I can be reached at the Auditorium Hotel, Captain. Shall I write the hotel name and address on my card?"

"Lived in Chicago all my life, Mr. DeVere. No need."

"Thank you, Captain," I said, rising from the chair.

"No need for thanks, ma'am. The Chicago Fire Department does its duty for the city."

With that, we returned to the hansom that was pulled by the sad horse, and I cringed each time the whip cracked. "Roddy, I asked, "what are the odds that Cronon will contact Detective Michael Brady...and Brady follow through to reach us?"

My husband hesitated. In a flat voice, he replied, "If I were a betting man, I'd guess the chances to be fifty-fifty."

The cab hit a bump, jolted and tipped. We were thrown against one another. "Roddy," I said, "you are a betting man. You are betting against long odds that Lydia died accidentally. You are betting that Martin Coates or his brother or his late wife's friend did not murder Lydia."

Chapter Twenty

IF LYDIA COATES DIED in a tragic fall down a steep flight of stairs, so much the better for my husband. In rose-colored moments, I felt sure that Martin's wife must have died in a freak accident. In such moments, my Roddy would certainly follow his path into a partnership with Lydia's widower—a business that would operate on a basis of worker safety and good wages. The partnership would uphold Lydia's values, which her husband would honor as his solemn vow.

Then again, did Martin push her down the staircase to her death?

Or did Owen?

Or Sara Dow?

And if so, why?

By noon, we reached our hotel, freshened up, and prepared to go out. The front desk was asked to take a message that might come from Mister Michael Brady, a title that sounded better than Police Detective Brady. So we thought.

Against my wishes, Roddy was going to the Chicago Club for a confab with "red sealing wax." Against my husband's wishes, I started for the Crerar Library at the corner of Wabash and Washington Streets. Roddy had yet to hear about Hull House.

The Michigan Avenue bustle gave me safe passage. I had donned a two-piece forest green suit with a gored skirt that let me stride with purpose. If I stayed on the crowded sidewalks, all was well. The day was pleasantly warm. Spring clothing mixed with tired dark winter wools. Long gloves and three-quarter length sleeves seemed favored this season in Chicago.

Expecting a library with columns and a welcoming entrance, I stopped at a building that looked like a bank. Or an insurance company. Or were those people inside shopping at this corner of Wabash and Washington. The wrong address? Could this be a library?

"Excuse me..." I asked a young man preparing to mount his bicycle, but he pedaled off.

"Excuse me...." I caught the eye of a young woman walking arm-in-arm with a friend. She walked on.

"If you please...." Two nuns in full white habits paused but had no familiarity with the building. "Thank you, Sisters...." They swept into the crowd.

A cigar-chomping deliveryman paused to tell me I had reached the Marshall Field Annex building.

"Annex?"

"Up above...." He pointed his cigar to the upper floors. "Like a warehouse, lady...goods shipped all over creation."

He was gone, but a gentleman tipped his top hat, pointed his walking stick at the building, and said, "Marshall Field's Department Store is on State Street, Madam."

I rose to all of my five feet, seven inches to say that I was not shopping but seeking the Crerar Library."

"Ah, Crerar...." His walking stick pointed high. "The man struck it rich in railroad fittings, then put it into a library." He counted the stories with his stick. "I believe the sixth floor...perhaps the seventh. That would be the John Crerar Library." He said something about freight or fate.

He meant the freight elevator that clanked and bumped to the seventh floor of the Marshall Field Annex. The cage-like elevator opened onto a vast room crammed with jutting bookshelves and a few tables set by the windows, where two men pored over an enormous open book.

A wan woman with a timid smile hurried from their table with a greeting. "Good afternoon. I am Miss Hedrick. May I be of assistance?"

"I am Mrs. DeVere," I said. "This is the Crerar Library?"

"Temporarily," she said, "we are making do until the new building is completed."

She tucked a pencil behind one ear. "Such great demand at present for scientific books and journals, you see...engineers and attorneys and businessmen...for the latest issues of *Iron Age* or the *National industrial Review* or...."

She fingered the pencil at her ear. "Is there something in particular? Something for your employer, perhaps?"

"Actually…" I said, "I am seeking information for a memorial tribute for a family friend who has passed away. I understand that my late friend may have visited the Crerar Library in recent months. I would like to be exact…in tribute to my friend."

I tried to look demure. Librarians fiercely protected patrons' privacy. Their lips were sealed as to who read what, or why.

I kept a few of my papa's journals on minerals and metals, but it seemed unlikely that mentioning the Big Bonanza in silver would open the Crerar files on Lydia Coates.

Before me, Miss Hedrick gestured at the bookshelves. "We have eleven thousand volumes and numerous technical periodicals…science and electricity… medicine…."

"Medicine," I said. "I believe my late friend sought information in the medical field…and I trust that her name is recorded in the library's file of patrons?"

"That would depend," she said cautiously. "Our senior librarian is not here today. He is at the new building site. I am an assistant."

She had begun to sound wary of the new visitor who might not follow the rules. Who might be a problem for the assistant?

"Perhaps at the moment we are both 'assistants,'" I said. "I am here in place of the doctor who has also been a friend of the dearly departed…Doctor Alice Hamilton."

"Oh, yes, Dr. Hamilton. We sometimes see her in the evenings."

"Although a doctor's evenings are often spent at a bedside," I said, "tending to a sick patient. As we know, a doctor's work never ends." I paused to let the portrait of the beleaguered physician take hold.

"So," I said, "I agreed to come today. My late friend was Lydia Coates...Mrs. Martin Coates."

No recognition flashed in her slightly moist eyes, but a slow focus on me and a glance toward a certain shelf.

"Chemical hazards," I said, "in food...and in medicines too?"

"Medicines...." she repeated, then grew silent.

"So many pills and tonics on the market these days," I said.

A new wariness showed in a tilt of her chin.

"For instance," I said in a low, confidential voice, "the vegetable compounds that so many of us ladies rely on...to our shock, we have learned that they contain...."

I strategically paused. If she supplied the last word, I might have an ally, and so I paused. "Not vegetables at all," I said, but instead they are filled with...with....."

"Alcohol..." she said.

"Indeed," I repeated. "And along with alcohol, we often find the potent other drug...."

"Opium," she whispered.

We both shook our heads and shuddered. What now? Would Miss Hedrick open the records to show me the books and journals Lydia Coates had requested? Would a library assistant violate the code of confidentiality for this stranger?

One of the men at the table marched our way just then, interrupted us, and demanded the most recent issue of *Electrical Age* in a voice as rough as his tweed coat. Miss Hedrick excused herself, scurried to a back shelf, and meekly took the requested issue to the table.

Her step looked firmer on return, her chin thrust with resolution. "Mrs. DeVere," she said, "why don't you have a seat at an empty table with good light by the window, and I will bring books and other documents that might interest you today."

In moments, an armful of books and reports were set on the oak table in front of me. "Take your time, Mrs. DeVere. Our patrons often visit after their workday, so the Crerar Library is open until late in the evening." Stepping away, she said, "I am sorry for the loss of your friend. Do give our best to Doctor Hamilton. We always look forward to her visits...oh, one more thing...." She pointed to a thick, well-thumbed volume in a dark brown cover and pressed it with her thumb. "I suggest," she said, "that this title might be especially helpful."

I first delved into government reports and encyclopedic tomes, some in foreign languages. If Dr. Hamilton sat at this table, she could probably decipher the German. If Cassie were here, she could translate the French, but I bumbled through "*des falsifications des drogues, simple et composée.* At last, I reached for the volume that Miss Hedrick thumbed, then spent the next two hours with the book I was certain had been in Lydia Coates's hands. Its title: *Drugs, Medicines, Chemicals as to Their Purity and Adulterations.*

❧

"You did not see her actual name in a registry?" my husband asked.

"Not her signature, Roddy, but the librarian sensed that I was eager for the books and papers that Lydia Coates had seen. I feel fairly certain she understood me and chose to help."

"Fairly certain?"

"Confident," I said. The atmosphere in our suite's sitting room felt dim and rank. Roddy was already at the hotel when I returned from the Crerar Library to recount my exploit, proud of my wiles and ready for a compliment.

Instead, Roddy's right eyebrow raised to signal lawyerly skepticism. I regretted not taking notes from the book on adulteration. I would wager that Lydia had taken notes. I folded my hands. "Documentary evidence...what we need... what we lack."

My husband's nod meant that I had just restated his point.

"Roddy," I said, "you are perfectly free to visit the Crerar Library and to inveigle your way to the records." I might have stamped a foot if my stocking feet were not at rest on a hassock.

"Val," my husband said softly, "this is not a cross-examination, but we need the facts. Let's agree there's high probability that Lydia learned about the chemistry of medicines in the library, and not from her husband."

"Though Martin already knew the compound of Vitalene was toxic," I said. "He had vowed to shut down the distillery."

"But perhaps on his own schedule," Roddy said.

"...and alarmed when Lydia suddenly put the terrible facts in front of him," I continued. "...and confronted him in front his father too? With Sara Dow present?"

"Possibly."

"Then suppose," I said, "that Martin felt embarrassed... humiliated, especially if the two men and Sara were together when she faced them with her findings. Martin would have been caught between his wife and his father."

A powerful father, I thought, recalling the painting of Harold Coates glowering during dinner.

"And Sara Dow too," I said, "employed by Harold Coates to promote Vitalene...the good friend who discouraged Lydia from visiting the Crerar Library."

"How do you know?"

"I learned it at Hull House."

"Oh."

Slightly flushed, Roddy poured us water from a carafe on the table. "Val," he said, "I haven't given you the time to hear about your Hull House visit, which is selfish of me... so bruised by that scene in the distillery...and then the fire-house...and this afternoon on Van Buren Street."

"The Chicago Club," I said. "The red sealing wax...and I hope you have not agreed to a scheme involving better whiskey for the packinghouse workers."

"Most likely not."

"Most likely?"

Roddy drank water and sat back. "I have been invited to join...as a non-resident member, like several of our New York friends...George Crocker... Stuyvesant Fish."

"Mamie Fish's husband...oh, Roddy, may we not catch sight of them in Chicago...that woman." Mamie Fish's rapier tongue was feared and relished in Society. I had been her target in Newport.

Roddy paused for a long minute that brought me back to Chicago in the here and now. "It won't surprise you, Val, to learn that the Coates brothers belong to the Chicago Club."

"Both Martin and Owen," I said, "members in good standing, yes?"

Roddy nodded and sucked his lip. "It's a tough town," he said. "The men of 'Porkopolis' dine and do business at the club. Some take their ease, like old Augustus Swift who is dead certain that immigrant workers are ingrates and communists...and lots of talk about Pullman's failed experiment."

"What experiment?"

"His model factory town that pleased workers and their families until the country went into a bad slump and the rents and fees stayed so high the families were driven out. The Pullman strike was blamed on lazy ingrates. George Pullman is dead, but the lesson of the strike tolls like a funeral bell."

Roddy put his water glass down. "The mood of this city," he said, "could make it very hard for someone to go into business with different ideas about pay and safety."

"Roddy," I said, "your business idea also hinges on whether the 'maybe' about Lydia Coates's death can become hard and fast truth, the truth being her verified, accidental fall."

We sat with my pronouncement. I drank water for something to do, and Roddy refilled our glasses. We were about to discuss dinner when the suite telephone jangled. Roddy rose to answer it, and I heard yes...and another yes.

With the receiver cradled, he paused for a moment. "A message from Mister Brady," he said. "He will see us."

Chapter Twenty-one

BY 8:30 A.M., WE finished breakfast in the hotel dining room and eyed every man who might be Michael Brady. He agreed to meet us by 8:45.

"What does 'by' mean?" I asked Roddy.

"It means we sit here until he shows up."

"Or does not," I said.

Finished with eggs and toast, we sat over coffee and tea. Roddy signed the check, and our waiter disappeared. Salesmen with sample cases had left to start their day, and three men huddled over blueprints at a large table. Otherwise, the dining room was not occupied. We sat as the 8:45 hour became 9:00… 9:06…9:13. Plucked from his watch pocket, Roddy's time piece seemed to mock us with each sip of our drinks. And still we waited.

Facing the dining room entrance, we were startled when a large man in a nut brown suit burst from the kitchen door and beelined to us. "Mr. DeVere? Mrs. DeVere?"

"Mister Brady?" Roddy had risen as the man hovered over us. Roddy put out his hand, the two men shook hands, and I acknowledged a short bow.

"Won't you please have a seat?" said Roddy as a waiter hastened our way with a cup and saucer that he put at the detective's place and promptly filled his coffee cup.

"Two spoons of sugar, I believe, sir?"

The detective held up two thick fingers and winked.

Roddy shot me a quick glance, which the detective noticed and grinned. No one spoke until the waiter spooned sugar into the cup and walked off.

The detective took his time stirring the coffee. He looked both large and lithe, ready to anchor down or spring into action despite the snug suit and too-tight necktie. With gray eyes, a broad nose, full mouth, and cleft chin, his expression looked both wary and somehow genial. Clean-shaven, Michael Brady's balding head was barely covered with hair brushed carefully over the scalp. His ruddy complexion suggested an outdoor life.

"Regrets for making you bide your time this morning," he said, "but once again, the Auditorium has been searched for bombs."

"Bombs?" I said.

"Once again...?" said Roddy.

He looked from one of us to the other. "Your first visit to Chicago?"

"Yes," Roddy said.

"...but you paid a visit to Captain Cronon to ask for me."

"We heard your name," I said, "from someone in New York...a roundabout acquaintance."

"Meaning," he said, "that 'a little bird' told you. Isn't that what ladies say?'"

"Detective Brady," I said, "whatever ladies say, we do not expect to hear that our hotel has been searched for explosives."

"I suppose not." He sipped his coffee and looked toward the Michigan Avenue windows. "You have been guests for... how many nights?"

I held up three fingers.

"Perhaps you dined in this very room three evenings ago?"

"We dined at the Palmer House...," Roddy said, then broke off. "Actually, we changed our plans when a fracas broke out just outside...."

The strikers' parade and the chanting *"Arbeit"* came to mind, and the next morning's paper that reported a death. My husband shot me a quick glance.

The detective sipped his coffee while we stewed in the recollection. "This hotel," he said at last, "is a favorite of businessmen. Some prefer it to their club when bad weather or late meetings keep them in the city. Others make the Auditorium their longterm residence."

We nodded.

"So," he said, "when their workers get stirred up, they know where to come...to make their feelings known.

"Feelings?" I said.

He hesitated, lowering his eyes.

"Detective Brady," I said, "please do not soften your terms for my sake. If the 'feelings' are dangerous, please say so."

He sipped his coffee, then raised those gray eyes at me. "Some call the threats and violent acts a headache for the police." He took a sip. "They are far worse than a headache, Mrs. deVere. They threaten to crush the city with lawless anarchy."

His fingers clutched the handle of his cup. Had I given this man permission to voice extreme views?

"Today's leading businessmen risk assassination," he continued, "and elected officials too. You heard about Carter Harrison...Mayor Harrison?"

I had not. Roddy kept quiet but looked as though he understood.

"Six years ago, Mrs. DeVere, our Mayor Harrison opened his front door and was shot dead by a lunatic. The mayor didn't give him a job, so he knocked on the mayor's door and fired his pistol. He was hanged, of course, but the police had failed to protect the mayor."

"Horrid," I murmured.

"And it goes on," he continued, "because ladies enter into politics these days. The ladies insist on public speaking, and the threats mount up. Perhaps you know Mrs. Bowen... Mrs. Joseph Bowen?"

"I'm afraid not."

"...well known Chicago family, a lady very interested in juvenile protection. Every time she gives a speech about juveniles, a whiskey-drunk woman sits in the front row and flashes a pistol. The police can't do much because the gun is not loaded—so far."

He had my attention.

"You should call on her, talk to her...Mrs. Joseph Bowen resides on Michigan Avenue. She'll tell you about the letters that threaten to kidnap her children. She'll tell you about the bomb somebody put on her front porch."

"A live bomb?"

"Put inside a box, set to explode when the lid was lifted. The night watchman found it and got worried. The police took it away, put it under water to explode it. Had it burst, somebody could have died."

His gaze became earnest as he looked over the dining room where the men studied the blueprints. "Protection," he said, "is our foremost duty. Protection and prevention." He looked from me to Roddy. "To get criminals off the street and hunt them down, that is our mission."

The waiter appeared with refills for all of us. The new spoonfuls of sugar reminded me that the Auditorium was familiar to the detective, that he had roamed its corridors more than once in search of bombs meant for guests.

"Detective Brady," my husband said at last, "I appreciate your time this morning. I am in Chicago to explore a business proposition, and your name was suggested as a reference. An attractive idea has come to me from a businessman of this city, someone you might remember from your school days. I understand that you grew up

with him and his brother and sister outside of the city…
in Oak Park?"

"Sleepy village," he volunteered.

"And you knew Martin Coates…in Oak Park? And Owen
Coates too?"

A curt nod, and the man's palm suddenly slapped down
on the table. Jarred, we stared at a dead beetle the detective
flicked to the floor. Wiping his fingers, he said, "I did grow
up in Oak Park. My family operated a business…still has it."

"Some men are not drawn to business," Roddy said.

The detective laughed. "This one was not keen on nailing
slates on roofs. This one saw a cousin slip and fall and never
walk again. That was enough for me."

"But you knew Mr. Martin Coates and his brother,
Owen?" I asked to make sure.

"In Central School," he said. "The Coates brothers…the
little sister too."

"Were the Oak Park boys and girls in the same school?"
I asked.

He nodded. "At the time…yes."

About to introduce Lydia Gerstle's name, I felt Roddy
nudge my knee under the table and blink a warning.

"About Mr. Martin Coates and his brother…" my husband
said. "As a reference, Detective Brady, I hope you can recall
anything helpful in regard to my possible business arrangement. Mr. Coates and his brother, Owen, are members of the
Chicago Club where I enjoyed lunch just yesterday. But club
members get behind one another as a rule."

Roddy looked earnestly at the detective. "Anything you might recall could be most helpful." With eyes wide open, Roddy folded his hands on the table and waited.

The detective waved off the waiter who approached again with a coffee pot and a teapot. "You are here from... New York, isn't it?"

We nodded without speaking.

"Funny, how things go..." he said, "how New York lost out to Chicago for the world's fair...put itself in the running and lost out to our 'City by the Lake.'"

Roddy had told me how insulting New York's loss to Chicago for the Columbian Exposition, how Americans and international visitors sped directly to Chicago, snubbing Gotham.

"High times here," Detective Brady continued. "Millions came to play...and to work...carpenters, masons, day-laborers...and criminals. Chicago got itself drunk on the fair, but the party is over, and the hangover goes on... tramps, hoboes...killers."

Reaching into a pocket, he might have plucked a handkerchief or notebook. Instead, a Bristol board card, somewhat bent, and he read, "Roderick Windham DeVere, Esq."

The man had Roddy's card all along. He either visited the firehouse or else Captain Cronon came downtown to hand it over.

"Those three letters mean you are a lawyer, Mr. DeVere... Esq. for Esquire."

"I am a member of the New York bar," Roddy replied.

"A gentleman's practice of the law, I presume?"

"A practicing attorney," Roddy said.

"In an Eastern city that has traditions, old ways...settled."

"We hardly think so," Roddy said, but the detective held up his palm to silence my husband.

"Mr. DeVere, your streets are paved, are they not? Asphalt? Stone cobbles? And your bloodlines reach back to colonial times?"

Roddy could only nod.

"You drive carriages in your Central Park."

"We do." Roddy's voice tightened.

"In Chicago," he said, "we have Lincoln Park, named for President Lincoln." His lips curled. "What would Abraham Lincoln think if he knew the park named for him started as a cemetery? The bodies were dug up and moved, but even today, people find bones."

I shuddered. Our Central Park had its own twisted history, but nothing so macabre these days.

"And some Chicagoans remember cattle drives up Wabash Avenue to the stockyards...dust and mud. People got gored...and trampled."

Roddy cleared his throat. "Detective Brady," he said, "the history of this city need not concern us just now."

The man snorted "To the contrary," he said. "You can listen to the gentlemen at the Chicago Club if you wish, Mr. DeVere, but others from the East have come here, to their lasting regret. Some say Chicago is 'rough at the edges,' but the fact is, this city is rough to the core. People are gored. People are trampled."

He rattled his coffee cup. "Interesting thing about the Auditorium building," he said. "The hotel is fireproof, but Chicago is a tinderbox."

Chapter Twenty-two

THE WRITING DESK IN our suite featured creamy Auditorium stationary, inks in crystal jars, pen point nibs, and a blotter. The center drawer, however, was empty. We had just come up from the meeting with Detective Brady, and I pulled out drawers of the chiffonier, of a small chest in a corner, and the writing desk too.

Roddy watched me sprint around the carpet and asked what I was seeking. To me, the answer was obvious.

"A time-table for the New York Central Railroad," I snapped, "for the next train to New York."

"Val...." Roddy reached for my hand but grasped my wrist. "Let's sit down for a moment."

"We are forever 'sitting down,'" I said, "...sitting at break-fast, sitting with that detective.... We have had our fill of Chicago. It is time to take the next train out."

Roddy took a seat on the brocade sofa and patiently outlasted my fuming. Which irked me more.

"Roddy," I said, "this trip was well meant, but Chicago is not for us. Blessings on Miss Jane Addams and her devoted followers. The future may yet be theirs, but to us, this city is angry and depressing."

"Rough and tumble," my husband said.

I shook my head so hard my hairpins came loose. "My far West is 'rough and tumble,' Roddy. The Rocky Mountains... the Washoe Zephyr winds of Nevada...they are 'rough and tumble,' but Chicago is downright mean. The telegram said it, **Chicago Kills**."

I had not finished. "A hotel that boasts conveniences," I said, "ought to provide railroad schedules. I want to know when we can board a train for New York." I folded my arms and dared my husband to disagree.

He patted the sofa cushion and said, "Val...I will go to the desk downstairs to see about trains, but let's take a few minutes to quiet down."

Roddy's tender glance bordered on pity, and the tightened hairpins jabbed my scalp. Another few seconds, call me ridiculous.

Reluctantly I took a seat at the end of the sofa. "Roddy," I said, "you warned me with a wink and a nudge not to ask the detective about Lydia. I thought that you planned to ask about her. Why didn't you?"

"I changed my mind, Val," my husband said, "when Brady recalled the Coates brothers and possibly their younger sister too. And he said both boys and girls went to the same school."

My husband crossed his legs. "But Brady held back about Martin and Owen when I said that Chicago Club members are a closed circle and gave him his chance. Brady is...how old, would you guess?"

About the same age as Martin and Owen," I said "...and the younger Lydia Gerstle was also their schoolmate."

Roddy nodded. "Do consider..." he continued, "that the Coates brothers were the sons and grandsons of leading businessmen, prominent figures in Oak Park. The son of a roofer, however...."

"Social class," I said, "...the rungs of the social ladder." I would not recount girlhood in mining camps that put my Irish immigrant papa and me on the lowest rung. Nor say aloud that the top was still dizzying. "So," I said, "Brady and the Coates children attended the same school but lived in different worlds."

"Very likely," Roddy said, "and Brady might have worshipped Miss Lydia Gerstle from afar...though we know so little about her."

"She came from a genteel family," I said, "...fully at home at her summer garden parties." I eased a hairpin in place. "And we know that she had money of her own, that she bequeathed sums to Hull House and to Sara Dow...the mysterious Miss Dow."

I sighed. "Roddy, let's go home? Chicago is not for us."

My husband did not reply. We grew quiet, but not at peace. His eyes lowered as if he coped with dispiriting news. His face became stoic.

It struck me that Roddy was coping with a city that infuriated and frightened me but deeply disappointed him. The love of my life had counted on the business partnership that now felt ashen. I had thought only of fleeing Chicago at the earliest moment, assuming he would share my fast and furious feelings ...impetuous me.

I reached for Roddy's hand and moved beside him on the sofa. "My dear" I said, "your partnership...the business venture.... You have cared so much. I am so sorry."

"Not a problem," he said, rising to stand at the window and look out for a long moment. "The lake is cement gray today," he said, at last, "no shimmering blue for the visitors."

He turned. "I will see about reservations for the next train to New York," he said, "so, if you will please begin to gather up a few of our things...."

Alone in the suite when the door closed, I put Roddy's extra shirt studs in a leather box monogrammed R.W.DeV., then plucked the necktie he had looped over a wall sconce and held it to my face. I gathered my husband's flannel nightshirt and breathed my Roddy's scent while reaching for my silk nightgown.

How jarring when he burst into the suite rattling an envelope and sheet of note paper. "Martin," he said, "he insists that we dine with him."

"He what?"

"Dine." Roddy sounded like a man rescued from the sea by a pirate ship, alive but anguished. "At the Grand Pacific Hotel.... He apologies for any 'misunderstanding.'"

"But the train..." I said.

"Val, today's Lake Shore Limited is already reserved… unless you care to sit up all night and half of tomorrow on a bristly chair in coach."

"Bristly chair…" I began while hugging the soft nightclothes.

"All night long sitting upright," Roddy chided. "Tomorrow, however, we can enjoy a private compartment in comfort."

Comfort…. My husband had never been without it. My mind filled with memories of stagecoach rides over ruts and rocks. And nights in a scratchy wool Union suit under a bearskin in the subzero Colorado winters.

Suppose that sitting upright in a railroad car would somehow do us good, the sleepless hours on a train as a lesson for Roddy and reminder of my past?

No, it would be pointless, like dinner with Martin Coates. "Roddy," I said, "what could Martin possibly say that would make a difference in the situation? An evening with that man in yet another hotel dining room in Chicago, and…and a man who possibly killed his wife. That runaway horse has put you in a terrible bind, Roderick DeVere. Your pact with that man might be a pact with the dev…."

At that moment, a sharp, startling knock at our suite door. Another, insistent knock, and my husband went to the door. I heard the words "flowers" and "Mrs. DeVere."

In moments, two bouquets of American Beauty Roses were brought into our suite and arranged in vases on tables that Roddy thought best.

My husband read the card: "'In hopes that you and Mr. DeVere will join me for dinner.' Signed 'Martin C.'"

Roddy paused for a long moment before saying, "Dinner, Val, at the Grand Pacific Hotel?"

A deep breath and deep sigh, and I finally replied, "Dinner, then...dinner with the devil?"

Just past seven p.m., the maître D'hotel led us to a table in the Grand Pacific dining room. My mauve crape dinner gown was a good guess for the décor of the room, where Martin stood to greet us with a deep bow to me and cordial handshake with Roddy. Our host's shirtfront gleamed and his formal suit looked new. Was it worn at his wife's funeral? His moustache had been trimmed and accented his craggy face and those dark eyes.

"Mrs. DeVere, so very good of you to spend another evening with me. I cannot allow the DeVeres to depart without dining in Chicago at its best."

"Mr. Coates," I said, "the roses are beautiful."

"This city rises to the occasion when it must, Mrs. DeVere." The waiter poured champagne, and the three of us toasted the springtime.

"This is one of Chicago's very first premier hotels, the Grand Pacific," Martin said. "Recently redone, but my father remembers the famous wild game dinners. Saddle of antelope, loin of Buffalo." He smiled. "Roast elk was my late father's favorite, but never fear, Mrs. DeVere, this evening's menu has been tamed. A few roasted ducks continue, but visitors to this city expect beef at its best."

He turned to Roddy. "I cannot vouch for the bitters, Roderick, but would you care to risk a cocktail? A Manhattan in Chicago?"

"As you suggest, Martin."

"And Mrs. DeVere…champagne?"

I nodded, galled at the sight of ladies at nearby tables who sipped wine while their male companions enjoyed cocktails with distilled spirits. In drinks, Chicago was no better than New York. No votes for women, no cocktails either. I would soon move to change the beverage preferences, even if the votes were not yet in sight throughout the U.S.A.

Manhattans were presented to Roddy and Martin, and my champagne glass refilled. The men ordered oysters. I chose a whitefish cake. The dinner proceeded with beefsteaks for the men and roasted canvasback duck for me. Red and white wines were poured, and we agreed the creamed spinach was delicious.

All the while, I awaited Martin's apology for the "misunderstanding" in the morning note and guessed Roddy felt the same way. As our host, Martin must take charge of the timing and the topic. By the apple charlotte dessert, we had chatted about carriage traffic and the future of transportation in Chicago.

Martin finally put down his spoon, leaned toward my husband, and said, "Roderick, I have been mulling over your ideas for the distillery...putting our new bitters business on a different basis."

"Oh?" Roddy's tone hovered between hope and doubt.

"And laying groundwork," Martin said. "First of all, I am about to be free of the witch-hunting detective. I have taken care of that bad business. He is longer a problem," Martin continued, "because a contribution to the Chicago Police Force settles the matter."

His eyes shone. "A reduction in pay and the loss of rank can work wonders, and a certain sweetener works almost every time."

Martin rushed on. "I avoid Chicago's civic affairs as a rule, though dear Lydia took a great interest." He pushed away his dessert plate. "My wife felt that a better day was in sight." He paused. "However, as my brother Owen said, that charity in the slums filled her head with ideas."

"Hull House?" I said.

Martin frowned. "A 'second home,' Lydia once called it. My wife could never get enough of that miasma and filth."

He lowered his voice. "Sara took me aside to complete the picture. It seems sentimental ladies plough family fortunes into that place. Maybe they yearn for buildings named for them...a dance hall with a plaque...a gymnasium named for Bowen."

"Bowen?" I said.

Martin blinked. "You know that name? A Chicago banker whose wife meddles in a system for juveniles. The woman has stirred up a hornet's nest. We have no such thing in Oak Park, thankfully. Sara tried to interest Lydia in the choral society or the protection of birds, but no...."

He turned to me and to Roddy. "Does this make sense? It made no sense when Lydia was alive. We had words over Hull House."

Words? The term ranged from a tiff to a full-blown feud resulting in her death.

"To my everlasting regret, Mrs. DeVere, we had words over my dear wife's plan to donate money."

I took a quick sip of water. In New York Society, the "M" word was not spoken aloud in company. One spoke of "resources" as Cassie advised.

"Gerstle money," Martin said, "from her family. Owen and I worried sick that Lydia would plunge into the fairy tale of the slums, sign away every dollar. And my wife's health became a constant worry."

I glanced at Roddy. Did he share my thoughts at this moment? Lydia had bequeathed sums to Hull House and to Sara Dow. What about her husband? Their children? Did Martin benefit from his wife's death?

Roddy said, "Martin, if we might turn to the new business idea that you began to explain?"

Our host rubbed his eyes. "More in line with your proposal at the distillery, Roderick. Exactly the sort of thing I heard more than once from my dear Lydia's lips, a new movement that calls itself progressive." He paused. "That is the actual term, 'progressive.'" He spoke the word as though trying out a foreign language.

"To my father's way of thinking," he said, "progress meant railroads to ship Coates's products. To me, the chemical laboratory shows the way forward."

His lips puckered as if with a lemon. This new 'progressive' idea is slippery...mostly do-gooders. For all practical purposes, the 'Progressive' people are in line with the Pure Food folks. Together, they will push new laws."

"And so," Roddy said, "we are back where we started... the Vitalene elixir could be legally banned—"

"—and properly so," Martin snapped.

"And laws into effect about workplace safety and wages...." Roddy let the notion hover.

Martin did not respond.

The moment belonged to the men, but I piped up, foolishly as Roddy and I later agreed. "It happens," I said, "that I belong to an organization that promotes a Progressive agenda, the National Consumers League."

Martin stared, and Roddy squinted in chagrin.

"An organization," I continued, "that campaigns for workplace safety and good wages for workers. We who volunteer agree to inspect businesses and file reports. And not only that, but...."

My foot felt Roddy's boot press, and I stopped, eye contact not needed.

Speechless at that moment, Martin drummed his fingers, signaled the waiter, and ordered coffee. "Mrs. DeVere," he finally said, "I have full confidence that your activities are meant for the good."

The coffee arrived, and liqueurs were offered. Roddy refused with a quip about "utmost sobriety" and our early train tomorrow morning.

I began to gather my gloves, but our host had not finished. From an inside coat pocket, he produced a paper folder. "Artwork from my daughter, Mrs. DeVere," he said. "It seems you made quite an impression on my Tansy, and I promised this to you."

Taking the folder, I smiled, conveyed my pleasure and admiration for the talented young lady, and let Roddy tuck the gift into his inside pocket, all the while Martin went on, "Departing Chicago so soon...but we will see one another in the near future to socialize...and to continue our plans, Roderick. Your letter of intent is locked in my office safe. Could we shake hands on it?"

"On the promise of further discussions," my husband said. The men reached across the coffee cups for their handshake."

"You are the witness, Mrs. deVere," said Martin. His eyes almost twinkled. A glimpse at his cufflinks showed wild boars' heads.

"And Mrs. DeVere," Martin continued, "I hope you might do your good works for the Coates family...to help Sara."

"Miss Dow?"

"...who makes every effort with our Celia but needs an ally before my sister's spending gets out of hand. And Roderick," he continued, "you will hear of Owen's scheme to revive jousting. You will hear of chain mail and lances. I ask you to withhold judgment for my sake."

"For your sake, Martin?"

"For the sake of all concerned," he said.

We stood, and Martin took my hand and bowed. In days to come, I would remember his boar's head cufflink that gleamed with ruby eyes and tusks that thrust like tiny spears.

Chapter Twenty-three

AS WE WOULD LEARN, Chicago had not finished with Roderick and Valentine DeVere, who would depart "The City by the Lake" with fair warning and a threat.

We accounted carefully for the hours from our dinner with Martin to the New York Central train that we would board the following morning. Planning a good night's sleep, we took a hansom from the Grand Pacific Hotel to the Auditorium. The lobby was quiet, and the desk clerk nodded as we stepped into the elevator to be whisked to the eighth floor. Arm in arm, we walked softly along the carpet, hearing no voices from the rooms on either side of the corridor. Once inside the suite, we undressed and quietly began gathering up our things, having decided to forego the evening maid and valet service. Working side by side, Roddy and I folded and packed. Tomorrow, we agreed, would be time enough to talk over the dinner with Martin.

We slept fitfully, as is often the case when travel looms. Neither of us was to recall any sound outside our suite door that night. I heard no one in the corridor. Nor did Roddy.

At dawn, we washed and dressed quickly, and my husband telephoned for a bellman, who was to come promptly with a luggage cart. When he knocked, we expected our luggage to be loaded, but instead the man called us into the corridor, where a box lay on the hallway carpet just outside the door. Tied with red ribbon, the box was topped with one single red rose. The wrapping paper sparkled.

"Roddy," I said, "a gift. Someone has...."

"Madam," the bellman said sharply, "you must not...."

"Not touch it," Roddy said.

We three stared at the box.

"I will summon the watchman," said the bellman. "Please do not touch the box. We fear it might be...." His lips quivered. "Might be...."

Roddy said aloud what we all thought. "Might be," he said, "a bomb."

Chapter Twenty-four

WE MIGHT AS WELL have sat upright on bristly seats. Tense, both of us watched farm fields and small towns roll past. Over and again, the question—was it a bomb? If so, who meant us harm?

And why?

The telegraph to start the trip.

A bomb to end it.

And why?

We left the Auditorium before the box was touched. The watchman came to the suite, and police were called, but Roddy and I had left the hotel and boarded the train before we knew what was inside the mysterious gift box.

"The red rose on the lid," I said, "suggests something from Martin ...perhaps a gift to flatter me."

"To encourage the partnership," Roddy said.

"Or not to stop to it," I snapped.

Then again, in my darkest thoughts, perhaps wives were too inconvenient. One dearly lamented late wife had troubled an Oak Park household. Could a bomb remove a possible obstacle to Roddy's alliance with Martin?

Disposable wife?

Was I that rattled? My mind gone rogue? Gazing outside at the farm fields, I yearned for tedium.

Instead, fear.

"Val," Roddy said, "would you care to take something?"

We both peered at a handkerchief in my fingers. Heedless, I had shredded it. "Something...? You mean medicine?"

"The steward probably can get you something for nerves."

"A sedative," I said in scorn. "The 'ladies' doses soaked with opium. Absolutely not. But Roddy, that box was meant for me. For you, the lid ornament would have been...a cigar."

My husband could only say the box probably held a small gift and that we would know soon enough. He squeezed his eyes shut and glanced downward, clearly worried.

We sat in silence, tried to read, and put the books aside. The steward brought coffee, tea, and juice and suggested that we choose our seating hour in the dining car for luncheon and for this evening's dinner. I could not conceive of dining.

"Roddy," I said at last, "do you suppose that Detective Brady was called to see about the box? He would learn whose suite was targeted."

"He would...if he was not already reassigned."

"By Martin's bribe," I said, "...to guarantee that Brady's rank is stripped and his pay cut. Chicago, it seems, has learned a good deal from policing in New York City."

Roddy winced. It was all too true, as we had learned last fall in the city, dealing with Officer Colin Finlay and Chief Devery, whose fleshy hand I had shaken.

I would barely remember the next hours, the click of the wheels on the track. Seated across from cordial strangers, we dined and made polite conversation, though I recalled nothing of what was said. Roddy later mentioned to me that he had recently consulted about a special cocktail for the railroad.

We reached New York at midday, met by Noland on the box seat of a large barouche carriage in blustery weather. Atlas and Apollo high-stepped to 620 Fifth Avenue. Noland mentioned that our saddle horses would soon arrive from the South. The private stable we shared with the Forsters would be ready for Comet and Justice, my quarter horse and Roddy's Arabian gelding. Our homecoming was brighter with the cheerful prospect of the bridle paths.

Sands met us at the entrance, and Mrs. Thwaite managed a tight smile, but warm and wriggly Velvet was our best "welcome home" as she rolled over for a tummy rub. She looked well cared for in our absence, perhaps too well fed for a French bulldog.

"Home," said Roddy.

"Home," I echoed without joy. The Auditorium already felt like a month ago, and Chicago another country—except for the gift box in the corridor.

"Roddy," I said, "will you telephone the Auditorium? Or shall I?" We sat at lunch in a nook off the dining room.

"Sands says the telephone is not in service. The outside wires are under repair."

"Then, a telegram?"

"I'll send a Western Union wire after lunch." Roddy tilted his head. "The household air, Val...not paint, more like...plaster? Val, it's the *Empire* room, isn't it?"

"Probably." Would we quarrel? He reached for my hand across the table, and I recalled his handshake with Martin. Suddenly, the Coates' family seeped into this space. The detective too.

"Roddy," I asked, "do you think Brady can be bought off?"

"Can be? Or will be? If the man is obsessed, then I'd guess a break in rank won't budge him. Nor will a pay cut. He might dig in his heels. Martin might find that he made a big mistake." Roddy reached to pet the dog. "He's a tough nut, that Brady.... He admitted he went to the same school as the Coates boys and their younger sister. But not one word about Lydia Anne Gerstle Coates. We made every effort, didn't we?"

"Every effort," I said. "We saw Jackson Park, and I watched you race after Officer Jakub Polachek...and then the long ride to a firehouse, and the next morning, voila, Detective Michael Brady marched out of the hotel kitchen door to warn us to get out of Chicago."

I put down my spoon. "And still, we have no idea why the detective believes that someone in the Oak Park household killed Lydia Coates."

"Nor whether his belief is backed up by evidence," Roddy added. He stroked Velvet's ears. "Or a motive. Those are the big ones...motive and evidence. Sometimes they intertwine. So far, we have neither."

"Neither..." I murmured.

"I'll wire the Auditorium." He took my hands in his. "I have faith, my dear, that we will learn of a small parting gift meant for you upon our departure, a gift the hotel clerk will wrap up and forward in a day or two."

My husband's strained voice undercut his message. Our lunch was finished. "One more thing, Roddy.... You shook hands with Martin, and your handshakes are never trivial."

My mouth felt dry. "Could we agree," I said, "that I will look in on Celia in Washington Square, if I must? And you will pay a call on Owen in whatever stable or barn he frequents? And as for the partnership...."

Roddy crossed his arms. "Val, l am ready to dismiss the whole idea. I agreed to further discussions, but the business plan is suspended and can go no further."

The moment so decisive, the pledge so firm, but the promise could be broken as so many promises broke when events came crashing into the best laid plans.

Perhaps I sensed the irreversible errors in the offing, but household tasks shook off inertia when Calista lifted a pair of stiff and wrinkled boots from my baggage. "And these boots, ma'am?"

Caked with Chicago mud and sunk in puddles in front of Hull House, they looked ruined, yet meaningful.

"Calista," I said, "put the boots in a muslin bag for the time being."

"And these papers, ma'am? Important papers?"

I smiled. "Children's art," I said. "Let me show you the drawings that brightened our hotel suite in Chicago."

On the bedspread, I smoothed Charlie and Bea Forster's colored sailing ships and Tansy's horse and lamb.

"The ships are by Mrs. Forster's little children," I said, "and the animals were drawn by a young girl whose father hosted us at dinner in their home...a very talented girl, as you see."

"Indeed, I do," Calista said as she opened the folder that Tansy's father passed on at dinner. I had slipped it from Roddy's coat pocket and put the art together when we packed up.

"I expect we'll see other animals," I said. "The child said she only draws animals these days."

My maid and I peered at the three extra drawings that I spread alongside the others. "The young lady likes horses," Calista said, "and lambs too."

Once again, Tansy's charcoal pencil drawings showed a horse atop a ladder and a lamb asleep on the ground below.

"Looks like the same black horse, ma'am."

"And the same snow-white lamb," I said. "...probably the artist in search of perfection, drawing and redrawing whatever catches attention and won't let go."

Somehow disappointed, I put the drawings on a side table. Tansy's art felt like a sad keepsake, like the wrinkled boots.

"Ma'am," Calista said, "just a few more things to sort out, and you will be fully at home."

Home—the word always echoed from the far West to New York, but Chicago, thankfully, could pass out of mind.

So I thought.

Roddy's telegram to the Auditorium was acknowledged in a reply that failed to give specifics about the gift box. My husband spent the afternoon visiting his parents in their apartment. I sent warm regards.

I approved the dinner menu and spoke to Sands about curbing Velvet's snacks. Avoiding Mrs. Thwaite, I peeked into the *Empire* room to glimpse new lightweight chairs and sunny wallpaper. The room was not yet completed, and I closed the door.

At five o'clock, Roddy and I went upstairs to our favorite green Bergere chairs, and he summoned his "bar cart," the converted tea wagon now featuring bottles, barware, glasses, an ice bucket, and a bowl of fresh fruit.

"Val, to celebrate our return to New York, I propose the Manhattan cocktail." At my nod, Roddy faced the cart, and I admired his deft movements until he turned with stemware glasses for each of us and said, "Salud, Val."

The Manhattan

Ingredients

- ½ ounce Irish whiskey
- ½ ounce Italian vermouth
- 2 dashes orange bitters
- 2 pinches refined sugar or teaspoon simple syrup.
- Ice

Directions:

1. Add whiskey and vermouth to ice-filled tall glass or shaker.
2. Add sugar
3. Add bitters
4. Stir and strain into martini glass.

The cold zinged to my head, and the whiskey steamed at my throat. "Delicious," I said. Roddy remarked that Chicago could use help at its cocktail bar.

"But Chicago is on its own," I said, "because Mr. Roderick DeVere has no plan to join the Chicago Club nor to distill bitters in league with Martin Coates. So, let us drink to that!"

With the ring of an ultimatum, my words prompted sips and silence. The early evening darkened, and our dinner was announced. For once, I did not mind changing into a dinner gown, a silk brocade trimmed with tiny glass beads. Roddy's tuxedo and black tie always lured me close, and we dined slowly, speaking little but saying a good deal with glances that were filled with after-dinner promise.

From the table, Roddy took my hand and led me upstairs to his study, where he lighted a candle, sat us on the pearl-gray sofa, and began to unhook my gown. I gently tugged at the bow tie and nipped at his shirt collar until my lips reached Roddy's bare, warm neck, and our lips met in the kisses that drowned all else in the world. My gown and underthings slipped off, and his tuxedo seemed tailored just for tonight, a breakaway coat and trousers. We lay pressed against one another, warming each other with bodies that rolled and thrust in a rhythm both well understood and yet new every time. The vocal gusts, the crests and collapse against one another let time suspend itself.

We might have spent the night here, but Roddy gently wrapped us in throw blankets, gazed into the hallway to see no servants in sight, and led me to my boudoir here we made love all over again.

Had I kept a diary, this night would be recorded with constellations of stars. Had Roddy and I been left to ourselves, what's more, this spring season could have blossomed and leafed out just for us, with the recent turmoil over and done.

Was this too much to hope for? Was Roddy's promise to me so fragile that it would shatter so soon and easily? Did the world need to crash in the very next day?

These questions were moot. No diary would record the fact that the world crashed in, and Roddy's promise broke wide open.

Chapter Twentyfive

MY HUSBAND WOULD SURELY join me at breakfast.
I counted on his smile, his loving eyes after such a night as
we had together. I had sipped the usual feeble coffee when
Sands entered the breakfast room to say that Mr. DeVere
had gone out very early this morning.

"Early? How early?"

The unflappable butler looked as flustered as I suddenly
felt. "At first light," he said.

"First light?" That was not the dawn, but what was it? I
could not remember. "At what hour, Sands?"

The butler thought perhaps four a.m.

"Where did he go?"

On an "important errand" was all Sands knew. Or would
tell me? The master of the house was the master. "Sands," I
said, "this is highly irregular."

He cleared his throat. "Mr. DeVere would wish to assure you that he will return as soon as possible. He would wish you not concern yourself but enjoy the morning."

Too many *woulds*. The butler's wing collar was not quite winged. His rare appearance in the breakfast room signaled disruption.

"Why was Mr. DeVere awakened?" I asked. "Was someone at the door?"

"I believe, ma'am, the cook heard the telephone."

On a baking day, the cook lighted the oven at an ungodly early hour. "Sands," I said, "whoever used the telephone or managed to wake up Mr. DeVere...just tell me about the message?"

"Ma'am, all I can say is that Mr. DeVere dressed without assistance and departed promptly."

"On foot?" Was Roddy around the corner in his parents' apartment? No, the senior DeVeres refused to install a telephone.

"Did he order a carriage, Sands?"

The butler admitted that a carriage awaited Roddy at the front curb, but not one of ours.

"And who saw the carriage out front...?" He paused. "Don't tell me...the cook, yes?"

Sands's short nod tucked his chin nearly to his neck. He bowed and withdrew.

The Junghans clock struck ten, and still I sat. Both footmen hinted that I might breakfast by myself. Their household duties were stalled, so I set them free with a toast request. From her bed by the table, Velvet gazed expectantly at Roddy's chair. "Girl," I said to her, "I am as confused as you are." We waited. Velvet first sensed her master's presence after 10:30 when she dashed from the room, disappeared, and returned in my husband's arms. "Roddy, where have you....?"

"Val...." My husband's tousled hair, rumpled shirt, and crooked tie measured the day's discord. He sank into the chair across from me. The dog's eyes looked brighter than Roddy's. A footman appeared at his elbow.

"Tea, Chalmers...just tea." Lowered to the floor, the dog was satisfied that her pack was intact. She napped as Roddy rubbed his whiskery cheek, and we waited until his steaming cup of tea was sipped. And sipped again.

"Coming up for air," he said at last.

"I'm all ears."

"Val, just listen for a few minutes. No questions...."

I nodded.

"So," my husband began, "at around 3:30, I was rousted by Norbert, and bless my valet, he walked me downstairs to the telephone. The cook—"

"—I know about the cook.... Sorry, Roddy. Go on."

"The manager of the Traveler's Club telephoned, and the man was barely coherent...something about a member and guests who dined and took violently ill. A carriage was sent for me, and I was to come at once. A doctor was at the club."

My husband saw my puzzlement. "I know...why telephone me? I vaguely recalled that Father was once a member, but I never joined the Traveler's Club. Anyway, the man sounded desperate, insisted I come at once.... I thought it might involve Father's friends, so I threw on these clothes, and the carriage was at the curb."

Roddy sipped his tea. "Surly driver," he said, "not a word out of him. The carriage went straight down Fifth Avenue... nothing stirring but milk wagons on cross streets... Finally, number 124 Fifth Avenue... the building with evergreens in the window boxes. You've admired them."

I had?

"We pass it all the time."

I kept quiet.

"Anyway, the manager met me at the entrance. He apologized for the haste but would not say what happened. He looked rousted from his own bed, probably by the night clerk. He took me upstairs to a room and knocked on the door. I waited in the hall until Strether Kimball came out to speak with me."

I nearly exclaimed the name in surprise, for Strether Kimball, M.D., was Society's own physician, a man whose medical skills allied with a suave bedside manner. "Kimball was called because four men dined last evening and suddenly fell ill...a resident member and three of his guests. Kimball was called when the club management became alarmed. When I arrived, he had been treating them for hours...almost nightlong."

Roddy stopped. Perspiration beaded on his forehead, and he fumbled for a handkerchief.

I handed him mine.

"The men," he said at last, "are not friends of my father. They are strangers to me.... The club member hosted three guests for dinner, and they dined in a private room...now an infirmary. Kimball fears that one man might not pull through."

Roddy patted his forehead. "The first thought was food poisoning.... The Traveler's is not known for fine dining, but the kitchen is well managed. They searched the kitchen, and food poisoning was finally ruled out."

"Then, what...?"

Roddy's glare beseeched me to keep still. He swallowed hard. "Val...what it comes down to is their drinks...their cocktails. Kimball is quite certain the alcohol was bad."

What did 'bad' mean? "The cocktails they drank," I said, "what was in them?"

"In 'it,' Val. They all drank the same whiskey cocktail. The drinks could have been corrupted any number of ways."

"What was in...it?"

"The recipe calls for whiskey, dashes of absinthe, gum syrup...and bitters."

"Bitters..." I echoed.

"And ice. Though I doubt the ice was impure."

"And you were summoned," I said, "because you are known for your skill...?"

Roddy took a deep breath, folded his hands, and gazed straight at me. "I was summoned," he said, "because I devised the club's signature cocktail. The secret recipe for 'The Traveler's' is my very own."

❧

We decided to walk in the park. We could talk, and Roddy was too upset to nap or rest. I dressed while he was shaved and changed into a gray sack suit. We took the dog. I held her leash while Roddy carried a walking stick. The uncertain spring weather threatened showers, but we refused the umbrella that Sands offered.

Just past noon, we started into Central Park at the Fifty-ninth Street entrance. Pedestrians strolled around us, and policemen patrolled on foot and horseback. Several pedaled bicycles. A few carriages were visible along the drive, but we took the path toward the Green Gap. No horseback riders were in sight, perhaps because rain threatened.

"So, Roddy," I began, "you spoke with Dr. Kimball."

"We talked briefly in the hallway. His patients needed him at their side. Kimball thought a move to a hospital would be too risky, so the club settled the men on the floor with pillows and blankets...and pails. Nurses were called."

"And he feels certain the men were poisoned by the cocktail?"

"Quite certain."

"Perhaps," I said, "they drank so many that they became ill?"

"No. The bartender said each man drank just two Traveler's cocktails. He was on duty when the men took ill, and he remembered no one else ordered a Traveler's last evening."

"But isn't whiskey a mainstay for many cocktails?" I asked. "Surely other members ordered whiskey cocktails last evening."

"They did," Roddy said, "but the bartender sets aside a certain brand for the Traveler's. He keeps those bottles separate."

"And the others? The absinthe?"

"Imported from France. *Le Tourment Vert Absinthe*... very expensive, also reserved for Traveler's cocktails and a few others."

My husband poked his walking stick at a pebble. "The gum syrup," he said, "is sugar water... pure water piped from the Adirondack Mountains and refined sugar crystals from Hawaii."

"And that leaves...."

"Bitters." Roddy nearly spit the word. "The Traveler's calls for two dashes of orange bitters, and the bartender uses whatever brand is at hand."

"So, it could be—"

"—could be, yes, but we do not know." We paused while Velvet sniffed a shrub. "Before leaving the club," Roddy said, "I arranged for the ingredients to be tested in a laboratory. The whiskey, the absinthe, the gum syrup...and four brands of bitters because I doubt the bartender would recall which bottle he used. He was long gone by the time I was called."

"Roddy, why were you called? Your skill is known, but you devise cocktails in secret. You never let your name be attached to them. So...why you?"

My husband sighed. "The club bartender's notebook," he said, "listed my name...penciled. I don't know why. The irony, Val, is that a fatality could bring a lawsuit against the club...the sort of litigation that usually finds me on the side of defense."

"So," I said, "you would defend the Traveler's Club... while defending yourself?"

Roddy's harsh laugh startled the dog. "I would bow out of the case for ethical reasons, Val, but probably be called as a witness."

"For the defense?"

His harsh laugh once again, and Velvet eyed him. "Most likely," Roddy said, "cross-examined by the prosecution."

I shuddered. "What shall we do?" I asked.

"Pray to Heaven that the men survive and that none of them feels litigious."

"They could sue?"

"For bodily harm...false pretenses...." Roddy sucked his cheek. "However it goes, my reputation would be ruined. Every tavern or club would shun me, and I would lose my law license."

At that moment, the skies opened, a soft shower that became a cloudburst before we could pivot and hustle home.

Before we had reached our front door, however, it became obvious that the promised "further discussions" about the Coates distillery must reopen immediately—for Roddy's sake. My husband's well-being was suddenly snarled with Martin Coates and the mystery of his wife's death.

Chapter Twenty-six

WE DECIDED TO STAGE A dinner. At our dining table, we would host Owen and Celia Coates and Sara Dow too. A small, cozy dinner would let us paint our Chicago visit in pleasant colors. A softened atmosphere could tempt our guests to say more about the late, lamented Lydia. We would pump them all for revelations in unguarded moments. "

"Our one desperate measure," Roddy said.

"But, will it work?"

We had no answer. Our footman was dispatched to the Louis Sherry building and to Washington Square to see about open dates on the Coates' and Miss Dow's social calendars. He returned with dates and a remark about live peacocks that he feared might attack him. ("Indoors, ma'am... large birds one imagines best suited to a menagerie.")

Celia's peacocks and Owen's devotion to black blooded horses aside, we found a convenient date. I wrote the invitations, and acceptances arrived promptly. I requested a menu that would not overwhelm body or mind. Roddy would see to the beverages. We had four days to prepare.

Roddy's daily telegrams to the Auditorium about the gift box brought return wires of apology. A change in hotel personnel and procedure was blamed for the confusion and delay. The hotel regretted the unfortunate "miscommunication" and offered a complimentary night's stay.

"Not on your life," I said, then grinned at the grisly literal meaning. "We could get in touch with Detective Brady—"

"—who would demand to know who might wish us harm. And what would we tell him, Val?" The only answer: the Oak Park schoolmates he suspects of murder.

"Roddy," I said, "my mind went crazy on the train from Chicago...the bomb meant for me but sparing you. The only reason to pursue the point...you would be open to new pressures."

My husband did not dismiss the "crazy" thought. For the time being, we said no more about my death or the pressures. Martin's name was not spoken, and we avoided mention of the terrible telegram. Two postal cards arrived from Theo showing an erupting Old Faithful and a log lodge that could make me homesick if I let my mind go back in time. Theo scrawled, "Wild Wonderland" with exclamation points.

Roddy had two court cases to prepare, and I surrendered to Mrs. Thwaite's lament about the the *Empire* room.

"Oh, the plumes of dust, ma'am. We might have lost a parlor maid."

"I trust the household used face coverings," I said, "...bandanas."

"A slang term from the West, ma'am? Do you mean kerchiefs?"

Snide swipe. "Kerchiefs, Mrs. Thwaite." The housekeeper had doubtless scurried to Roddy's mother to bewail the *Empire* room catastrophe. I did not know exactly when Miss De Wolfe would finish, but Cassie was eager to see the progress, and an afternoon with my close friend and her spirited children would be a spring tonic. So I thought.

Cassie and the children came to tea, and the house rang with their cheerful cries when Sands opened the door on a cool afternoon. The dog sprang to Charlie and Bea, wriggling and sniffing at their ankles.

"Velvet!.... It's Velvet!...."

"Now, children...manners...."

The familiar ritual, the children's spontaneous cries and the affectionate parental nudging,

"Good afternoon, Auntie Val.... Good afternoon, Auntie."

"And good afternoon to you, Charles," I said, "and Beatrice, welcome to you. May we take your coats?" I admired Bea's plaid kilt, Charlie's indigo shirt, and Cassie's high-collar lilac suit, though her pallor doubtless meant sadness at her husband's absence.

"Dudley cabled from the ship," she said. "The high seas are fair, and he sends his love." Cassie smiled bravely for the children and for her own poised self. "We can't wait to hear about the 'City by the Lake,' can we, children?"

Busy with the dog, the children could not have cared less. "The lake was beautiful,' I said to Cassie, "and the days were...interesting. Shall we have tea?"

We went into the west-facing drawing room, where I poured apple tea for the children and Darjeeling for Cassie and me, while Bea and Charlie ogled the cookies. My friend's voice was both soothing and firm, "One at a time, children... on your plates, please...no cookies for Velvet." The dog licked the little fingers, and we sipped our tea.

"Cassie," I said, "we last had tea at Washington Square."

"With Chinese steamed buns," she said, "a specialty of Miss Dow, a taste of the Orient" My friend reached for a cucumber sandwich. The children patted Velvet. "And will you see her again?"

"Miss Dow? I very much doubt that we will become friends." I avoided the fact that in days, Sara Dow would dine in this house.

"And Miss Coates," Cassie continued, "will you have her to tea?" My friend averted her eyes. She seemed to shiver. "Cassie," I said, "the Washington Square household is farthest from my thoughts...miles from my thoughts." My fib felt harmless. I had not meant to stray into the Coates family imbroglio. This afternoon was a respite from them and from the gnawing worry about Roddy while he awaited the laboratory test results and news of the men stricken at the Traveler's Club.

My husband's court cases had become his reprieve, as this little tea party was mine. Lively children, cookies, a lovable

French bulldog, and a close friend—what better recipe for a happy afternoon? Cassie and I would soon cap the occasion with a peek inside the *Empire* room to see what Elsie De Wolfe had accomplished. Approval would be likely, and celebration too. For the moment, the world felt in balance.

I could not have guessed that young Charlie Forster's off-kilter questions about picture frames would set things awry and bring this tea party to a crashing halt. I would not have expected my own well-intentioned enthusiasm to become the updraft to trouble my friend.

We had all sipped our tea when Charlie remembered the pictures that he and his sister sent to us in Chicago. "We drew pictures of Daddy's ship for you and Uncle Roderick," he said.

"And we put stamps on the envelope that cost two cents," Bea added.

"Yes, you did," I said. "And when your pictures arrived in Chicago, I put them on the mantel in our hotel so that Uncle Roderick and I could enjoy them every day." The children nodded, and the afternoon would have glided nicely if I had not added, "We brought your pictures home with us to New York."

"Did you put them in a frame?" Charlie asked. "Daddy says art belongs in a frame." He pointed to the drawing room walls, landscapes and seascapes of no special significance, each one lushly framed.

I said, "You are right, Charlie. Your art deserves framing. In the meantime, your pictures must be displayed on that mantel." I pointed to the marble mantlepiece and announced, "Ships at sea by artists Bea and Charlie Forster... right up there, in a jiffy."

I had no inkling of trouble. Why would the moment be fraught? The footman was sent upstairs to retrieve the children's art. ("Quick, Bronson....Calista knows") The folder was retrieved, and the children drew close as the footman spread the drawings on a table.

"I did not draw that!" Bea's voice pierced the space. "Or that! Or that either! I never draw a horse. That is not my lamb!"

"Where are the ships? Where are they?" Charlie's woeful voice joined his sister's furious high-pitched squeal.

I hurried to the table and peered over the children's shoulders at the charcoal pencil drawings. "Oh, no...not yours. These are a mistake...someone else's pictures, another young...."

"Children...children...." Beside me, Cassie was staring at the drawings and beginning to clutch at her throat. "Children...." She gripped my shoulder for support and seemed to struggle to speak.

"Cassie, are you all right? The tea...?"

My friend turned with her back to the table. "We must go...." Her voice was barely audible, a whisper. "We must...."

She faced me. "Val," she whispered, "please help...please." Her eyes looked faraway, her vision beyond the room.

With one arm around her shoulders, I calmly but firmly said, "Children, it is time to go home right now. I will find your pictures and put them in frames and invite you to see them very soon. I promise you."

The footman helped, and Sands appeared at the door To assist my friend and her children into the Forsters' phaeton carriage that stood waiting at the curb. I believe that Cassie's fingers clawed as the carriage door was closed, but I was not certain that she waved good-by.

&ro;

"Roddy," I said, "if you had been here…. She could barely walk to the door. Sands and Bronson helped her to the carriage. The children saw their mother come close to fainting."

My husband had returned to face my tumult and a tea service left untouched in the drawing room. He eyed the teapots and leftover sandwiches on a pedestal cake plate.

"I wanted you to see this, Roddy. Cassie ate one cucumber tea sandwich, and a few minutes later, she took ill…right over there." I pointed to the side table where the footman had spread Tansy's drawings. Calista had already apologized for the mix-up.

"Sands offered to telephone the Forster home," I said, "but I asked him to go in person for a butler-to-butler word with the Forsters' Hayes, who will speak to their housekeeper. So, Sands went on foot to Madison. He ought to be back any minute."

I pointed to the treats. "We both drank Darjeeling, so it can't be the tea. The kitchen can't account for it. I thought you ought to see it…perhaps send the sandwiches to a laboratory for testing."

"Val...really, now, Val...."

My husband's low, even voice had a steadying effect that I relied on...sometimes too much.

"Let's sit down for just a minute." Roddy led me to a tan camelback sofa. "Now, then, if you'll start at the beginning...."

My husband listened, asked a few questions, and finally said in his gentlest voice, "Val, aren't you avoiding the obvious?"

"What 'obvious?'"

"For one thing, Cassandra's scientist husband is suddenly far away, and she is probably tense and excitable. And Dudley is not here to dampen...." Roddy cleared his throat. "...to damp down her superstitions."

I had not told Roddy of Cassie's resolve to banish her otherworldly feelings. He did not know about the threatened treatment in Switzerland. "I hope you're right," I said. "Anyway, why would Cassie become 'superstitious' in our home? She has been here on countless occasions. That awful dinner honoring Dudley...she felt no 'superstitions.' Nothing has changed in this house except the *Empire* room, and Cassie was too faint to see it."

Roddy rubbed his cheek. "Let me propose, my dear, that our friend, Cassandra, is apt to neglect proper meals without her Dudley at the dining table. She probably felt faint from not eating."

"So, you don't think the tea sandwiches...?"

"Absolutely not." He took my hand. "The footmen can clear the room, but first, a few minutes to report on my afternoon?"

So engrossed in these doings I had not thought about Roddy's last hours. "You were in the courtroom…" I said.

"In court records, preparing for cases," he said. "But I also stopped at Strether Kimball's medical office. Good news… thanks to Kimball, all four men have pulled through." He bit his lip. "But no thanks to the orange bitters in their Traveler's cocktails."

"The laboratory results are in?"

"The report right here." Roddy patted his coat pocket. "The whiskey is pure…and the absinthe and gum syrup also tested true."

"But the bitters?"

"Three of the four bottles tested true…. The fourth had wood alcohol, Val. It's toxic…orange flavoring added to water and wood alcohol…technically, methanol. If ever this country outlaws alcoholic beverages, the criminals will resort to it and won't give a hoot who lives or dies."

My husband blinked. "I sped to the Traveler's Club and ordered the bartender to get rid of *Captain Roy's Best Orange Bitters*. I watched him pour it out." Roddy's expression became as grave as I could recall. "No telling how many toxic bottles are in circulation. I'll do my best to sound the alarm. And Val…one other thing."

"Yes?"

"This dinner, Val…. We need traction…about Martin Coates, about the future. You know what I mean. I need not spell it out. Let us plan together. This dinner party we have scheduled…let's make it count."

Chapter Twenty-seven

INVITED FOR 7:00 P.M., our guests would arrive at ten minutes past the hour if they obeyed social custom. Our footmen had spread a carpet from the front door, down the outdoor steps, and across the sidewalk to the curb. We had decided against an overhead canopy, but our footmen in dress uniforms would assist Celia and Sara from their carriage and escort Owen upon arrival. Sands would be stationed at the door, and Calista would assist with pre-dinner primping in a side room where a dressing table and mirror had been placed. The weather promised to be pleasant, a bit cool, perfect for light wraps.

All afternoon, aromas wafted from our downstairs kitchen, dishes baked and roasted, simmered and sautéed. No scorching or burning tonight—not in the kitchen.

Roddy's **Punch au Kirsch** was part of our plan, a beverage offered to ladies since it was not technically a cocktail. "A flaming ice-breaker," my husband said. The draperies would be closed, the reception room dimmed, and the guests treated to the sight of blue flames dancing atop the punch bowl.

"When a flaming match is touched to liquor, Val, even prim ladies and taciturn gentlemen light up...as did a certain Valentine Mackle a few years ago."

He winked. "No Blue Blazer tonight, my dear, but a quart of *kirsch* ought to help us make this evening count."

We kissed on it.

From a window overlooking Fifth Avenue, I watched the carriage come to a stop at 7:15. Our footmen sprang to the door and assisted two ladies up the front steps. Wearing a caramel taffeta gown edged with seed pearls, I quickly took my place in the Corinthian reception room, waited until Calista tended both ladies' coiffeurs, and heard Sands announce, "The Misses Celia Coates and Sara Dow."

"Celia, welcome...and so good of you to join us, Miss Dow...and how lovely are your gowns, ladies." We exchanged compliments. In floor-length turquoise velvet trimmed with white lace, Celia had chosen matching turquoise earrings that almost reached her shoulders but dangled unevenly. She approached with mincing steps, almost halting as she entered the room. Celia was most likely coping with ill-fitting new shoes, or so I thought at first. I would soon think again.

Beside Celia, Sara Dow kept a fixed smile as she eyed the Louis furniture and seemed to count the Corinthian columns. Her deep red satin gown outlined a low neckline, and her onyx jewelry flashed like black diamonds. Once again, her lacquered hairpins thrust at bold angles in her raven dark hair. Her small steps seemed to throttle back her energy.

Roddy came forward for introductions to Miss Dow. His sapphire cuff links gleamed as he bowed to the ladies, my gift on his last birthday. We began chitchat about spring flowers but stopped as Sands announced, "Mister Owen Coates."

Striding my way, Owen ceremoniously bowed to me, shook hands with Roddy, and nodded to his sister with familiarity edged with caution. Owen's suit looked tight enough to burst a seam as he bowed to Sara Dow. His injured wrist apparently had healed. His cologne could be mistaken for cognac.

"Miss Sara, how time flies," he said with mocking warmth. His lazy brown eyes swept the room in nonchalance. "And my dear sister...to dine with the DeVeres on Fifth Avenue." He grinned, and I guessed that brother and sister had not seen one another since the virulent dinner that Martin had hosted weeks ago, when Roddy and I endured the family quarrel.

"To the punch bowl, shall we?" Roddy drew us to a round table in the center of the room, where the glass punch bowl with crystal cups were arrnged beside a decanter of clear liquid.

Roddy took charge. "Let there be no mystery about the ingredients or preparations for our pre-dinner libation," my husband said. "So, I hereby pronounce that this punch bowl contains only hot tea and a goodly amount of sugar... which I shall now stir with this silver spoon. Are you ready?"

We nodded like children as Roddy stirred the punch in exaggerated circles. My reserved husband seldom dramatized, but just now he resembled a magician about to perform a trick.

"Hot tea and sugar," he stage-whispered. "...and are you prepared for the finale?"

Celia murmured, "Ready as rain," which sounded meaningless but pleasant.

"Then, for your pleasure...." Roddy lifted the decanter, displayed it to the right and left, poured the colorless liquid into the bowl, and spelled aloud,

"K-i-r-s-c-h." Distracted by the spelling, we were not to see the friction match flare, at which the punch bowl came alive with blue flames.

Celia cried, "oohh," and Sara murmured, "very nice." Owen said, "Neat trick, DeVere...if I do say so."

Sands appeared to ladle the punch, and in moments we sipped, smiled, and chatted about the upcoming summer season.

I had written down the punch recipe and could recite it if need be:

Punch with Kirsch

Ingredients:

- ½ ounce loose tea
- 1 quart boiling water
- 1 pound refined sugar
- 1 quart *kirsch*

Directions:
1.	In boiling water, add tea.
2.	Steep for ten minutes.
3.	Put sugar in punch bowl.
4.	Strain infusion of tea into bowl.
5.	Stir with silver spoon until sugar dissolves.
6.	Add *kirsch* and set it alight.
7.	When flames extinguish, ladle punch into handled cups and serve.

Promptly at 8:00 p.m., Sands reappeared to announce, "Dinner is served." Owen took Sara's arm, and Roddy escorted Celia and me into our dining room. Roddy flashed me a glance that said, "Let the Show Begin."

A clear consommé was served, champagne poured, and Owen asked about Chicago. "I mean, did brother Martin put the touch on you, DeVere?"

Roddy hesitated, but Owen pushed on. "The Vitalene works, did you see it? High volume, national distribution... big opportunities abroad. My brother will end up rich...if he plays his cards."

Celia said, "Now Owen, this is social...." She looked rather pale, perhaps from the lighting. Her harp-like voice sounded thin as she said, "Manners, please, Owen."

"Manners?" He snorted. "Our punch bowl hour is over, dear sister, and our host and hostess got an earful about the Coates bunch a few weeks ago at Sherry's restaurant." He chugged his champagne. "I need to tell Mr. DeVere a few things about the newest doings."

He glanced my way. "I hope you won't object, madame."

"Not at all, Mr. Coates," I said.

"Then, hear this…I have committed five million dollars to the distillery. My brother wants to produce cocktail bitters, and there's no reason the distillery can't do both… bitters and Vitalene."

Roddy's jaw tightened. He sipped his wine.

"Different vats and boilers," Owen continued. "Different bottles and labels. So, two for one…or one for two. You get the point."

"I believe your brother," Roddy said firmly, "plans to abandon production of the elixir."

Owen drained his glass. "Five million dollars," he said, "can change a man's mind." A footmen refilled his champagne. "And we shall see."

Conversation paused as the filet of sole was served, a pale fish in a pale sauce that seemed to stymie Celia until she heard whispered words from Sara, at which the young woman poked at the fish. The mistress of Washington Square seemed subdued this evening. Perhaps it was just as well.

"Mr. Coates," I said, "I hope you are finding New York City to your liking."

"A fine town for horses and those who love them," he declared. "But one sport has yet to see its new day…jousting."

"Jousting, Owen…" said Sara. "You are serious, after all…?"

"Stone cold serious," he said. "The Medieval sport of knightly warfare is ripe for our modern age. Coats-of-arms, lances...tournaments in season. I have visited your favorite jeweler, sister dear."

Celia murmured, "Tiffany?"

"The newest department for 'Blazoning and Designing of Arms.' The laws of heraldry will be rewritten. I have also seen Oliver Belmont's collection of armor and found a blacksmith who can hammer out breastplates and helmets. Lances too. And I have a man who makes chain mail, thanks to Gordon Bennett's blunder."

"What 'blunder?'" I asked, seeing Roddy's warning too late.

"Don't you know? I thought everybody in New York knew why Bennett wore a chain mail undershirt." He grinned. "Seems the man was under fire for a wee-wee in his fiancée's front parlor fireplace.... Thought her furious brother might shoot him, so he wore a chain mail shirt."

Sara's lips curled in amusement. "Owen, such naughty dinner table conversation."

"Never mind naughty, the chain mail is the point." He turned to Roddy. "So," he said, "I need horses that can run and carry the extra weight. Good of you to invite me to the private sale, DeVere, and I now keep several saddle horses, every one as black as midnight. But for jousting, I am as yet undecided." He paused while our fish plates were whisked off and cutlets served. Red wine was poured. "Burgundy, DeVere?"

Roddy said, "Claret, I believe."

Sara sipped but touched Celia's wrist when the young woman reached for her wine glass. Celia nodded and drank some water. As the hostess who must defer to her guest, I too sipped water. Owen's sister seemed fatigued. Her gray-green eyes did not flash tonight. Perhaps she did not feel well.

Her brother took no notice as he drank and drank again. "Not to bring up a sore point," he said, "but a New York City Police detective called on me."

It had to be Finlay. My husband did not return my glance, but looked at Sara, whose wry smile seemed meant to draw us into a conspiracy.

"What have you done this time, Owen Coates?" she asked. "And what 'sore point?'"

Owen raised his forearm. "This was plenty 'sore'...very bad sprain. We thought it was broken." He looked at Roddy. "Tell them, DeVere."

Roddy sipped his wine to gain time. At last, he said, "A ruffian wrestled Mr. Coates to the ground at the Coaching Club parade earlier this month. Fortunately, you fended him off, sir."

"Did what a man must do," Owen replied. "But the scoundrel lost his cap, and a detective tracked me down to have a word. The cap, you see, is the sort that stable hands choose. So, the detective questioned the hands at the riding school where my saddle horses are stabled...looked for a grudging fellow that might have it in for me."

"And was the culprit found?" I asked.

"Probably the greedy one that bullied the others to demand outlandish wages. I told the detective that I fired him on the spot. Gave the detective his name, but I doubt the villain will be caught. The detective's name is Finlay, doubtless Irish, so what can you ex—"

"—Owen, please." For the moment, Sara's hard glance stopped him.

"No offence intended, Mrs. DeVere," he said, sounding remarkably contrite.

"None taken," I said, smiling and thankful that the footmen appeared just then with vegetable dishes, asparagus and braised celery they offered to each of us in turn."

"Divine..." Sara whispered to us all, her fork poised over the plate. "And may I take this moment to recall that my beloved late friend, Lydia, adored such dishes as we enjoy at your table, Mr. and Mrs. DeVere...and the children, especially poor Tansy, tried so to learn their manners. The situation was at times...I should say, tragicomic."

I did not know whether to smile. All children struggled to master utensils. Maybe Sara simply meant to bring up Lydia, lest the evening pass without mention of the deceased. Why would she do this?

"I assure you, Miss Dow," I said, "that we found Tansy to be well-mannered and polite when we dined in Oak Park. The child gave us a gift of her artwork...a talented young lady."

"She is soon coming to visit," said Celia, who had been so quiet that her voice almost startled the table. "School vacation," she continued, "...or maybe school will be recessed. I can't remember which it is, but soon."

"And we will board the peacocks elsewhere," said Sara, "but most of all, we will get our Celia's health back first... won't we, Celia?"

The young woman's pale cheeks colored as she nodded. Her turquoise earrings dipped unevenly.

"I am sorry," I said, "to hear that you are not feeling quite yourself, Miss Coates."

Celia gazed wistfully in my direction. "Sara is nursing me," she said.

"...back to health," Sara said, "as I nursed dear Lydia in her last months."

"You have training as a nurse?" I asked, keeping my voice mild and neutral.

"Mrs. DeVere," she said, "For years, I represented Vitalene as a saleslady, and so it became necessary that I learn the American medicine cabinet. Top to bottom, I learned every shelf by heart. And so," she continued, "when dear Lydia's health declined, I was on hand to administer her medicines...in consultation with her doctors, of course."

"Of course," I murmured.

"And a perfect coincidence that I am able to be in New York to help our Celia at this trying time. And now, if you would be so good as to excuse us, Mrs. Devere...Mr. Devere... it might be best that we take our leave...Celia's dosage is due."

"Of course," Roddy said. "Let me call our carriage to take you...."

"No need, DeVere," said Owen. "I have a jump seat phaeton outside, and we three will fit nicely. Topping of you to have us here, but the knights of old bowed to the ladies in every tournament. Call me Lancelot."

Chapter Twenty-eight

"LANCELOT, RODDY.... THE MAN is a pompous fool." My husband had gone to the front window, watched Owen and the ladies drive off, returned to the table, and reached for his glass of wine.

"Pompous fool," I hissed, "...but maybe we have been the fools."

Beside me, Roddy and put a finger to his lips to signal, silence. With effort, I kept quiet as the butler eyed the place settings and deftly swept away signs that three others had dined here, although three spots of claret had dribbled from Owen's glass to the damask cloth, and a few crumbs lay on Celia's place. On Sara's place at the table, nothing whatsoever.

"What do we know about Sara Dow?" Roddy asked.

"Not much.," I said. "At Washington Square, she led Cassie and me to believe that her father was in a diplomatic service. She said 'legation,' but it could be anything...a clerk, an attaché. She claimed to have traveled the world, including the Far East. At tea, she served us Chinese buns she claimed to know from Peking."

I pushed up a hairpin. "Sara Dow could have lied about her past, but we know that she worked as a Vitalene traveling saleswoman. She outsold the salesmen and was hired by Martin's father to be a companion to Lydia...and a household cheerleader for Vitalene."

I sipped the wine that I had not touched in deference to the subdued Celia. "Something else, Roddy," I said. "At Hull House, I learned that Sara discouraged Lydia from becoming friendly with a woman doctor who researches toxins. Dr. Alice Hamilton lives at Hull House, and she encouraged Lydia to visit the Crerar Library."

"Which she did."

"Over Sara's objections."

My husband stroked his chin. "At the Crerar, Val, how deep did you get into medicines?"

"Not very deep. The book on adulteration included medicines from A to Z, but I can't remember them. I went there to verify Lydia's visit. She went to the Crerar Library to learn whether Vitalene was poisonous."

Roddy sat back and crossed his legs. "Suppose," he said, "that Lydia went to the library for another reason as well."

"What other reason?"

"It's just this, Val," he said. "At the Oak Park dinner, Martin told us that doctors frequented the house to treat

Lydia, but he added that Sara learned to administer medicines and injections to his wife. I especially remember the injections."

I did too.

"We know that Lydia's health declined swiftly in her last months," Roddy said, "but suppose that she began to feel ill much earlier? Suppose she sensed that the medicines she took might be impairing her health? If so, would she suggest such a thing to her doctor?"

"The ultimate male authority? Highly doubtful."

"And would she broach the topic to her companion and 'nurse,' Sara?"

I saw Roddy's point. Would Lydia challenge the woman who claimed to know the American medicine cabinet from top to bottom? "No," I said, "Sara would go to the Crerar Library to research Vitalene—and the compounds that might be making her ill."

"And if her suspicions were born out," Roddy said, "what would she have done?"

The question hung, unanswered and unanswerable. I said, "Nothing Martin told us suggested that Lydia resisted the regimen of pills and powders."

"Or the injections."

The room grew quiet. The wine stains had dried as brown as blood. The candles flickered and guttered. "We must not leave the table," I said, "until we talk about Celia. You remember her at Sherry's."

"Spunky," my husband said.

"Not 'spunky,' Roddy. She was bossy and combative. And impulsive. I saw her twice again at Washington Square and then at Maillard's confectionary. She would have ordered every item on the menu if I hadn't reined her in. And she desperately sought an invitation to the coaching parade… threatened consequences…lightning would strike."

I sipped my wine. "I braced for an outburst when you brought up the parade at dinner. Instead, silence." I shook my head. "Roddy, from the minute she walked in, Celia was a different person. Her gray-green eyes looked hazy. Now, I think that she was probably drugged."

A footman peered briefly at the entrance, then disappeared. Roddy said, "Two women drugged…. For what reason? What motive?"

"Suppose they are different reasons, Roddy. The Washington Square house is chaotic…frenzied decoration, hare-brained schemes. Sara is there to curb Celia's spending, but did she foresee the daily turmoil? Did she expect live peacocks to fit Celia's color scheme? My guess is, Sara is drugging Celia to quiet her down."

"And you think Celia would submit to medication?"

I reminded myself that Roddy had not seen the Washington Square house, nor did he see Celia's eyes flash at the menu of treats. "Roddy, "I said, "if Sara promised that a drug could make Celia feel on top of the world, she would take it in a heartbeat."

"And Sara could continue dosing…" Roddy said, "until the young woman became addicted." He rubbed his chin. "If

Sara Dow did spend time in China, she would have learned about opium, wouldn't she?"

"Definitely." I recalled that Virginia City had its share of opium dens on "D" Street on the far edge of Chinatown. Papa said opium smokers moved no more than dead men. A few miners were lost to the dens.

"And Lydia?" Roddy said. "She, too, addicted by Sara...?"

"Yes, I'd guess for a different reason," I said. "Roddy, you saw Lydia at the Law School reunion. How did she look?"

"I wish I could say, Val. She was slender and wore a big hat. We spent a very few minutes together. If Martin's wife was addicted to drugs, I would not have known." He rubbed his eyes. "But if she researched medicines at the Crerar, she could have found her drugs to be harmful."

"And addictive too...but still dosed to her by the faithful dear friend and companion, Sara. And so," I said, "let us consider the situation of Sara Dow, the former Vitalene saleswoman who sold so much of the elixir that Martin's father brought her into the Oak Park household so her sales skills could win over his son and daughter-in-law."

"We know all this, Val."

"But we haven't thought about Sara's feelings when she found herself living with a wealthy family in Oak Park... and trapped."

Roddy's eyes narrowed.

"In the Coates house," I said, "Sara became a hired companion, no longer traveling, no longer the queen of sales. She was now the nursemaid to the mistress of the house, a woman whose health was delicate...and what's more, a wealthy woman in her own right."

I sipped my wine. "Sara strikes me as calculating, Roddy. Suppose she took stock of her situation...a servant in the Coates household for the foreseeable future. For her, time was passing yet standing still. Let's say that she started off obeying the doctor who prescribed pain medications. She knew that opium was refined as morphine. Let's presume that she decided to increase the doses on her own. All the while, she thought about drawing so close to Lydia that she could become a beneficiary of her friend's will if her health should fail.

"But the friendship," I continued, "must first become so solid that the wealthy Lydia would prepare a new will to protect her friend's future with a generous bequest. It would not surprise me if Lydia confided the terms to her dear friend."

"Which Owen implied were quite generous," Roddy said, "since Sara did inherit money upon Lydia's death, as we know."

A hall clock struck the hour. "When she tumbled to her death," I said, "Lydia could have been so groggy that she lost her balance and fell. Or her dear friend could have given her the fatal push. Either way, Sara's happy ending required Lydia's tragic 'accidental' death."

Quietly and firmly, Roddy said, "Sara could be prosecuted...premeditated murder...manslaughter including a 'causal link'...." He muttered about 'contributory negligence' and other terms that flew past me.

"Evidence, Roddy," I said. "Where is the evidence? We have a motive, but how in the world could the evidence be found?"

"From Martin..." my husband began. "If it's true, Martin could help us. But if it is not true—"

"—then Sara would be framed," I said, "with Martin's 'help.' And we might find ours ourselves liberating the homicidal husband. We would have played into his hands."

"Then again," I said, "it is entirely possible that Lydia's death was accidental." I finished my wine. "Roddy," I said, "we are one thousand miles from Chicago, but the 'City By the Lake' keeps calling. My question is, must we answer the call? Must we?"

The wine had gone to my head, and I might have flown into "must we' arias, but Sands appeared in the doorframe with an "a-hem" and a telephoned message.

"Sir...ma'am...a call from a police detective. Officer Colin Finlay hopes to meet with you in the morning...at your earliest convenience."

Chapter Twenty-nine

OUR BREAKFAST WAS SHORT, our conversation curt. We dressed for the day in gray flannels and merino woolens, his and hers. Neither Roddy nor I slept well.

My husband rose when Detective Finlay was announced by Sands at 8:30 a.m. in the Corinthian room where dinner guests had sipped punch last evening.

"Mr. DeVere...ma'am." Finlay bowed to me.

"Mr. Finlay," I said. "Do have a seat."

We all perched on the Louis XV furniture. Finlay's blue suit showed a handgun "bump" at the breast, which I not seen on other visits. I always looked.

"Good news, Mr. DeVere, and I'll get right to it. We found the still that boils off the wood alcohol...just over the bridge, on Long Island. Our squad shut it down, smashed the operation, arrested three men...and so, no more *Captain Roy's Best Orange Bitters.*"

"Fine work, Finlay, but all over New York—"

"—doing our best to track it down, Mr. DeVere. Saloons, hotel bars, gentlemen's clubs...and you, sir, could give us a hand with the clubs. You could man the topsail for us... handle that line."

My husband said that he already wired clubs that might have the toxic bitters. "Depend on it, Mr. Finlay," Roddy said. "And allow us to thank you for putting us in touch with your former shipmate, Officer Polachek. Mrs. DeVere and I met him in Chicago. He sends his warmest wishes. And his family...his family...."

Roddy broke off when, somehow, the name of his old friend moved Colin Finlay to gaze into the distance and say, wistfully, "Good man, Jakub Polachek.... He wanted me on the big lakes, but I'm a high seas man...or I was."

He tugged his necktie, cleared his throat, and blinked his watering eyes. "Now then...here and now," he said, "let's get on with it." He grabbed a pocket notebook. "Couple of things," he said, "about the assault on May 6, Central Park... Mr. Owen Coates."

Roddy's glance meant we would not say that Owen had just been in this room hours ago.

"The day of the attack," the detective said, "the Park Police got diverted, I'm sorry to say. Seems a bunch of women carried on...banging drums and so forth. They were let off with a warning, except one was arrested...a public nuisance."

"Which woman was arrested?" I asked. "The one with the hurdy-gurdy?"

"The what?"

Roddy shot me a look. "Never mind, Mr. Finlay," he said. "You mean the Park Police were too engaged with the women to patrol the parade route."

"That's it, sir."

The detective looked at both of us, then back at his notes. "So, then," he said, "I spoke with Mr. Coates. He guesses that a former stable hand might have attacked him. He gave me a name and directions to his stable and grounds... also on Long Island, which is not my territory, but courtesy was extended."

"And the paddock cap?" I asked. "Did it help?"

"No, ma'am...no bare heads to claim the cap, but a sight you see all over...beautiful horses groomed to a fare-thee-well, oats and hay galore, stalls clean as a whistle...but the hands thin as rails, down at the heel and ragged all the way. They're a close bunch, the stable hands, and they said Mr. Coates is tight as a tick with a penny, unless it's for the horses."

He flipped a notebook page. "They knew the name Mr. Coates gave me, a man they called Flask. They said he was fired for mouthing off about wages. The Central Park attack was news to them. They doubted Flask would dare to thrash Mr. Coates, but they liked the idea."

He brought the notebook close to his face. "Flask," he said, is "Peter Cromb," and I found him in a roadhouse, rip-roaring drunk." I will see about him another time, but I did some digging around Five Points." He looked at Roddy. "Five Points, Mr. DeVere?"

"Gangsters..." Roddy answered.

"Plague upon the city, but it spreads scuttlebutt from time to time, if you know where to look, who to ask."

We waited. Finlay closed the notebook and tugged at his cuff. "We are not one hundred percent sure of what we hear," he said. "We have men on the beat that pick up a word now and then. They pass it on, we follow it up."

"Mr. Finlay," I said, "we have helped you, and you have helped us. If useful information has been provided, please say so."

"Crosscurrents, ma'am," he said. "A problem when one crosses the other. Which is the main? Which the cross?" He tugged his other cuff. "Thing of it is...looks like a man was paid to beat Mr. Coates to a bloody pulp, and worse. Which is one swift current. But then...."

"Then what, Mr. Finlay?" Roddy sounded harsh. "Then what?"

"Then, sir, you ought to be watching yourself. The cross-current lingo says it might be you."

Chapter Thirty

THE DOG FOLLOWED RODDY and the detective to the Corinthian room doorway. Velvet eyed them like the dog in the gramophone picture. When the butler closed the front door, she pawed at the basket where her leash and harness promised a walk.

"Shall we go outdoors, Val? Take the dog? The weather is good."

Reluctance in every syllable, I said, "It's not about the weather, Roddy. You know it's not about the weather."

"I know. But let's go."

We walked up Fifth Avenue while carriages passed on the asphalt roadway, but the jingling harnesses and soft clop-clop of hooves were too pleasant to be trusted today. We let Velvet sniff and scratch.

"Roddy," I said, "you huddled with Finlay in the doorway. What did he say?"

"We did not 'huddle,' Val."

I tugged the dog across 63rd Street, startled when my husband said, "Finlay suggests we hire a watchman?"

"A watchman?"

"To keep a lookout at night."

"A lookout for the man that meant to strike you...but attacked Owen?" I tightened the leash. "I saw him, Roddy. He burst from the bushes, masked and fierce. I saw him crouch down and look back and forth from our landau to the Regency coach in front of us. Then he lunged." I paused. "If he comes after you again...."

"That's why Finlay recommends a watchman."

A few of our neighbors employed night watchmen. It was not unheard of. "Roddy, why would anyone attack you?"

"Or why attack Owen?

We stood aside for an elderly gentleman in a thick winter coat who walked with the help of his manservant. I pulled Velvet close.

"All your courtroom work defending bars and saloons," I said, "...do you suppose a Temperance fanatic...?"

"It's possible," my husband replied. "A man inflamed by fiery sermons and driven to a 'holy righteous' act... 'Vengeance is mine.'" Roddy pulled at his lapels. "If so, Owen got the whipping meant for me."

"And that knife?"

Roddy did not answer. We had We crossed 69th Street. "Then again," he said, "I have another idea." The dog sniffed a fallen twig. "That dog collar, the diamond-studded collar that Celia sent as a gift."

"As a bribe," I said. "A failed bribe...no coaching parade for Celia. She was roaring mad, but crazed? Hired a thug to attack you? Attack us?"

Roddy's grim little smile had no mirth. "Val, think a bit further. Think of Sara...the companion who might enjoy owning a house on Washington Square...and plan how to get it."

Slow on the uptake, I finally said, "So, Sara would gauge Celia's fury at not being invited to the parade. And she would get the idea that the fury could be useful to her plan...that Celia's outrage could help her take over the house?"

Roddy's smile turned sly. "Go on."

The dog chewed the twig. "An act of vengeance to be pinned on Celia?" My husband nodded. "But how...? Oh, I see, hire a man that's good with his fists and a knife...the sort that fills the newspapers."

Roddy's smile widened. "That's it," I said, "Sara would read newspaper accounts of brawls and knifings...where they happen. She would go there to find her man."

"And then...?"

"Then...she would make it known that she was merely a messenger on an errand." I swallowed. My mouth felt dry. "Sara could hand over the cash in her employer's name, wouldn't she? She would spell out Celia Coates. The attack would happen, and Celia would get the blame. Meanwhile, you would be recovering—"

"—or not."

"Or not," I repeated in a whisper.

We stopped at the corner of 71st Street. Roddy took the leash and faced me. "It would happen fast. Finlay would get Celia Coates's name from the Five Points scuttlebutt. He'd question you and build a case against her."

"And Celia's brothers would quickly step in, wouldn't they? They would send her abroad before a case was filed."

"They would. And the house would go to Sara, and probably a handsome thank-you sum from Owen.

"The tight-fisted climber," I said, "who would pay up to rid himself of scandal...so he wouldn't get stuck on a low rung of the social ladder. And so," I said slowly, "Sara would have a Washington Square townhouse and money from Owen, plus the bequest from her dear late friend, Lydia. Sister Celia would roam around Europe. And Martin would go along with all this?"

"I'd guess he would."

We paused near the Inventor's gate to the park but decided to turn back. Roddy wrapped the leash around his hand. At 70th Street, I said, "What about Owen, Roddy? Maybe I was never meant to be your widow. Maybe Owen was the intended target all along? If Dudley hadn't driven him off...."

Our dog picked up the pace, eager to get home. "Roddy, if that knife was meant to do its worst to Owen, and did so, who would inherit the Coates fortune? The next of kin would be Martin, wouldn't it?"

"It would."

"And so," I said, "It is possible that the attack was planned by Owen's brother. It is possible the attack was Martin's scheme."

I kicked at a loose pebble. "We are going in circles...up and down Fifth Avenue in circles. By all means, let's hire a watchman. But do not hedge with me, Roddy. A knife blade flashed when Dudley wrestled the man. The blade was meant for Owen—or for you."

The next days became a jumble of tasks, errands, and obligations in a tense time. Roddy hired the watchman, a retired soldier who claimed to be a night owl and carried a pistol that looked like a museum piece. A burley man with a weak chin, Ezra Fehling would patrol our property from dusk to dawn. Our butler and Mrs. Thwaite were told to inform the household that the watchman was not a prowler.

Did we feel safer? We avoided the question.

We still had no answer from the Auditorium Hotel about the gift box I feared could be a bomb. Roddy's daily wire brought apologies that offered complimentary meals along with the night's free lodging. Our humor at inept management had turned to suspicion.

"Could it be a plot, Roddy? Suppose it was a bomb, and they won't tell us? Suppose Detective Michael Brady is involved. Will the hotel stall us every day until you stop wiring?"

My husband had no answers. He did not dismiss my questions. Each day, he sent a new wire.

Roddy also visited clubs to make certain that the toxic bitters had been disposed of, and he heard exasperated beverage managers flatly state that products they purchased must be reliable, including bitters and garnishes. (Maraschino cherries, he learned, were infused with formaldehyde.)

I had hoped my husband's fervor for the bitters business would lessen and free us from the Coates household forever. Instead, Roddy's visits to the clubs steeled his resolve. He met the Traveler's Club member who was sickened and learned the harrowing details of the man's struggle to survive. He visited Dr. Strether Kimball's medical office and learned about organ damage, blindness, and death. He met with the prosecutor who would handle the case against the three men arrested for *Captain Roy's Best Orange Bitters* and offered to be a witness at the trial.

At home, the two of us avoided mention of the Chicago distillery, a topic too scorching to touch. The more we avoided it, the wider our divide.

I noticed that Roddy bypassed the hallway leading to the *Empire* room, another topic best avoided. By chance, I was at a Consumers League meeting downtown when Elsie De Wolfe popped in to inspect her work. She was gone when I returned to hear Mrs. Thwaite relay the decorator's words on "finishing touches" for "the trio of light, air, and comfort."

The housekeeper's tinny monotone could not kill the pleasure, especially when I stepped in to see new draperies seemed to float, and wallpaper softly glowing, while the furniture of pale woods and soft cushions invited seating and lounging. I went inside by myself for cheer, though the *Empire* room door was kept closed. One day soon, Roddy would join me in the transformed space. Please, may it be a celebration, not a reckoning.

Two bright spots these days. First, the woman arrested in Central Park for the suffrage demonstration during the coaching club parade was not Annie Flowers. A skilled clerical worker, Miss Flowers had taken notes at the Consumers League meeting and told me that Leona, the bass drummer, had spent a night in jail. ("t'wasn't me this time, Mrs. DeVere, so I can soon crank the hurdy-gurdy for Votes for Women. I'll be in touch, count on it. You find me in Central Park very soon.")

Not quite yet, I hoped. The park would soon find me on the bridle paths with Roddy, for our saddle horses had arrived from the South, which was usually a great pleasure, though Roddy felt his Arabian gelding had not been sufficiently exercised.

"Justice is barn sour, Val," he said, meaning the South Carolina stable had kept the horse too much in the comfortable barn. "Next winter, we must find another stable. Justice needs a daily run. I will see to it. Noland and the groom can tend the Hackneys, but Justice will be saddled for me. I trust we will ride together, as always."

"As always," I said.

My buckskin quarter horse, Comet, appeared heavier, which was concerning, although I said nothing about it to

Roddy. The breed, favored by western ranchers, was more heavily muscled than the preferred Arabians and thus an oddity here in New York. My saddle, equally odd, had caused a scandal when I forsook the treacherous lady's sidesaddle and straddled my horse. Safety won out. Roddy approved.

We planned an afternoon ride. "A good trot, Val, but no cantering today."

"No cantering," I agreed.

At lunch, we barely spoke, the tension between us unrelieved over the last several days. Perhaps we were "barn sour." I should not bring unopened mail to the table but laid envelopes between our placemats. Roddy plucked out a postal card I had not noticed.

"From Theo...says he is 'geysered' and heading home. Will 'enlighten' us with Yellowstone photos."

"We'll make an evening of it," I said. "We'll sit in the new *Em*...."

Roddy scowled and picked up another envelope. "Speaking of Chicago...a letter from Vitalene."

"No...."

"From Martin," my husband said. "Oak Park School is recessed...Tansy coming to visit Aunt Celia and 'Aunt' Sara."

"And Uncle Owen?"

"Strange...no mention of Uncle Owen."

"Maybe not strange...such an oaf."

Roddy nodded. "...hopes to see New York...the theatre, the Liberty statue. And Central Park."

"Timing is with her," I said. "The park is opening for the season. Is she too old for the carousel? I hope not. And so...will she stay at Washington Square?"

"She will."

"And she's coming by train with a chaperone?"

Roddy frowned. "She's coming with her father. Martin is bringing her."

I hated this news.

"He plans to stay in the city for a few days," Roddy said.

"Must you see him? Must we? Are we obligated?" My husband did not answer.

"I suppose he'll stay at a club, Roddy, as he did before?"

My husband looked grim. "As before," he said, "but different club this time around." Roddy's eyes narrowed in a hawk-like gaze. "This time," he said, "Martin has made a reservation at the Traveler's Club."

Chapter Thirty-one

"HOW MANY MEN'S CLUBS in New York, Roddy? One dozen? Two?"

We lingered at the luncheon table. "I'm sure it's a coincidence." My husband's choppy voice meant he was not sure at all.

"Roddy," I said, "that man is hounding us."

"Let's not jump to conclusions."

"My conclusion," I said, "is that Martin Coates is pursuing you. He heard about the wood alcohol episode and hatched a plan. He's coming here with his daughter, but you are the reason Martin is coming to New York."

Roddy asked the footmen for coffee. "Val...take a step back. The Traveler's is one of the oldest and most revered clubs in the city. Nowadays, the club lives on its reputation and relies on gentlemen from faraway. For them, the club is a point of pride...like Martin's daughter seeing the Bartholdi statue in the harbor."

"You'll meet with Martin," I said, "for courtesy...a courtesy call with a murderer?"

At the twisted notion. Roddy lowered his eyes, and I gazed at a painting on the wall, a meadow with sheep and lambs that reminded me of Martin's young daughter.

The daughter of a murderer? The coffee arrived, kept warm from the morning but just as sad. I shut my eyes to recall the fact that Letitia (Tansy) Coates was an innocent young girl who had lost her mother and deserved good times in New York. She ought to meet other children, but Cassie's Bea and Charlie were too young to be playmates. Still, I could offer an afternoon's sight-seeing, preferably without Celia or the conniving Sara, let alone Uncle Owen.

"For Tansy," I said to Roddy, "perhaps an outing. She might like to see Cleopatra's Needle."

"Good idea...ancient Egypt in the park."

The Egyptian obelisk in Central Park drew enthusiasts who marveled at the red granite monument that came from the Nile. Visitors puzzled over the hieroglyphs and exclaimed about Pharaohs and Cleopatra.

"Maybe Tansy would bring a sketch pad and pencils. We could make a day of it." I lifted my coffee cup. "Here's to Cleopatra's Needle."

"And to the bridle paths," Roddy replied. "I will telephone the stable to request that Comet and Justice be saddled. So, my dear, if you will...."

I rose, Roddy stood, and the afternoon stretched before us for the first horseback ride of spring, 1899.

Tuesday, May 30, dawned bright and cool with wispy clouds and the promise of a warming day. Our watchman, Ezra Fehling, was already off duty when I peered from the windows each morning. So far, the watchman reported seeing nothing out of the ordinary in the nighttime hours. I suspected he napped through the wee hours. Roddy spoke to Sands about extra locks for every door.

My invitation to Miss Tansy Coates was accepted on her behalf by Aunt Celia, who invited me to Washington Square for an early luncheon before I "swept our dear girl to Ancient Egypt."

I replied that I looked forward to seeing Miss Celia Coates but declined the luncheon invitation. My note did not include mention of Sara Dow, though I expected to see her when Noland reined the Hackneys to a stop at Number 14 Washington Square.

The peacock-blue front door was opened by a maid who took my card and led me to the townhouse dining room, where Tansy sat stiffly at the table with her aunt and "aunt" Sara, both of whom lounged in glistening teal robes embroidered with dragons. Plates and breakfast remains lay scattered on the table.

"Won't you sit for a moment, Mrs. DeVere? And may we use first names at long last? Let me be Sara...and here is our Celia. And from Oak Park, Illinois, Miss Tansy Coates."

She winked at the child, who smiled shyly. Her blonde hair had been pulled into one long braid down her back, leaving her narrow face to appear somehow unprotected.

Celia had not spoken. Her complexion in the blue-on-blue surroundings looked sallow, her manner listless. Two capsules lay beside her teacup saucer.

I perched on a cushioned chair. "Tansy and I are eager to be tourists today," I said, nodding at the child whose green corduroy jumper over a white shirtwaist readied her for the day. She reached for a jacket and rucksack on the back of her chair. Her fingernails, I saw, were bitten to the cuticle as they were when we met in Oak Park.

"I hope you have a sketchpad and pencil in that sack," I said, pleased when Tansy said, "Yes, I do."

"No need to rush off," Sara said. "Ancient Egypt will wait, won't it, Tansy?"

The child let go of the jacket.

"I told Tansy," Sara said, "what a pity she could not sail on the Nile River, as I did in years past...from Aswan on the sailboats, the feluccas. So picturesque, and perfect for an artist like our Tansy."

The child bit a thumbnail and stayed silent.

"And we hoped to see a drawing of the statue in the harbor when we went to see it, didn't we, dear? 'Liberty Enlightening the World'...they call it the Statue of Liberty. It would have been a fine picture."

"A picture from our visiting artist," said Celia.

"And the peacocks we went to see in the shed near the river where they are cared for these days while Tansy is with us." Sara smirked. "We hoped Tansy would paint the peacocks, didn't we, Celia?"

"We did. Yes, we did." Celia thumbed her teacup.

"Especially when one fanned his glorious feathers," Sara continued. "And so, we have made certain that art supplies are here...peacock blues. We have had more than enough drawings of the same horse and the lamb. Don't you think so, Celia?"

"I do, yes."

"And that rucksack of yours," Sara said to the child, "You will have to say bye-bye to that plaything pretty soon. It's unsightly for a young lady."

The woman sounded taunting as she turned to me. "Morning, noon, and night...beside her on the pillow all night long."

"Perhaps you might sketch Cleopatra's Needle today, Tansy?" I said, trying to change the subject. I recalled her sweetness with the white kitten in Oak Park and the dining room photograph with her mother, the devoted daughter at age nine? Ten? The child was blushing. Her bitten nails most probably marked the mourning for her mother.

I started to rise, and Tansy reached for her jacket and rucksack, but the maid appeared at that moment to ask, "Are you receiving, ma'am? Are you at home to Mr. Owen?"

Before Sara or Celia could respond, I rose, and the child rose faster to grab the rucksack and jacket, just as Owen brushed past the maid and filled the doorway.

"Well, well…seems two ladies off to the carriage at curb-side…and two at their ease over cold tea and cold toasts."

"Owen, where are your manners?"

"In safe keeping, dear Sara" he said with a bow to all of us and then a wink at Tansy, who shrunk back.

I remained standing. Tansy clutched her rucksack and jacket, ready to spring for the door. Etiquette would guarantee a graceful pivot, but Owen flatly demanded a few minutes of my time.

"But first, Mrs. DeVere," he said, "let me ask about my sister's health, which is why I have come to Washington Square this morning." He turned to Sara. "And would you prepare my favorite brain duster?"

I recognized the drink, something with vermouth and absinthe for morning drinkers. Sara disappeared from the dining room, and Owen bent to one knee beside his sister's chair.

"Sister Celia," he said, "how goes it?"

Those gray-green eyes looked blurry when she turned her head. "A little bit better," she said, "Sara tells me to be patient and give it time." She touched the capsules. "All these pills…."

"Sara knows best," Owen said, "but maybe a New York doctor—"

"—what New York doctor?" Sara stamped into the room with a short glass she thrust into Owen's hand as he stood. "My opinion," she said, "is the peacocks are not healthy.

Celia breathes better without them scratching around in the house. I say, let us donate them to the menagerie."

"A discussion for another time," Owen said. He sampled his drink. "Although I understand they are better than watchdogs...screech at every stranger."

"Then maybe we ought to bring them back, after all," Sara said. "They can screech at that man that prowls around."

"What man?" Owen drank as if thirsty.

"Some tramp...lolls around daytime and after dark too. Big man, hat pulled down low. Celia saw him at night, didn't you, Celia?"

"Parted curtains," Celia said.

"The police will drive him off, so never mind," Owen said. "For the moment, I must ask Mrs. Devere about the carriage horses out front...Hackneys, your coachman tells me."

"Mr. DeVere's choice," I said.

"Great stamina for the saddle too," he replied. "I have a weakness for a strong black horse...understand the breed goes back to medieval times."

Flattened against a wall, Tansy took short beaths. "Mr. Coates," I said, "this subject is best taken up with my husband. The Hackneys are our carriage horses. On the bridle paths, Mr. DeVere prefers an Arabian gelding, and I enjoy a quarter horse."

"Work horse, isn't it?"

"In the West," I said. "And now, if you will excuse me, Tansy and I have an appointment with ancient Egypt."

Never did a child look more relieved than when we walked to the carriage, climbed inside, heard Noland flick the reins, and felt ourselves underway from Washington Square.

We spoke little at first. Tansy asked permission to look out of the carriage side window to see the city. The sights held her rapt as we drove north up Broadway and then Fifth Avenue. Seldom had the child seen Chicago's downtown, she said, because her father thought it best to avoid the noise and traffic.

I wanted to ask whether Tansy ever accompanied her mother to Hull House. If not, what did Lydia tell her daughter about Halsted Street…or the Crerar Library?

Could I inquire? Subtlety was not my gift. If Cassie were here, she would know exactly how to inquire about life in the Oak Park household with Lydia and "Aunt" Sara, the self-appointed nurse. Perhaps I could find out whether Tansy's brother, Lester, was in the picture, or forever at prep school or summer camp? Or visiting school friends' homes during vacations?

The questions pulsed, but I must not ask. Not today. Roddy and I understood that Tansy would be at Washington Square for ten days, having arrived last Saturday. This was day number four. Her father was settled in the Traveler's Club and was in touch with Roddy for a meeting this Thursday.

At 79th Street, we left the carriage and walked into the sun-dappled park where birds chirped in mulberry trees that bordered the Great Lawn. The rucksack looped over Tansy's head and shoulder with a strap, and I resisted temptation to take her hand, fearing to insult a child who was soon to be a young lady.

Tansy asked, "Have you seen Queen Cleopatra's Needle many times, Mrs. DeVere?"

I admitted I had not, not even once. "But Mr. DeVere filled my head with facts," I said, "and I promise to give out a few of them...not too many." We smiled.

The obelisk rose like a spike in the sky between the Great Lawn and the Metropolitan Museum of Art, another landmark that might attract the young artist at my side, depending on her mood. A crowd clustered. Churchwomen in dark wools laughed as if embarrassed by the monument to heathens. A young man in a bowler hat held his Kodak high to capture the granite tip. Visitors on all four sides of the obelisk held opened guidebooks and murmured as they looked up, then down at the books.

Tansy and I saw them look up and exclaim, "...almost seventy feet...two hundred tons...from Egypt and Rome too...thirty-two horses hitched in pairs to bring it here from the East River...took 112 days... oldest thing in America...."

"Are you listening?" I whispered. "It seems that I need not give you Mr. DeVere's facts."

She nodded and smiled, and we stepped closer to see the hieroglyphs. "So many birds, Tansy," I said. "Ancient Egyptian birds. Some look like storks, don't they?"

"They do," she said.

"Maybe you will draw the birds? Or maybe..." I said, "you'd like to draw Cleopatra's Needle, the whole monument." I pointed to a bench at some distance from the crowd. "Would you like to sit over there and sketch?"

She gripped the rucksack and said, simply, "I must."

We walked toward the bench. "Some artists enjoy company while they work," I said, "but others insist on privacy."

At the bench, Tansy looked searchingly into my eyes and said, without apology, "I must do it by myself."

I nodded and promised to keep a distance. I would stay in sight and wait for her signal to return.

On the grass, midway to the obelisk, I shifted from foot to foot, swatted bees and overheard bits of chatter from the walkways. Regretting not bringing a snack for us, nor water, I kept watch on Tansy, who bent over a tablet she had taken from the rucksack. Her pencil moved decisively, and she did not look up once. Finally, she raised a beckoning hand, and in minutes I stood over her at the bench.

"Finished?"

"Would you like to see?"

"If you will allow me," I said.

Sunshine beamed on the tablet paper the child presented for my view, though a lone dark cloud suddenly cast a shadow as I leaned forward. Expecting to see the obelisk or birds, I squinted, blinked, and bent closer to make sure that I saw correctly, that no stroke of the pencil referred to the scene at the park.

"Oh…" I finally caught my beath. "Oh…not again…." Before my eyes, the too-familiar shaded lines of a black horse atop a ladder while a white lamb slept in the straw below. "I thought…" I said, "I thought…."

Tansy's eyes darkened as she looked up. "You thought I was finished, Mrs. DeVere, but I never, ever can finish."

Chapter Thirty-two

"RODDY," I SAID, "I think the child is not in her right mind...she is disturbed."

We sat upstairs in the Bergere chairs, though comfort depended on feelings as well as cushions. The cocktail hour did not tempt me this evening as we sat before a cold fireplace in a room whose late spring sunlight promised cheer I did not feel.

"She is fixated on that same horse and lamb...and a ladder. She sat on a bench, pulled out a tablet and pencil in full view of the Needle and began to draw. I watched her. She did not look up once."

"Maybe she feels better drawing the same thing, especially after losing her mother. And New York is new territory."

"I thought so, Roddy, but I have serious doubts. This morning, Celia and Sara teased her, and I was annoyed.

Now, I am concerned. They took Tansy to the harbor to see the Liberty statue, and they showed her the peacocks and bought art supplies. But still, the same drawing. She hugs a rucksack the way little children hug plush animals."

"Maybe it's comforting." Roddy poured himself a glass of sherry. "What's inside it?"

"The rucksack?"

"Besides the tablet and pencil, what else?"

I had not thought to ask. "No idea. I'll say this, I took the blame for the art when we returned to Washington Square. I told Celia and Sara the Needle was so crowded that we could not get close. I said all the benches were filled, and the grass was too wet to sit down. Sketching Cleopatra's Needle was impossible, I said.

"And they believed you?"

Probably not. But Tansy looked grateful. She insisted that I take the picture."

"Making how many?"

"Five," I said.

"All alike?"

"Every last one."

I declined my husband's offer to pour me a sherry. "And I refused a glass of wine at Washington Square this afternoon. It seems Sara Dow now tends bar. She mixed a brain duster cocktail for Owen this morning, and she offered me wine when I brought Tansy back. The child vanished the minute the door opened, so I sat down for a few minutes for politeness...awkward minutes. Sara chattered, and Celia struggled to say a few words."

"You think Celia is drinking alcohol?"

"I don't know. She took a powder that Sara mixed in water. No idea what it was. We sat in the parlor."

"Without the peacocks?"

"No peacocks, but Sara seems ready to bring them back from the shanty near the river. Owen said they are better than watch dogs because they screech."

I paused while Roddy put his glass down. "These last few days...did you notice crimes reported around Washington Square? Anything in the newspapers?"

"No. Why?"

"Sara spotted a big man on their block, hat pulled down low. She saw him in the daytime and night too. She thinks he might try to break in."

"Washington Square is very heavily patrolled, Val. They shouldn't worry."

"It's not the women I'm concerned about, Roddy. It's Tansy," I said. "That troubled young girl needs help. At least I can offer one more outing that might lift her spirits and not require artwork. I'll see what Cassie can do...maybe another afternoon in the park with the little children. Tansy could help with Bea and Charlie on the goat carts and pony rides. The Carousel is running, and everyone enjoys Carousel rides. Maybe kites...."

I broke off. "You will see Martin...Thursday?"

"Day after tomorrow at a club, but not the Traveler's. I suggested the Union League where we met in February to plan our partnership."

"Roddy," I said, whichever men's club, you must tell Martin that his daughter needs a counsellor. Tansy will soon return to Oak Park with him, and he must hear that his daughter needs someone to help her. I now think that Lydia's death can be explained as an accident. It is highly likely that Tansy bumped her mother... bumped her while they both stood at the top of the stairs. Those compulsive drawings are too much. The child is in mental shock, and her father needs to know that she desperately needs help. Whatever the two of you say about the partnership, promise that you will make Martin understand the importance of life."

Roddy promised.

The next day passed quickly as Calista helped me sort out my wardrobe for the changing season. Cassie agreed to an afternoon in the park with her children and Tansy this Friday afternoon. Washington Square seemed relieved to get the child off their hands for another day. The note from Celia said her niece "moped" with her sketchpad and could use fresh air. The note was probably penned by Sara, then signed in Celia's quavering hand.

At midday on Thursday, Roddy left for his meeting with Martin, and I decided to go to our stable to see about my horse, Comet. I suspected she was over-fed in South Carolina and would speak to Noland, our coachman, about her feed. Understandably, Noland paid closest attention to the Hackneys, and the saddle horses were at times given over to the groom, Zachary, who was Noland's young second cousin. He was cleaning out the stalls when I arrived in a hansom cab.

"Ma'am..." he said, "if I did know that you were to come...."

"Zachary, about horses...what goes in front must go out...." I smiled.

The freckled, blushing young man put the shovel and rake aside and walked with me to the stall with a nameplate reading COMET. My buckskin quarter horse nickered as I stroked her back and withers. If she expected an apple or carrot, she would be disappointed on a day when I came to discuss overfeeding.

"Fed her and cleaned out her stall first thing this morning," Zachary said. "She's been exercised and brushed too. So, if you're wanting her saddled, ma'am...?"

He frowned at my streetwear, and I said I only wanted a word about Comet's feed. "She looked heavy when she came home, Zachary."

"My thoughts on the mark, ma'am. First time I saddled her, the girth buckles got let out a notch. Too much sweet feed down South, I'd say. We are cutting back on the oats and bran mash, but taking it slow, ma'am."

"Good."

"And Mr. DeVere's Justice is getting his exercise. Too much time in that barn in the winter." He stroked Comet's back. "She's apt to kick since coming home. Maybe you noticed?"

I had.

"Checked to see nothing prickly at her legs, ma'am. She's kicking at her stall. Likely started it in the winter."

"We'll work it out of her," I said. "Sweet horse."

"And maybe Comet and Justice will keep company with the Hackneys next winter?"

He pushed a hank of dark red hair from his eyes. "And maybe your gentleman friend will go for Hackneys for himself."

"Gentleman friend?"

"He talked to Mr. Noland this morning, ma'am. Mr. Coates, I believe."

For horses, it had to be Owen. Had Roddy suggested he visit the stable?

"Came to see about the Hackneys, he did. He talked about knights and armor and how Hungarian horses are not black enough. He's dead set on the blackest horses he can find, ma'am. Strong and black as pitch, he said."

The groom shifted his feet and eyed his tools. "And will you need anything else, ma'am?

"Not just now, Zachary. Not just now."

Roddy had not invited Owen to tour our stable, he said, but would speak to Noland about the conversation, especially to learn whether Martin's brother dared think our horses might be for sale. I was pleased by my husband's assurance that he had impressed on Martin how important that Tansy get the help she desperately needs. The two men had a firm discussion about the bitters partnership, Roddy said, and the dismissal of Detective Michael Brady from the Chicago police force was supposedly the end of the Oak Park case.

"Brady has been fired?"

Roddy nodded. "Fired. According to Martin, the matter is closed, and he almost apologized for sucking us into their household drama."

"That's what he called it, a drama?"

He said their household sorrow was ruined by the detective. He hopes Michael Brady starves on skid Row."

"And your pledge to help him, Roddy? You have done your utmost. You have repaid Martin in full from the runaway horse years ago. Does he recognize your effort...our effort? Does he?"

My husband shook his head. "I am not certain that he does."

"We were threatened, Roddy. That telegram...CHICAGO KILLS. Where is it?"

"In a bottom drawer in my suite."

"And the gift-wrapped box at the Auditorium...we still don't have an answer. And the attack at the coaching parade. It could have been you."

"But it wasn't."

"And Washington Square...Celia is being drugged. The woman is a ghost of herself. Sara Dow is malicious."

"Val...stop." Roddy took both of my hands in his. "We are not responsible for Washington Square. Whatever the strife in that house, we are not involved."

"But your partnership...the bitters business...."

"The business plan can go forward without knotting us in the Coates family affairs. It will be Martin's and Owen's job to deal with their sister and Sara Dow. We are not to be...what's the word for the new job you heard about?"

"Social work?"

"We are not social workers, Val. The Coates family problems are none of our business."

I kept quiet at the moment. I would remind Roddy of this conversation in days to come. I would say how much I wished he had been right. I would admit how wrong I had been—treacherously wrong.

Chapter Thirty-three

FRIDAY DAWNED SUNNY AND cool. I brought Tansy from Washington Square, and we joined Cassie and the children in the south end of Central Park, the children's area. I had told my friend that the child had lost her mother but her delicate condition might not be obvious. I also said the pictures shown by mistake at tea at our house were drawn by Tansy. And I I mentioned the rucksack with art supplies and warned the child could be upset if Cassie asked about it. My friend closed her eyes prayerfully and said the outing should be comforting and amusing.

We said no more, agreeing on a picnic, so I brought sandwiches while my friend's basket held other supplies and a quilt to spread on the grass. The nearby Dairy would be a good stop for ice cream in the late afternoon —so we thought. Our plan for a pastoral afternoon was to prove naïve in the extreme.

The outing began with introductions that turned awkward because the little children's sailor outfits almost matched the older girl's skirt and sailor blouse, allying Tansy with Little Beatrice and Charles who insisted they were to be called Bea and Charlie. Cassie's son looked up and blurted, "I never heard of Letitia."

"Then you may call me...Tansy," The child spoke with dignity.

"What's in that bag you wear?" Charlie asked.

Tansy said, "This is a rucksack. It is...confidential." Young Charlie backed away.

"Tansy," Cassie asked, "would you please help me unfold this quilt?" The child took the blanket ends quickly, partnered with Mrs. Forster for the afternoon.

"Shall we have our lunch first?" Cassie suggested. "And Tansy, would you please assist me?"

The Carousel was turning, and the pony rides open, but the children sat on the blanket while apple juice was poured and sandwiches handed out.

I had filled the sandwich bread with jam and ground up peanuts, which was a new idea promoted for good health. Bea pronounced her sandwich "yummy."

We all sat on the blanket. The sun was high and warm. Little Bea pointed to the Carousel and asked Tansy, "See the animals?"

"Going around," she said. "Yes I do."

"I see a camel and a lion. I want to ride the horse...the white one."

From nowhere, Charlie asked, "Do you draw horses, Tansy? Auntie Val showed us horses by mistake."

"And lambs," Bea said. "We drew ships. Our daddy is on a ship in the ocean."

My relief at the mention of their seafaring father was all too brief. Charlie asked, "Did you put our ships in frames, Auntie Val? Did you put the horses in frames?"

"The white lambs," Bea said. "I want a lamb like that."

"Uncle Roderick…" I began, but Cassie said, "Children, please…your manners." Cassie's creamy complexion turned paler, and she looked uneasy.

I said, "Who wants a pony ride this afternoon?"

"First, the Carousel," Bea said. "I want to ride the white horse."

"Charlie," I asked, "what is your favorite Carousel animal?"

"The lion," he said, and roared.

Cassie handed out sugar cookies, murmuring that her children would not sleep a wink that night. The next minutes found us swatting bees. "The jam…" I said. "They're after the jam from the sandwiches…and the sweet apple juice." We quickly wrapped up the stray sandwich crusts, drank the juice, and packed up. The bees buzzed elsewhere.

"Let's walk to the Carousel," Cassie said.

"Ten cents," Charlie said. "One ride is ten cents."

Near the Carousel gate, Cassie asked, "Tansy, would you like to help Bea and Charlie? You could be the big sister on the Carousel."

The child brightened. "Yes, please."

"But dear," my friend continued, "you will need both hands and arms free...nothing to get in the way when you help the children."

Tansy stopped still. Her fingers gripped the strap of the rucksack, her nails bitten to the quick.

"I can get on the lion by myself," Charlie boasted.

"I can get on the horse...I think so," Bea said softly. She looked up at Tansy. "You could help me."

"My dear," Cassie said to Tansy, "we could hold...everything. Mrs. DeVere and I have the picnic things, and we can stand right over there with...everything else." She pointed to a bench. "Right there."

"There..." Tansy gripped the strap tighter.

"I want ten rides," Charlie cried out. "Ten rides on the lion."

"I want ten too," his sister echoed.

"Three rides," Cassie said. "I will pay for three rides. Other children need turns too."

Actually, few children were here this Friday afternoon.

Should I offer to oversee them? Cassie's face was stark white. It ought to be me on the Carousel. Then again, if Tansy could break free of her fetish with the rucksack, the child would not be shamed when an adult finally wrested it from her. This was her moment.

We stood still, a tableau until Bea took Tansy's hand and softly said once again, "You could help me."

Time stopped. The Carousel entrance gate opened for the next ride, and in that long, hesitant instant, Tansy made her decision. Cassie was given the rucksack, and this afternoon's big sister took the little children to the Carousel.

"Look," I said, "Charlie on the lion."

"And Bea at the white horse. She could not get on by herself, Val."

"No. Tansy helps."

The charming moment, so good, so picture perfect.

Then I saw my friend's sheet-white face and trembling hands. "Cassie, are you all right?" My friend clutched the rucksack as the Carousel began to turn. "Are you ill?"

The children waved. I waved back. "Let's sit down." I held the picnic basket, and Cassie the rucksack. We sat on the bench. The Carousel turned faster. Cassie put the rucksack between us. I reached for my friend's hand.

The rucksack fell.

"I'll get it."

I reached down. Pencils spilled out, and a sketchpad. And a leatherbound book that was barely in reach. Cassie's arms had crossed as if she were chilled. The Carousel turned faster.

I snatched the pencils and the sketchpad. "I'll put them all back," I said, stretching for the book, which had opened. "It's handwriting..." I said. With the opened book in hand at last, I could not help reading the lines....

> *Our love is all, but disgrace overcomes me.*
> *His threat to kill me if I dare to lift this*
> *burden from my heart...and yet I must!*

"Val what is it?"

"I...I can't say."

"Quickly, Val. The Carousel is slowing. Put the book...."

"Away," I said. Sliding it to the rucksack, I saw the embossed word on the front cover—*Diary*. And just below, the initials I already guessed, *L. A. C.*

"What is it, Val?" Cassie's eyes looked faraway and troubled, the look I recalled when she felt the auras that were lifelong...the auras she vowed to banish.

"Val, here come the children." My friend's voice chocked. "What did you see, Val?"

"Nothing, Cassie. Nothing at all," I said.

And yet, I saw everything I needed to see, everything I needed to know."

Chapter Thirty-Three

I TOOK THE STAIRS two at a time to my husband's study. "Roddy...Roddy...." Breathless, I stood at his doorframe. "Roddy, I was wrong."

My husband's calm turned to confusion. At his desk with opened law books and an inkwell, he put his pen down.

"Wrong..." I said.

"Val, take a seat."

"Why did I not see it? Why didn't we?"

"See what?" He pointed to the chair by his desk. "Catch your breath."

I sat and reached for a glass of water on Roddy's desk, spilling some as I gulped. My heart thumped, and the sun glared through the window. I shifted in my chair. I had made certain that Cassie and the children got home safely and took Tansy back to Washington Square. The rucksack was returned to the child, intact. She knew nothing of the spill.

"You asked about the rucksack, Roddy. You asked what was inside. I can tell you...a diary, Tansy's mother's diary. It was Lydia's, with initials, *L.A.C.*...Lydia Anne Coates. The diary fell out, and I picked it up. Tansy was on the Carousel and did not see me, but the diary was opened...and Roddy, why didn't we see what the drawings have told us? Told us all along...."

My husband stared, puzzled.

"Listen to me, Roddy," I said. "I was wrong about Tansy. She had nothing to do with her mother's death. She did not bump Lydia down the staircase, but she knows how her mother died. She has tried to tell anyone who sees her drawings. She tried to tell me. Roddy, the drawing was staring at me from the Oak Park dinner. Tansy almost begged me to see it. Every one of those drawings...she beseeched.... Think of the black horse and the ladder—"

"—and the sleeping lamb?"

"Not sleeping, Roddy. The lamb is dead. The lamb is Lydia...pushed down the stairs by the black horse. The black horse is Owen, and the ladder is the staircase. Lydia was murdered by Owen."

"What makes you...?"

"Think so? The lines in her diary.... Lydia's romance with Owen started up again, probably in the afternoons when he read to her at her bedside. She was crushed with guilt... ready to tell Martin." I swallowed. "And Owen threatened to kill her." I reached for the water glass. "Roddy, he did kill her. Tansy saw it happen. Tansy saw it."

My husband rubbed his cheek. The sun glared. I shifted again. "And Cassie sensed it from the drawings," I said. "The day she brought the children to tea, she was not feeling faint from hunger. She felt...sensations."

"She told you so?"

"She was trying not to feel them, Roddy. She promised Dudley to try hard to be...to be normal. I think she struggled at the coaching parade. I think Washington Square brought on her...vibrations." My husband bit his lip. "I have the drawings," I said. "Do you want to see them?"

"No need." Roddy closed the blind. "But if it's true, Val.... If it's true, Tansy would be the witness."

"Yes."

"And has she told her father? Or Sara?"

"Roddy, everyone who sees those drawings has been told."

In the silence, a clock struck the quarter hour. "Val, one minute, please...." Roddy capped the inkwell, closed the law book, and shelved it. He moved the blotter and put his pen away and placed several pencils in his center desk drawer. My husband was buying time for himself and for me. He pushed back his chair at last.

"Two questions, Val. First, why would Owen threaten Lydia?"

"Because of Martin," I snapped. "Furious husband, heartsick...household tumult." My husband's impassive face told me he had another thought. "Why else, Roddy?"

My husband fingered a paperweight embedded with antique coins. "Oh," I said, "it's money, isn't it? Something about the father's will? The inheritance?"

"The codicil," Roddy said, "about 'family continuity.' My guess is, if the 'continuity' were disrupted, the will could be contested."

"And Owen's tens of millions...?"

"Would be subject to a legal challenge by his brother and sister."

"Celia and Martin would cooperate, wouldn't they?"

"As interested parties," Roddy said. "And during the legal proceedings, the judge might limit Owen's access to the money. He would not live lavishly."

"No jousting, no Camelot..." I said. The clock struck again.

"You had another question, Roddy. It's about Tansy, isn't it? If Tansy saw her uncle shove her mother down the staircase...?"

"Did Owen see her witness the fatal free fall?"

The two questions were now three, and we sat with terrifying thoughts. "Roddy," I said, "the child speaks in her drawings, but she will not come forward to tell what she saw. She was too shocked, and Owen counts on her silence. She cannot speak out. Not now, perhaps not ever."

"Unless," Roddy said, "the counsellor helps her in the months ahead. Martin agreed to find help for her, Val."

I clutched the chair arms, realizing what I had done. "Tansy's mental freedom could put her in jeopardy," I said.

"Owen will find a way to silence her. I will have put the child in danger, Roddy...unless...."

"Unless what?"

"The diary," I said. "Lydia's diary is inside Tansy's rucksack. I read just a few lines, but other entries would show Lydia confiding her passion and her terror too. The diary was her confessional, I'm sure of it."

"Do you suppose Owen knows?"

I shook my head no. "A lady's diary is her secret, Roddy, her feelings locked inside like a vault. Lydia's diary holds evidence, and we must get hold of it. Somehow, Tansy got her mother's diary and keeps it with her at all times, day and night. She will be in Washington Square for another four or five days, and we must plan another social event. Work with me, Roddy. We will get the diary. It will be a next step."

By dinner and dessert, we decided to invite Tansy to luncheon on Monday, along with Cassie and the children. My friend would offer to safeguard the rucksack so that Charlie and Bea would be in Tansy's "nanny" care for the afternoon. While the children were distracted, the diary could be retrieved. I sent our footman with invitations, hoping for the immediate acceptances that that he confirmed upon return. One more day, and the diary would be in our possession.

On Sunday afternoon, Roddy agreed to call on a hotel whose bar served a "not quite right" cocktail and asked for help. Roddy chose to ride horseback to the hotel, and I went as far as our stable. Comet needed to be fully reacquainted with her mistress and, I hoped, quit her kicking. She would snack on the apple and two carrots fetched from our kitchen.

"You'll indulge her," Roddy said.

"No, I will talk sweetly to my horse while brushing her gently from neck to thigh," I replied.

Roddy's Justice was saddled, and off he went downtown. Noland and Zachary had prepared to wash and polish our carriages in a nearby vacant backlot. "Too much springtime dust, ma'am," Noland declared. The groom, Zachary, looked unhappy but had no choice in the matter. The two men had pulled the barouche and the cabriolet to the lot. In the stable, Zachary filled oak buckets of water and selected brushes.

"Not riding this afternoon, ma'am?" He eyed my culottes skirt.

"Not today, Zachary," I said. "I'm hoping the dandy bush will help settle Comet down. She's still kicking?"

"Kicked her stall this morning, ma'am. Bad winter in that barn down South. You be careful, now…stand clear. You all right by yourself, ma'am? I'll be in and out for fresh water."

The stable felt peaceful, a space of stamping hooves and nickering from the stalls. The sounds were like musical notes, though I recalled that Lydia—the late Lydia—had met Owen in a stable where she spent the night to comfort an ailing horse. Her death was ordained in a stall like this.

Apollo and Atlas's whinnies were lullabies as I offered Comet her first carrot, careful to keep my palm flat. The apple, I decided, would be the last treat. "Comet, be a good girl this afternoon," I said, "and enjoy an apple after your brushing."

I patted her forehead and nose, then took up the long-handled dandy brush and lightly stroked her neck. Not that she needed my brushing. Zachary had cleaned her well with a curry comb. The brush swept along her left side when the groom's voice called, "Just here for fresh water, ma'am. Wouldn't want to startle you."

"No problem," I replied, hearing the splash in the buckets and the spigot squeak. I was alone again, brushing and brushing. The next time Zachary came for water, I would compliment him on Comet's grooming.

The time between the buckets...was it twenty minutes? An hour? "Girl," I said to my horse, "you ought to be at work on a ranch out West. You ought to help herd cattle." I fed her another carrot and started brushing once again at her neck.

The new footsteps, I thought, were likely our coachman Noland taking a turn with the buckets to give the groom a short break. Good for him.

The familiar voice, however, was not Noland's. Nor Zachary's.

"Mrs. DeVere...good afternoon."

I turned. "Mr. Owen Coates.... Good afternoon."

He wore riding britches, a bowler hat, and a bulky flannel shirt. "The Hackneys," I said, "are in their stalls."

"So they are," he said, "and this little filly is...Comet?"

"A quarter horse," I said. "Every stall has a nameplate." He stood foot to foot and leaned against a beam as if needing balance. Did I smell liquor?

"If you are wishing a word with my husband," I said, "or perhaps our coachman?"

"Actually, Mrs. DeVere, your housekeeper told me you might be right here."

"Mrs. Thwaite...." That woman.

"And so you are.... We are."

"Mr. Coates," I said, "I am brushing my horse, as you see. Perhaps another time?"

He stepped closer, nearly at the stall, liquor heavy on his breath. He grabbed another beam. Was he dizzy? "Just a few minutes," he said, turning to the tools on wall hooks. "A bedding fork and a shovel," he said, "and trimming scissors...very sharp."

"Our stable is supplied," I said. If only Zachary or Noland would come in for fresh water. Owen's eyes seemed glazed as he surveyed the stable. Slightly stumbling, he took a step closer. Comet neighed. "Easy, girl...easy." I stroked her neck.

"I am not here about horses," he said. "I was at Washington Square...seems my niece took a shine to you, Mrs. DeVere, you and your lady friend."

I would not say Cassie's name. "I have enjoyed your niece's company on two occasions in Central Park, Mr. Coates. She is a delightful young lady."

He rubbed his eyes. "Girl reads novels," he said. "Gets ideas."

"Youth is a special time of life," I said, mouthing the cliché I hoped would satisfy the moment.

"Girl with no mother," he said, pulling us to the topic I determined to avoid. I gave Comet a brushstroke on her flank. My horse sensed tension. Her neck muscles tightened.

"We had a fuss at Washington Square last night, Mrs. DeVere."

"Oh?"

"Sara said Tansy should get rid of that sack around her neck."

My horse felt me stiffen.

"Quite a time. Girl fought like a tiger till Sara settled her down.... Ether soaked in a rag stunk up the place, but Sara pulled off the sack, and I got what was coming to me."

"Coming..." I echoed.

"Not a pad and pencils, Mrs. DeVere. Something else in that sack...."

I shrugged.

"Don't suppose you and your friend nosed into that sack...or did you?"

"I don't know what you mean." Comet flicked her tail.

"Don't bluff me, Mrs. DeVere." A glance around, and he grabbed at the trimming scissors. Comet stamped her front feet.

"You would not know, Mrs. DeVere, I am wearing a chain mail shirt." He took a step into the stall, scissoring the blades of the trimmer. "Your little Comet," he said, "needs a haircut."

"Her mane," I said, "is fine."

"You need your hair cut, Mrs. DeVere."

"Mr. Coates," I said, "I believe you are very drunk."

He gripped the scissors, its blades open in a vicious V. "Chain mail shirt," he bellowed. "Knight of old...Lancelot's dagger. Dagger to the heart." His arm raised, both comic and fierce. He braced to lunge at me.

"Mr. Coates..." I called, "stand back...my horse kicks... Comet, no...no...."

It happened so fast, in the blink of an eye. A horse will kick to defend itself when threatened. Most dangerous, the back legs that thrust at lightning speed with power that can break bones. A kick can kill.

Comet's legs were again on the straw, all four feet on the stable floor straw. Behind her, Owen Coates also lay on the straw, flat on his back, face up.

"Ma'am...oh, ma'am....."

"Zachary...."

The groom's eyes met mine, and we looked down. "Oh, ma'am...."

"Zachary...."

I was to recall that our groom dropped both buckets and that wash water splashed on my feet. I remembered bending over Owen, seeing blood seep from his temple and drain from his ear. He did not move, and our groom could not listen for a heartbeat because the unconscious man's upper body was encased in woven metal.

I barked orders in a voice that was mine and not mine. Our coachman and groom saw to Comet and stood guard over Owen. The telephone summoned an ambulance wagon from Bellevue Hospital. In the melee, the Traveler's Club was notified that Mr. Martin Coates, a guest, must hasten to Bellevue where his brother was gravely injured. Somehow, I issued these orders. The telephone in our stable proved its worth over the hours. Or was it two? Three?

My husband returned to find me clutching the dandy brush. I had held it all along. "Roddy...finally."

"Val...." My husband slowly dismounted from Justice and gave the reins to Zachary for a cool-down walk. "Is everything all right? The groom looks dazed, and it feels somehow ...unsettled. And what's this in the straw?"

"Oh," I said, "...the shearing scissors."

Roddy picked up and closed the scissors. "Val," he said, "that looks like blood. Is that blood?"

"Roddy," I said, "I have a tale to tell...after I put down the dandy brush and give Comet her apple."

Chapter Thirty-four

OUR POCKET GARDEN WAS mainly ornamental with wrought iron furniture best enjoyed from a window inside the house. This afternoon, however, Roddy and I sought the privacy of the little back garden. "Where you and the footman exploded the firecrackers that came with the diamond dog collar," I said.

My husband flinched. "No harm done, not then. But if we knew what was coming, Val...in our stable, your life at stake...and I was not with you. Once again, your husband not by your side...truant, absentee...."

"Roddy, you must let it go. Owen was so drunk, he could have fallen flat on his face. I was afraid he would strike Comet. But instead—"

"—pure instinct," Roddy said, "she struck first."

"She sensed my tension," I said, "and her horse sense won out. She must be gentled to rid her of kicking, but

Comet has earned bunches of carrots and apples by the bushel."

Roddy patted Velvet, who found a patch of sunshine and lay down. The question that hovered between us—what else could we have done? Or done differently from the beginning?

We asked endlessly in the eight days that passed since Owen Coates was kicked by my horse, lingered briefly and died at Bellevue Hospital. The mail had brought us a black-bordered, engraved notification of death with **Owen G. Coates** in medieval script.

In these eight long days, Detective Finlay reported the arrest of a Temperance zealot who flashed his knife at a teamster with a wagonload of ale from a brewery. ("We think it's the scoundrel from the coaching parade, Mr. DeVere. Same sort of paddock cap. Looks like he got the wrong man...like he meant to go after you.")

A second arrest was reported to us in a note from Sara Dow, who wrote "for your information" that the loitering tramp with his hat pulled low was arrested by the police on her say so. When questioned, he purported to be employed recently as a police detective in the city of Chicago. He raved about surveillance in a murder case involving persons seen in and around Washington Square. Sara's note added the indigent man had no identification and was sent for a mental examination at Rikers Island.

"It's Brady," I said. "Roddy, it has to be Michael Brady. His 'witch hunt' drove him to New York. The man is obsessed."

Roddy smiled ruefully. "Val," he said, "I would not be surprised to learn that Michael Brady was long enamored of the lovely Miss Gerstle."

"Though he did not once mention her name at our interview."

"Exactly my point, my dear. I think it likely that he said her name by his silence...a 'flame of love' secretly burning in his heart since school days."

"And he would watch her from afar? The genteel Lydia as Mrs. Martin Coates, married and a mother...but forever Lydia Anne Gerstle in his mind? Any harm to her unthinkable?" Roddy nodded. "Can we do something for him? Rikers is no place for anybody."

Roddy agreed to help, especially given what else we learned in the last eight days. Martin had told Roddy that in the short time that he lingered, Owen's final words were, "got the diary" and "I pushed her."

"A deathbed confession?"

Roddy nodded. "Martin said the nurses heard the words from Owen's lips."

"An admission...for himself?"

"Or for his brother's peace of mind. And perhaps for Sara Dow too."

I plucked a dogwood blossom. "Roddy, I am convinced that woman was in tight with Owen...allied with him. I think those two sent the awful telegram when we went to Chicago. And that gift box in the Auditorium hallway...will we ever know? How many wires have you sent?"

"I stopped counting eight days ago, Val."

A silent moment passed. "Do you think," I asked, "that Sara was possibly Owen's mistress?"

"Possible, yes, but we might never know," my husband said tartly, "since Miss Sara Dow is suddenly nowhere to be found."

The woman had not joined Martin and Celia to accompany Owen's body from New York to see him laid to rest in the Oak Park Memorial Garden. Tansy went with them and stayed in the care of a neighbor for the time being. On return to the city, Celia had found herself alone in her house. The maid said that Miss Dow had departed in haste, that she carried a valise and left no information on her plans or whereabouts.

"A conniver," I said. "Good riddance."

"Especially for Celia," Roddy said. "Martin tells me his sister feels less 'foggy' since the funeral trip. She's jittery but more like herself."

Coming off the drugs, I guessed. "Roddy, will you see Martin soon again? About the partnership—delayed, I suppose?"

"Roddy sighed. "Delayed until financials are settled. With Owen gone and the next of kin being Martin and Celia, the allocation ought to be fairly straightforward. The codicil in their father's will complicates matters, but it ought to be voided by Owen's death. Nonetheless, the law takes its time...."

"But for now," I said, "Vitalene stays on the market, and little boys toil at the distillery?"

"A bright note on that, Val. Remember Owen's five-million-dollar investment for bitters and Vitalene?"

"I do."

"Martin is committing the money to convert the distillery, close out Vitalene, and prepare for bitters. And he will see about school for the little boys."

To my mind, the proof will be in the pudding. We shall see. "Martin is now closing down Owen's suite, isn't he?"

"He is." My husband gazed at the dogwood blossoms on a slender tree. "How they seem to float in midair," he said, then turned. "And yes, Martin is seeing about the suite. Owen's things...and Lydia's diary."

"You're certain the diary is in the suite?"

Roddy nodded and waved a bee away from our dog. "The question," he said, "is whether Martin will choose to read the diary?"

"Oh, he must not, Roddy. Please, forbid him to open the diary. The man must pull himself together for his children's sake...especially for Tansy. And his sister too. And Tansy should not lay her hands on it either. I say, burn it. Douse it with coal oil and light a match."

The dog jumped. "Mrs. DeVere," Roddy said, "I hear you loud and clear. Your advice sounds...sound. And where we go from here...."

"From here," I said, "Theo will return to regale us with tales of Yellowstone, and we will entertain him in the new *Empire* room, all light and air. And perhaps you will conjure a cocktail to be called...something to do with Yellowstone?"

"The cocktail," Roddy said, "for the occasion, it must be...The Geyser...."

"Then I salute The Geyser, the Roddy DeVere special for our Golden Age of Cocktails."

ABOUT THE AUTHOR

Cecelia Tichi is a native of Pittsburgh, the steel city of the Gilded Age, and is an award-winning teacher and author of numerous books focused on American culture and literature. Her most recent titles: *What Would Mrs. Astor Do? The Essential Guide to the Manners and Mores of the Gilded Age* was followed by *Cocktails of the Gilded Age: History, Lore, and Recipes of America's Golden Age* and the sequel, *Jazz Age Cocktails: History, Lore, and Recipes from the Roaring Twenties.* The "Val and Roddy DeVere" mystery series premiers with *A Gilded Death.*